SILVER MOON

GREAT NOVELS
OF
EROTIC DOMINATION
AND SUBMISSION

NEW TITLES EVERY MONTH

www.silvermoonbooks.co.uk

TO FIND OUT MORE ABOUT OUR READERS' CLUB
WRITE TO;

SILVER MOON READER SERVICES;
Suite 7, Mayden House,
Long Bennington Business Park,
Newark NG23 5DJ
Tel; 01400 283488

YOU WILL RECEIVE A FREE MAGAZINE OF EXTRACTS
FROM OUR EXTENSIVE RANGE OF EROTIC FICTION
ABSOLUTELY FREE. YOU WILL ALSO HAVE THE CHANCE
TO PURCHASE BOOKS WHICH ARE EXCLUSIVE TO OUR
READERS' CLUB

***

NEW AUTHORS ARE WELCOME
Please send submissions to;
The Editor; Silver Moon books
Suite 7, Mayden House,
Long Bennington Business Park,
Newark NG23 5DJ

Tel; 01400 283488

This edition published 2012

The right of Kim Knight to be identified as the author of this book has been
asserted in accordance with Section 77 and 78 of the Copyright and Patents Act 1988.
All rights reserved.

ISBN 978-1-908593-27-6

All characters and events depicted are entirely fictitious; any resemblance to anyone living or dead is entirely coincidental

THIS IS FICTION. IN REAL LIFE ALWAYS PRACTISE SAFE SEX

SLAVES ON SCREEN

by

Kim Knight

Chapter one: Mia

'I can't outrun them in this heap of junk.'

'I told you not to even try,' Mia yelled angrily at the driver, her hand gripping the door handle, 'I've had enough shit from the police. I don't need this!'

'You don't need it?' the driver demanded, glaring sideways at her, 'I've got a bag of fucking smack in my pocket. D'ya think I need it?'

Mia was even more furious, 'You bastard! What are you doing? I asked if you were clean, I told you I'm trying to stay out of trouble!'

'Well, aren't you just squeaky clean these days?' he snarled, glaring at her again.

'Watch the damn road!' she shouted but it was too late. The car spun, sliding sideways across the road and slamming into a barrier at the side of the country lane. Mia was temporarily stunned, shaking her head to try and clear the lights that were dancing in front of her eyes. A blast of cold air filled the car as the driver's door was thrown open. 'Mickey?' she asked and looked up through the cracked windscreen in time to see him vault the barrier and disappear into the darkness. 'You bastard!' she yelled and undid her seatbelt. She tried to open her door and found it jammed. Cursing angrily, she climbed across to the driver's side in time for a hand to reach in and haul her out of the car. She was pushed back against the rear door and a bright torch shone in her eyes.

'Police officer, don't move.'

She couldn't see the man beyond the light but she knew immediately who it was and her heart sank.

'Well, well, well, if it isn't Mia.' He didn't lower the torch as he spoke but she knew he was smiling nastily, 'Mia – no surname, no fixed abode. Car theft is a bit of a step up from shop lifting, isn't it?'

Mia tried to swallow her fear, 'Oh, come on, Sergeant Kent, you know I wasn't driving.'

'I just pulled you out of the driver's seat.'

'Yeah – I was trying to get out. Didn't you notice that there was a passenger in the front?'

'So, you were the passenger?'

'Spot on.'

'Well then, what a shame that your client didn't hang around to corroborate your story.'

'Client?' Mia sighed angrily, 'I'm not a prostitute, Sergeant Kent.'

'What have we got here?' It was another familiar voice, PC Jameson, Kent's usual partner.

'Either a joy rider or a slapper who's trick has just legged it.'

'I told you, I'm not a prostitute.'

Kent lowered the light to run it down her body, studying her slim lines beneath the battered leather jacket, faded t-shirt and ripped jeans. He gradually moved the light back up until he could see her face and long, straight brown hair. 'Tell that to the whores you hang with.'

'Yeah,' Jameson snarled, 'if it walks like a duck, sounds like a duck and fucks like a duck, what is it?'

Mia shrugged, 'A cat?'

Kent moved fast, slapping her hard across the cheek and knocking her down to one knee. 'Care to answer that again?' he sneered as she lifted herself to her feet.

'What was the question?'

He back-handed her, knocking her to the ground. She lay there for a moment before finding the strength to lift herself to her knees. She looked up at him, 'Is this how you get your rocks off?' The look in his eyes made her instantly regret her words and she hauled herself to her feet, 'Alright, look, just give me a ticket or a summons or wha -' He knocked her down again.

'I prefer you down there.'

She stared up at him. She wanted to move, wanted to stand up and show that she wasn't afraid of him. But she couldn't – she was afraid. She could, and would, stand up to anyone on the streets and had developed a reputation for being someone who would fight to their last breath. But this – this was different. This wasn't street punks looking for an easy bit of cash or a fast fuck – she had no power here and they both knew it. She couldn't fight back and hope to win. Even if she managed to get away, Sergeant Kent would find her and it would be so much worse then. He must have seen the resignation in her eyes because he smiled and it wasn't pleasant.

'That's right,' he announced, 'you know your place.' Slowly, making sure that she was watching his every move, he unzipped his fly. She closed her eyes, turning her head slightly to the side. 'On your knees.' he ordered. She did so, opening her eyes but keeping her head turned to the side. 'Come on then,' he half laughed but there was a tone that made his laugh threatening.

Mia swallowed and then turned to face the half erect cock before her. He was stroking it between his thumb and forefinger and she could see nicotine stains on the edges of his fingers. She grimaced, she couldn't help it. He stank of sweat and cigarettes. He saw her reaction and reached down to grab a handful of her hair, twisting it in his fist and making her gasp as he pulled her head up.

'What's the matter? I'm not good enough for you?' he snarled and then pushed her away. She hit her head against the side of the car and fell sideways. Her hands and feet scrabbled at the road as she cried to get away from him but his foot pushed down on the small of her back and pushed her down, trapping her there. A distinctive sound followed and she knew what was going to happen next. It was Jameson who yanked her arms behind her back and cuffed her wrists. For the barest of moments she dared to hope that they were arresting her and that they would now be off to the station for a night in the cells. But that was too much to hope for. She was picked up and thrown into the back of the car. She didn't know how long they drove for but when she was hauled out of the car she could see that they were on some high waste ground. The lights on the motorway glowed far beneath them.

'That's right,' Kent announced as he saw her looking round, 'it's lovely and quiet up here, no one will disturb us.' He undid her cuffs, 'And, in case you're thinking of playing us up, there's a truck stop a couple of minutes from here and I just know that they'd love you.' Mia stared at him, desperate to see him bluffing but he wasn't. He would take her there and no doubt enjoy the show of a dozen truck drivers having fun with her. Such an image flashed past Mia's mind's eye and she was thankful for the darkness that covered up the flush that crept up her neck. A familiar tingling nestled in the pit of her stomach, she tried to ignore it but it abruptly grew worse when Kent suddenly said, 'Strip.'

'Sergeant Kent, please, I –'

'Jameson,' he said curtly with a sharp nod.

The constable moved in on her, grabbing the back of her jacket and yanking it down her arms, tossing it away into the shadows. He ripped the t-shirt from her – just shredded the material between his hands and threw it away without even looking where it was going. She was wearing a bra beneath and he struggled with the clasp, pulling her harshly as he struggled to undo it.

Jameson held his hand up to stop him and stared at Mia, his eyebrows raised, 'Well?'

Shivering, Mia reached up behind her to undo the bra and slipped it down her arms. Kent held his hand out and she gave it to him. He studied her tight, smooth breasts while he rolled the bra into a ball and then tossed it away.

'If you want to have something to wear when we're finished with you, I suggest that you take your jeans off.' He didn't wait to see if she agreed with him and just walked to the car and leant against it. Jameson joined him and the two policemen lit a cigarette each and then watched while she stripped out of the last of her clothes. When she was standing naked before them, Kent lifted his hand to circle his finger. Taking a deep, shaking breath, she turned full circle so that they could get a good look at her whole body.

'Again.' Kent smiled and sucked on his cigarette. She turned three more times before he told her to stop. 'Not bad,' he commented to Jameson who nodded his agreement.

'Not bad at all for a street whore,' Jameson agreed. 'Those truck drivers don't know what they're missing.'

'The night is still young and the slut might still be paying them a visit,' Kent replied as he finished his cigarette and flicked the butt away. 'Come here.'

Mia wanted to turn and run but she had no idea where she was or what was around her. Slowly, reluctantly, she approached the men. She felt patches of grass and dried mud under her feet, she flinched as sharp stones dug into the soles of her feet. Once she was standing in front of Kent he lifted both hands to pinch her nipples. She gasped in pain, closing her eyes for an instant and biting her lower lip.

'Don't worry about making a noise,' he told her, 'no one is going to hear you out here. In fact, he pinched her nipples harder, I think I'd like to hear you some more.' He rolled her nipples between his thumb and forefinger, a nasty smile creasing his lips. 'Shall we get started?'

Jameson grabbed her arm and dragged her to the car, using his weight to push her against the side. She felt the hardness of his crotch pushing into her back and the full realisation of what was about to happen hit her. She tried to push back from the car but he held her tightly and whispered in her ear, 'Truck drivers.'

The thought of how bad things could get made her head swim. She leant her cheek against the cool roof of the car and tried to steady her breathing. She was shivering uncontrollably and barely felt Jameson's hands on her sides as he slid her along the car until she was standing in the middle. She looked up as she felt something being tied around her wrist and realised that Kent had found some rope. He was leaning across the roof of the car to tie one end around her right wrist. He pulled it over to his side and through the window to loop it through the handle above the door. He then fed the rope through the driver's door and tied it securely around her other wrist before feeding it back through the window and securing it to the steering wheel. He tested the rope, nodding with satisfaction when he found it taut and her arms tightly stretched over the roof. The car was cold where her body pressed against it and increased the shivers that ran through her body. She gasped as her ankles were suddenly pulled apart and rope slipped around them. Jameson and Kent worked at the same time to secure her ankles, pulling her legs apart and keeping them wide by looping the rope around the front and back bumpers. The two men then stepped back to admire Mia who was stretched painfully across the side of the car. She was stretched so tightly that the quivers of cold and fear were now little more than ripples running along her skin. She should have known what was to come next but was perhaps too numbed by everything else to fully believe it. Kent had slipped his belt from his trousers and wrapped the buckle end around his wrist. The rest of the length of leather was delivered across the centre of her tight rump with a resounding snap that drew a shocked cry from Mia's lips. Another blow and Mia screamed as fire seared her buttocks. She managed to look over her shoulder in time to see the third blow as it found the backs of her thighs. She screamed over and over as blow after blow fell upon her smooth, virgin buttocks. The belt became like a knife slicing her flesh and driving hot needles into her skin. But even as her arse and thighs were engulfed in flame, a freezing chill ran up her spine and down her chest. It became impossible to tell one blow from another as her bruised buttocks succumbed to the wide belt. When he finally finished she sobbed with relief, only to scream again when his open palm found her buttock with a loud smack. Kent moved round to the other side of the car and leant his forearms on the roof, a cigarette hanging out of the side of his mouth as he studied her tear stained face. Suddenly the belt found her buttocks again and she screamed loudly, her eyes pleading with Kent who merely smiled back as his colleague beat her mercilessly. When he finished Mia had the fleeting hope that they were finished with her but then she saw the hunger in Kent's eyes and she knew that there was more to come.

The two men untied her wrists and ankles. Once she was free she looked around for her clothes but Kent just laughed and pushed her against the car again. 'Stupid slut, you don't really think that we're finished with you yet?' He laughed again and then forced her hands behind her back, trapping her wrists into a pair of handcuffs. He yanked her away from the car and pulled the door open. He pushed her onto the back seat and then slowly unfastened his trousers. Mia tried to back up, crying out as the seat scratched her battered buttocks. Kent grabbed her ankles and pulled her towards him until her arse was on the edge. He dropped to his knees and freed his hard cock from his trousers before pushing between her legs. She cried out at the first touch of his cock against her sore pussy and struggled to get away, twisting from side to side. He dug his fingers into her thighs to keep her still as he drove himself forward, burying himself as deep as her could go. He grunted as he thrust back and forth, lowering his mouth to her breast so that he could harshly suck the smooth skin there. She cried out again and then again as he thrust forward, her hips rising up to meet him. He was as surprised by her reaction as she was and smiled down at her. 'You like that?' he asked and thrust down again, crushing her against the car seat. She cried out again but it was more than just a pained reaction. 'Well?' he demanded and thrust again.

'No!' Mia cried but the uplift of her hips told them

both otherwise and he laughed before grunting again and thrusting as hard as he could. Suddenly he gripped her breasts and made her cry out as he drove forward and held himself deep inside her. He held himself there for a moment and then pulled free to tuck himself back into his trousers. He climbed to his feet and turned to Jameson, 'Your turn, mate.'

Jameson tucked his phone back into his pocket. 'Cheers,' he replied and dropped to his knees. He gripped Mia's thighs, turning her over so that she was on her front. After slapping her bruised arse a few times, he pushed forward into her semen soaked pussy. He gripped her hips painfully, pulling her back onto his cock as he thrust forward, slapping the backs of her thighs with his own. He was quicker than Kent and after just a few moments he pulled free to milk his semen over her welt striped buttocks. Mia was left quivering on the back seat while he tucked himself away, trying desperately to fight the urge to slip her hand between her thighs and finish what the men had started. She bit her lip and tried to ignore the burning arousal.

They left her lying on the back seat and she closed her eyes, trying to ignore the heat at her pussy.

She had no idea how much time had passed before she heard Jameson say, 'Here they are.'

She cried out as she was grabbed and dragged out of the car and forced to her knees on the harsh ground. Mia looked up in time to get a flash of headlights across her face, gasping and closing her eyes. She turned her head from the glare that remained on her as the engine died and then the sound of four doors opening and closing.

'Very fucking nice.' It was a man's voice and Mia squinted against the glare of the headlights to try and see who had spoken but all she could see was a blur of silhouettes formed by four or five people. As the men separated to move closer and study her, she was able to count five altogether and her heart sank as she saw them staring at her with that same lust-filled stare that Kent and Jameson studied her with.

After studying her, the newcomers collected in a group by their car and seemed uninterested in her for the moment – she knew that it wouldn't last but was grateful for the short reprieve.

'Harper is going to love her,' one of the men announced.

'Yeah, that's a point, Clive, where is she?' Kent asked, 'I thought she was coming.'

'She is,' Clive responded, flicking his cigarette butt away, 'she just wanted to stop by her home and pick something up.' Clive glanced over his shoulder at the sound of a car approaching, 'Speak of the devil.'

An unmarked car pulled up alongside the second police car and an attractive woman, dressed in a WPC's uniform, climbed out. She smiled at the men and moved round to the rear of the car. Mia's expected the policewoman to retrieve any of a number of torture devices from the boot but she wasn't prepared for the lithe, young woman who was hauled out. The woman was about Mia's age, nineteen or twenty, and she was gorgeous. Her long blonde hair and startling blue eyes were incredible and for a moment Mia forgot everyone else and where they were. She was dragged back to reality by the sight of the leather straps that stretched around the woman's breasts, throat, stomach and thighs. Metal studs glinted along the lengths of the straps when the woman moved beside Harper as they went round to the front of the car.

'I'm sure you all remember Kelly,' Harper said as the slave fell to her knees beside her, apparently unconcerned by the rough ground under her bare legs. 'And I brought this along for an extra bit of spice.' Mia had no idea what the woman was holding up but all the men recognised it instantly and appeared to be delighted. Kent took it from her and held it up, flicking a switch at the side and smiling as a blue spark shot across the two small points at the top. 'I've had the voltage adjusted slightly,' Harper announced.

'Why?' Kent queried as he handed it back.

'I got sick of my whore passing out every time I used it on her,' she replied and then, as if to demonstrate, she lowered her hand until the end of the tazer hovered over Kelly's breasts. The slave tensed but didn't move as her Mistress flicked the voltage on and the blue spark shot across her nipple. She screamed loudly and fell backwards, sobbing. 'Of course, it still fucking hurts,' Harper laughed.

'That gives me a great idea,' Kent announced and waved for Harper to bring her slave. He approached Mia who tried to shrink away from him but he just grabbed her hair again, hauled her out and pushed her against the side window of the car. She struggled against him when she realised what he had planned for her. 'Someone give me a hand!' he yelled and Jameson wandered over with another of the men.

They pushed her up against the driver's window. She glanced sideways when she sensed someone next to her. Kelly was leaning against the rear side door, her breasts pushing against the window. If she had an idea of what was to come it didn't affect her as she stood obediently, her Mistress's hand on her shoulder. Kelly was studying Mia with a look that was a cross between pity and understanding. She was perhaps wondering how Mia had come to be here and Mia couldn't help but wonder the same thing … about both of them. Thoughts of the slave beside her were forgotten as she felt the glass of the window sliding down. She struggled again but there was no point as her breasts were pushed through the opening. She felt Jameson's fingers pulling on her nipples and easing her soft flesh through the window. Kent's hand pushed against her back, holding her in place while the window was closed up. Mia grimaced and then cried out as the edge of the glass dug into the underside of her breasts.

Her cry turned into a scream and she struggled anew but her efforts only increased her discomfort and she relaxed, sobbing softly.

'Your turn,' Harper announced and reached in front of Kelly to lift her large breasts through the open window.

'Look at the size of those beauties,' Mia heard Jameson say from inside the car as he closed the window. The slave struggled slightly at the first bite of the window and then cried out as her breasts were squeezed painfully. Once they were both held firmly, their hands were cuffed behind their backs and their legs spread. Mia felt her shin resting across Kelly's calf and she was grateful for it, taking what little comfort she could from that small contact. Kelly glanced at her, a strange look in her eyes. It was a look that was similar to the one she had seen in the men's eyes that it startled Mia to see it in the slave's expression. It was a look of pure hunger – of pure lust and need. She suddenly realised that the slave's need was as great as the men's – she needed them to abuse her. The cuffs at her wrists suddenly felt heavy and the tight squeeze of the window pinning her breasts was suddenly a heat that spread throughout her body, settling at her cunt and flaring like a contraction of warmth. She looked away from the slave, afraid to see a mirror in the slave's eyes. She heard a strange crackle, distant and muffled. She realised what it was a moment before the tazer found her nipple. She screamed loudly, her pain intensified by the crush of her breasts as she struggled from side to side, her bruised flesh sawing between the glass and the window housing. The spark found her other nipple again and she screamed pitifully. She struggled as before, despite the additional discomfort that it caused her, because it was impossible not to. She heard herself screaming for mercy and the men laughing at her.

'Mind if I have a piece of arse?' someone asked and Mia prayed that the man who had spoken wasn't talking about her.

'Be my guest,' Kent responded, dashing Mia's hopes.

'You sure, you not got anything planned for this one?'

'Not tonight. This one is being thrown back for now,' he replied.

'Fantastic.'

Suddenly she felt hands pushing at her buttocks and she cried out, struggling again as the tip of a hard cock pressed against her tighter opening. She had never been fucked there before and she tried to tell them, tried to beg them to stop the man.

Kent appeared on the other side of the car and studied her, 'I do believe our little slut is an arse virgin.'

'Really?' the man behind her asked, 'Shit, that's gonna hurt.'

'Stick your cock in her cunt, 'Harper announced, waving at Kelly, 'You'll find plenty of lubricant there. That tazer would have made her cream.'

'Thanks.' His fingers delved into Kelly's pussy and scooped her juice onto his fingertips to spread the thick, musky come around Mia's anus. He pushed his finger into her and Mia gasped at the sudden entry into her virgin hole. He curled his finger and Mia quivered, gasping as waves of pleasure coursed through her. Kelly watched them, quivering with something akin to jealousy.

'She likes that,' Harper announced and looked at Kent, 'Did you realise that she was such a submissive?'

Kent shook his head, still standing on the other side of the car, 'Not until after we had beaten her.'

'Has she come yet?'

He shrugged, 'I don't think so.' He glanced at Harper, 'What are you thinking?'

'I was just thinking that we should let Kelly show her a good time.'

'Now?' Kent sounded disappointed.

'Oh no. Kelly hasn't had the tazer on her tits yet.'

If anything was said after that Mia didn't hear it because suddenly the man's cock was pushing at her virgin hole and she screamed loudly. The thick dome of his helmet pushed hard against her resisting arse and she shook her head from side to side. His helmet was forced in and she cried out as her arse closed around the hard rod of his cock. He groaned as he forced himself in, there was a pained tone to his pleasure and his fingers gripped her buttocks as he was squeezed harshly in her tight passage. He held himself there and then suddenly, with a disbelieving cry, he shuddered and came deep inside her.

Kent raised his eyebrows and looked over Mia's shoulder at the man. 'Impressive,' he half laughed, 'she's that tight, eh?'

'Uh, huh,' he grunted in response and pulled free, making Mia cry out again.

'I gotta have a go at that then,' someone said and then two other voices agreed. Mia stared at Kent with pleading eyes, even though she knew it was pointless.

He just stared back at her, tilting his head slightly so that he could see over her shoulder, 'Form an orderly queue.'

Mia gasped and managed to turn to look over her shoulder at the three men who had lined up behind her.

'Please,' she said to the first man who didn't even hear her as he stepped forward and parted her buttocks. Her anus was still open from the man who had just had her, his semen lubricating her tight hole so that the second man's entry was easier but no less painful. She screamed again and then looked sideways as another female cry joined hers. Kelly was sobbing next to her, struggling as Mia had and she knew that the tazer had found the slave's nipples. The sight of the screaming slave beside them was too much for the man who was fucking her arse and he came as quickly as the first. The next man took his time, ploughing her bruised arse carefully, enjoying the strokes. Jameson continued to play intermittently with Kelly's nipples and Mia couldn't help but watch the slave's reactions. Once he had come inside her the last man stepped forward and slid easily into her now well-used arse. He tapped on the window and waved for Jameson to use the tazer on Mia who screamed and struggled. He pushed her against the window, using his own body weight to hold her firm while Jameson ran the electricity over her pained nipples. Mia screamed louder than ever before she swooned. She came to a moment later with the man fucking her arse violently, lifting her feet off the floor and causing even more pain to lance through her breasts and bruised buttocks. He suddenly pulled free of her and she felt hot splashes explode across her arse cheeks.

When Jameson opened the window, she fell backwards but was caught by a strong pair of arms. The world shifted crazily as she was lifted up and pushed onto the roof of the car. Her ankles were grabbed and she was hauled towards Kelly, her legs on either side of the slave's head. She tried to sit up but hands grabbed her shoulders and held her down.

'You know what to do, Slave,' Harper announced as Mia was pulled closer to the slave's mouth.

'Yes, Mistress,' she responded. Her voice was smooth and deep and Mia felt her pussy react to her instantly. The first touch of her tongue was almost as electric as the tazer and she gasped loudly as pleasure swamped her in a warm blanket that grew hotter as the slave's tongue explored her pussy. She groaned and gasped, her hips circling as the slave drew her pleasure out like a musician playing an instrument. It was with her tongue buried deep inside Mia's pussy that Jameson put the tazer to Kelly's nipples again. The slave's shocked scream filled Mia's cunt and she cried out, her pleasure equalling the slave's pain. The tazer drew scream after scream from the slave but she worked on and soon Mia was panting with pending climax. She expected them to stop the slave at any moment, expecting them to torture her further by denying her pleasure. But they didn't and as her pleasure crested and the most incredible climax broke over her, she almost screamed her thanks to the men who had abused her and let her have some release.

She would have thanked them had her pleasure not stolen every ounce of breath that she had, leaving her shuddering and gasping on the roof of the police car.

They left her on the roof while two of the men took it in turns to fuck Kelly. They fucked her cunt mercilessly, making her scream, pant and groan in equal measure. When they had both come, they left her in an agony of arousal while Jameson opened the window and released her marked breasts. The slave was forced onto her back, crying out as the harsh ground dug into her skin. Mia was dragged down from the roof and made to kneel between the slave's legs.

'You have until we have finished our fags to show your thanks to the slave,' Harper told her and then wandered off to join the men.

Kelly was groaning with unspent lust, her lips pulled back in a grimace as she looked desperately at Mia. 'Please,' the slave whispered.

Mia slowly lowered her mouth to the slave's cunt. She had never pleasured a woman before and had been pleasured herself, by one, for the first time just a few moments before. She smelt the musky scent of the two men that had had her and licked tentatively at the sticky juice. She thought she would be repulsed by the taste but she wasn't and, if anything, it was intoxicating. She lapped the juice from between and around the slave's cunt lips, cleaning her outside and within her outer lips. When there was none left to clean, she delved her tongue inside. Kelly cried out, bucking her hips up to meet the thrust of her tongue, grinding her pussy onto the tentative organ. She needed more and tried to convey her need without speaking, for fear of the punishment that would follow. Mia understood her need but with her hands still cuffed behind her back there was little that she could do. She pushed her mouth hard against the pussy, forcing her tongue as deep as she could. Then she pulled free and lifted her tongue to the sensitive nub above. She pushed hard, closing her lips around the fleshy button and sucking hard, running her teeth gently around the nub and making Kelly scream. She sucked as hard as she could and then quickly drove her tongue into the cunt beneath. The slave's back arched as her climax bowed her spine. Her scream was more of a sob as she relaxed and rolled sideways to curl into a ball.

Once the slave had come, Mia was dragged her to her feet and forced over to the car that Harper and the slave had arrived in. She was made to lie down with her feet towards the car while Kent tied some more rope around her ankles. Two of the other men then lifted her up while he tied her ankles securely to the roof rack of the car. Once she was secured, they let her down and she gasped as her shoulders rested on the floor, her head bent at a painful angle. She managed to adjust her position slightly by pushing her elbows under her but Kent kicked her arms away, 'If I wanted you to be comfortable I would have fetched you a cushion.' She looked up at him as he raised the whip and then she screamed, even before the strands had found her exposed cunt. The leather sliced along her pussy lips and inner thighs, forcing a painful shudder to ripple through her body. He lifted the whip and waited for the shudders to ease before he struck her again. Mia was screaming and sobbing openly by the time he had delivered ten blows to her burning cunt. He stopped and she gasped with relief, only to scream again as Clive stepped forward and forced a truncheon into both of her holes. He rolled them between his fingers and then slowly began to move them in and out. Unbelievably, Mia felt her body reacting to the stimulation and she groaned loudly as her holes were fucked. He drew her to the point of climax and then suddenly pulled the wooden phalluses from her, leaving her shuddering with unspent lust. The whip found her cunt again and her tears soaked her hair as she was beaten again. She couldn't count the lashes that befell her pussy, it was one long agony that had her screaming for mercy. When Kent had finished the beating he handed the whip back to Harper and then let Mia down. He pushed her, face down, across the bonnet of the car and pulled her hips back so that he could painfully impale her on his throbbing cock. Mia cried out, throwing her head back. In the windscreen she could see the reflection of Harper as she raised the whip. She couldn't see the slave but she heard her a moment after the wet leather strands found her breasts. Kent fucked her harshly, his fingers digging into her hips and sliding her up and down the cold bonnet. His fucking became more and more painful and when she started to struggle he had her hands tied to the two wing mirrors. He had said that he would fuck her into unconsciousness but he didn't manage it and she gasped as she felt his come filling her. She slumped forward across the bonnet but there was no respite as she felt another man moving into her. The sound of the whip falling across Kelly's breasts and her resulting cries were a constant accompaniment through the fucking.

After the man had finished with her, Mia was aware that the beating had stopped. She felt the car move and then suddenly a pussy was presented to her mouth. Harper leant back against the windscreen and slid her pussy onto Mia's mouth. 'Well?'

Mia tentatively licked between the pussy lips but that wasn't enough for the Mistress and she grabbed her hair, pulling her face painfully into her cunt.

'Pete, give this slut some encouragement.' Mia struggled as the meaning of the Mistress' words sank in but there was no escape and she screamed against the pussy before her as the whip found her buttocks. 'Again,' Harper instructed and then gasped as Mia's mouth was forced against her pussy. 'Again,' she spat, 'the stupid whore hasn't got the fucking message yet.' The whip fell across her buttocks again and Mia screamed before she quickly drove her tongue into the musky tasting cunt. Harper cried out and ground her hips forward, 'Ahh, yes! Again, whip the fucking slut ... ahh! Whip her until she makes me fucking come!' Harper continued to spout obscenities, twisting Mia's hair in her fists, until she suddenly screamed loudly and Mia felt her juice gushing into her mouth. She climbed from the bonnet and Mia slowly lifted her head, the breath catching in her throat as she saw the reflection of all the men behind her. It seemed that they all wanted to enjoy her again and Mia had no defence against them. She stared at the reflection as the first of them moved in on her cunt. He slid his cock into her pussy and then pulled free to slam it into her arse. She cried out, flattening herself against the bonnet as she was violently mounted. Kent had wanted to fuck her into unconsciousness and although he had failed once, he was the one fucking her, an hour later when she finally succumbed to the abuse of her arse and pussy that had continued without pause. The darkness that surrounded her rode on the back of an unbelievable climax and was as great a release.

When she came to, she was alone and the first rays of sun were glinting off her naked body. She moved, as if in a dream, and dressed in the clothes that they had left her. She searched the surrounding area but couldn't find her underwear or t-shirt. She walked slowly down the road. She wanted to be grateful that she had survived the night. They had beaten and abused her but she had remained intact – they hadn't broken her. She was still Mia. Mia. Mia. Mia. She said it over and over again. Perhaps trying to convince herself that she was the same person who they had dragged up here to abuse and enjoy. But she wasn't, was she? She wasn't the same person. In the same way that she couldn't deny that they had changed her, she couldn't ignore the fact the niggling feeling that they hadn't finished with her. Mia wanted to cry but refused herself the luxury. Things had only just started – if she cried now then she would never survive whatever came next.

Chapter 2: Out of the Frying Pan …

Three months later

Mia gritted her teeth against the heat of pain burning her breasts. Her nipples had been cruelly clamped and tied with string that had then been tied to the steering wheel behind her. Her squashed nipples and normally perfect breasts were stretched to either side, distorted and painful. Her discomfort was made all the worse by two things – she had been ordered to keep her hands on her head and Kent was fucking her mercilessly. His fingers dug into her naked hips, lifting her up off his cock and then dropping her down again as he thrust upwards. He lifted her again, higher than before, making her cry out as her breasts were stretched. He laughed at her pain, filling her face with the stink of his breath – alcohol and fags. A few more thrusts and he leant forward to untie the string that secured her nipples. Sighing with relief, she allowed him to push her out of the car. He used her hair to drag her to her feet and forced her onto the bonnet of the police car, pushing her knees up with his rough hands. He spread her thighs as far as he could and then, still holding her knees, he thrust into her. She cried out at his cruel invasion and struggled uselessly, stopping when he grabbed the string hanging from her nipples. He twisted the string in his hands and then grabbed her behind the knees again, laughing as she tried to lift herself to ease the painful stretching of her nipples. He started to fuck her again, pushing himself deep and holding himself there for a moment before slowly withdrawing. His cock had a horribly familiar feel and she knew that he was close to coming but she could see that he was prolonging the moment, enjoying the build up. Suddenly he sped up his thrusts and as he hammered into her she groaned at her own response. He was fucking her so harshly, so deeply, that there was no way that she could not succumb. Groaning and sobbing at her own worthlessness, her pussy throbbed around his cock as she climaxed. She was aware that he didn't notice when she came – he never did and for that she was thankful. He pushed himself in deeply and held himself there as his cock twitched and then shot come inside her. He groaned his release before pulling back and leaving her to slide off the car. She had barely hit the ground before Jameson moved over to her. He clicked his fingers and she lifted her face to him, presenting her mouth to his hard cock. She waited to see what he wanted and when he started to thrust into her throat, she tried to relax and allowed him to fuck her mouth like a wet pussy. She heard a lighter strike beside her and then the smell of cigarette smoke drifted over her as Kent leant against the car beside her.

'Harper was asking after you today,' Kent announced. The sound of the WPC's name made a cold shiver run down Mia's spine. The female officer could be as spiteful as Kent was vicious – the only saving grace was that she allowed Mia to be distracted by Kelly. 'She's got a little job for you.' Mia almost choked on the cock that was thrusting into her throat at the thought of what could be planned for her. Jameson laughed and stopped his fucking, slapping the side of her head when she didn't start working on him immediately. She started to slide her mouth along his cock, flicking her tongue over his smooth helmet. Jameson was always cleaner than Kent and she was grateful that it was the younger copper who preferred the attentions of her mouth.

In the three months that had followed that first night of abuse, Kent came to find her at least twice a week to have some fun. PC Jameson was often with him and sometimes she would be taken somewhere to be enjoyed by others – such as WPC Harper. She had told no one about it, not just because he had threatened her with worse if she ever told anyone, but because she didn't want anyone to know. How could she explain the way that they left her feeling? Who could possibly understand? Mia had only one hope – she had to get away. She was saving every penny that she could get her hands on but her savings were growing desperately slowly. She had even considered turning tricks to raise some cash but, despite everything that Kent had done to her, she just couldn't bring herself to do it. She felt Jameson's come sliding down her throat and wondered if turning tricks could be as bad if it meant she could get away from them.

'So, this job ...' Kent continued as Jameson pulled free of her mouth and tucked himself away, '... she wants you to get some important evidence for her.'

Mia wiped her mouth with the back of her hand and looked up at him.

'She's after a little shit called Gary Marshall,' Kent announced, 'and you're going to get the evidence she needs to sort him out.'

'You're not serious.'

He moved in front of her and grabbed her chin, pulling her face up, 'Do I look like I'm fucking joking? I tell you to fuck me, you fuck me ... I tell you to take me up your arse, you fucking get it up the arse ...' he let go of her face and slapped her cheek, '... and if I tell you to get some evidence for a friend, guess what you're fucking going to do!'

Mia rubbed her face, her eyes stinging with tears.

'Besides, it'll be easy,' Kent continued, 'all you have to do is find a blue file with a picture of a camera on it.'

'What?' Mia laughed, she couldn't help it, it sounded so ridiculous. Kent glared at her and she quickly added, 'How am I going to get it?'

Kent smiled nastily, her earlier comment forgotten, 'You're going to go to his club and get yourself into his office, the evidence should be there.'

'What if it isn't there?'

'Then she says it'll be at his home.'

'And how do I get into either his office or home?' Mia asked.

'All you have to do is make an impression, do it right and he'll invite you there.'

She stared at him, hating his smugness, his smell, everything about him. 'And how, exactly, am I supposed to make an impression?'

His smile grew as he slowly, deliberately, slipped his belt from his trousers. She tried to stand, to get away but Jameson grabbed her arm and threw her across the bonnet. He grabbed her wrists and pulled her round until she was lying across the car, her feet kicking uselessly.

'Keep still or this will hurt more.' Kent told her. She doubted whether her movements would actually affect the feel of the belt striking her breasts but she knew that if she didn't do as she was told, there would be more blows. She gritted her teeth as she stared up at him, waiting for the first blow on her naked flesh. Strange how, while they had been fucking her she had barely noticed that she was naked. But now that he intended to whip her, she suddenly felt horribly exposed and vulnerable. Her nipples hardened at that thought and a quiver of anticipation ran through her. She felt her pussy warming at the thought of what was to come and her last thought as the belt descended was, 'I have to get away from here!'

The belt landed with a loud snap followed by a piercing, pitiful cry. He hit her again, the strength of the blow banished any feelings of arousal as she sobbed for him to stop. He didn't just want to hurt her, he wanted to mark her. The leather strap sliced her breasts again and again, the harsh edge raising livid welts across her naturally tanned skin – welts that would bruise within the hour and would remain for several days. He delivered a particularly harsh blow to her nipples, dragging one of the clamps from her swollen bud and making her scream as it grazed the sensitive skin. She kicked her legs in anguish, knowing that Kent would now try to remove the other clamp in the same way. She kicked and twisted, making Jameson swear as he tried to hold onto her. He stopped her escaping but she twisted in his grip and managed to roll over. She pulled her knees up beneath her, hoping to get her feet under her so that she could jump from the car. The belt landed squarely across her buttocks, bowing her back and flattening her against the smooth bonnet. She screamed and struggled again but Jameson grabbed her arms near her shoulders and there was nothing she could do. The belt landed again and again across her quivering buttocks, drawing identical welts to those on her breasts that were now squashed painfully beneath her. Kent kept delivering the blows to her buttocks until she screamed that she could take no more and begged him to stop. Nodding to himself, he delivered another three blows before calmly putting his belt back on. Jameson let her go and she slipped from the car, sobbing as she curled into a ball, her arms crossed over her aching breasts.

She half looked up as her clothes were dropped in an untidy pile in front of her. Placed on the top was a scrap of paper with an address scribbled on it.

'Dress sexy tomorrow night when you go to see him,' Kent told her as Jameson climbed into the car and started the engine, 'And make sure he can see what I did ... he'll like that.'

The car pulled away, leaving Mia to sob pitifully as she slowly dressed. She didn't know what was worse, the burning at her breasts and buttocks or the burning at her pussy. Once dressed, she wiped her tears away and straightened. She pulled her scuffed leather jacket around her and then slowly headed out of the deserted car park and back towards the lights of the main street.

*

She was wearing her battered leather jacket when she entered the club but was ordered by a heavy-set bouncer to leave it with the cloakroom attendant. Mia knew better than to argue and slipped the jacket off her shoulders, revealing the clothes that she had borrowed from a friend. If the female attendant noticed the welts that were clearly evident due to the very low cut of the dress, she didn't react. She just took Mia's jacket and hung it up. Trying not to tug at the hem of the, incredibly short, dress Mia approached the main door of the club.

She had asked her friends about the Sun and Moon Gentleman's Club and had been surprised by their response. All of the working girls knew the club and they all knew to stay away but only one of them told her why. It had hardly been a revelation, after what Kent had done to her, but it was still a surprise to open the door and see it all with her own eyes. Her friend, Keeley, had taken her aside to tell her that none of the girls went there ever since a friend had gone in as an escort and had not been seen again. Keeley had told her that it was an S and M club, as the name suggested but Mia wasn't prepared for the sights that were on full display. To her left, as she entered the club, a Master was leading two slaves by means of a collar and lead around their necks. One male, one female – their mouths stuffed with bright red ball gags, their eyes wide with arousal. To her right, a female slave pleasured her Master with her mouth while she played with her exposed pussy lips. All around her were sights of Masters and their slaves and the more she looked, the more she realised that the slaves were enjoying themselves as much as their Masters.

She approached the bar, forcing a smile to her lips when any Masters looked her way. She had expected to feel uncomfortable in the borrowed knee high leather boots. The three inch heels were three inches higher than she normally wore and it had been difficult to walk at first. But as soon as she entered the club and the atmosphere of sex and arousal wrapped itself around her, she suddenly felt more comfortable than she ever had before. It was natural to wear the revealing dress and the high, tight boots that made her legs so shapely. The approving looks of the men were a boost and she could feel her pussy throbbing as she leant forward to rest her arms on the bar. The barman came to her immediately, ignoring the other customers who had reached the bar before her.

'Wine,' she told him. Her voice sounded different, almost sultry and she liked it.

'Red or white?'

'You choose.'

He smiled and poured her a glass of red wine which he placed on the bar. He clearly wanted to stay and talk to her but the other customers demanded his attention and, with a sigh, he wandered off. She sipped the wine and almost immediately felt the effects coursing through her adrenalin filled veins. She hadn't felt this good in a long time – perhaps had never felt this good. She could almost believe that there was nothing she couldn't do, nothing she couldn't face. Any thoughts of Sergeant Kent and the reason he had sent her here were temporarily forgotten as she savoured the moment, the feeling of just being ... right. She leant further over the bar, knowing that the skirt had ridden up to reveal the welts that smothered her buttocks. It was an invitation and one that was quickly accepted. She squirmed exaggeratedly as a hand slid over her bruised buttocks, gently stroking her skin. She wondered why she wasn't annoyed by the unknown man's attention but she wasn't, like so many other things, it was right.

'Looks like someone enjoyed you recently,' he said softly into her ear.

She leant her head back against his shoulder, her breath stirring the fine hairs on his cheek as she said, 'We both did.'

His stroking fingers lifted her skirt so that he could look at the welts more closely. 'It must have hurt.'

'It did ...' Mia breathed, circling the stem of her glass between her fingers as she tried to think of something to say next. Thoughts of Sergeant Kent and what he had done to her dampened her mood and made her remember why she was here. She forced herself to smile at the man, '... and I loved it.'

Had she not been so engrossed by the man stroking her buttocks, she might have noticed a handsome man further down the bar turn to look at her with sudden interest.

The man's hand pressed against the welts on her sensitive buttocks, making her gasp and his smile was lust-filled, 'D'ya fancy showing us some more?'

'Us?'

He turned to glance over his shoulder where a group of men, gathered around a table, was watching them expectantly.

She had no idea what they expected from her but she knew what Kent expected ... make an impression ... taking a deep breath she smiled at him again, 'What do you want, honey?'

'Let's start with seeing these wonderfully decorated buttocks more clearly.'

'If you like those,' Mia smiled, 'then you'll love these.' She turned so that he could see the curve of her breasts and the identical welts that lined them. Almost instantly she felt his hardness pushing against her thigh.

'Shall we?' he invited and took her arm, spinning her off the bar stool and slipping his arm around her shoulders, all in one swift movement.

His companions were practically jumping up and down as they approached and the man waved his hand, laughing, 'Easy now, boys, give the girl a chance ... she's new here.'

'Shall we break her in gently then, Paul?'

The man who had brought Mia gave a quick nod, 'Oh yeah, we'll treat this one nicely tonight – she's special.'

Mia felt her pussy warm at his words and as she looked at each of the men in turn she saw the sentiment reflected in their eyes. It was intoxicating. With the help of Paul, she stood on the table as the men quickly gathered around to get a better look. Their hands ran up her thighs and over her buttocks, stroked her waist and reached up further to stroke her breasts. Mia was below average height, which enabled the men to get good handfuls of her bruised breasts. The feel of eight pairs of hands roving over her body was incredible and her thong quickly began to feel wet and uncomfortable. She gently pushed the hands away and the men quickly moved back, giving her room. She slipped her hands beneath her skirt and hooked her thumbs into the waistband, slowly pulling the thong down her legs. A couple of her friends had clients who liked them to dance and they would often try out new routines in front of Mia to see what she thought. The routines had always aroused her and she was surprised to discover how much she had learnt. Her body moved in the way that she had seen, her hips twisting and her hands moving in time to music that only she could hear. She watched the men closely, their mouths were open and their eyes wide, not really believing their luck and perhaps wondering how far she would go. She looked over their heads and saw other men enjoying women … submissives … and realised just how far they were hoping she would go. She slipped her arms out of the dress and folded it down to her waist, revealing her lined breasts. The men groaned in unison, several of them slowly sliding their zips down and pulling their rapidly hardening cocks free. She cupped her breasts in her hands, moulding the flesh gently before digging her nails into the skin. She moved her hands to grip her nipples, turning slowly to make sure they could all see as she pinched and stretched her sensitive buds. After several turns she lowered her hands so that she could push her dress down, bending at the waist to make sure they all saw her lined buttocks. The groans that had previously accompanied the sight of her wounded flesh turned now into shouts and whistles. A sting of fear lanced through Mia's gut as she saw the hungry, animalistic looks in the eyes of the men that surrounded her. That fear gnawed all the more when she realised that she had gone past the point of no return and there was no way that she would be getting away from these men until they were satisfied. But even as the fear gnawed at her gut, her pussy warmed at the thought that she was, essentially, their prisoner ... their slave. Trembling hands cast her dress from her and it disappeared somewhere amongst the crowd. Crowd? She was suddenly shocked to realise that many others had joined the initial eight men and she was now the sole entertainment in the club. Even those who had no desire to take part were watching her intently, perhaps feeding on the lust that her naked, bruised body was generating. She stood, wearing nothing but her high boots, and studied the crowd who were watching her expectantly. She had no idea what to do next and her fear threatened to consume her.

Bang.

The sound made her jump and she looked down to see that one of the men had slammed a beer bottle down onto the table between her legs. She looked for and found Paul who was grinning at her. He nodded encouragement and then she knew that there was only one thing she could do ... only one thing that she wanted to do. She slowly bent her knees, looking down for the bottle and adjusting her position slightly. The crowd held its collective breath and watched, stunned, as she lowered her pussy onto and then over the neck of the bottle. She gasped and closed her eyes as the cold glass slid into her hot cunt. She took the neck all the way and managed to close her pussy over perhaps half an inch of the thicker length, holding herself there while the crowd erupted in applause. Two of the men stepped forward and stood in front of her while they slid their fists along their shafts. Mia stayed where she was, her thighs trembling with the effort of keeping herself in the squatting position. She rested her hands on her knees and stared at each of the men in turn. Within seconds of each other they suddenly groaned and shot their come over her spread pussy lips. Mia gasped as their hot spunk struck her sensitive flesh. The two men were slapped on the back and then led away before another two took their place. Mia couldn't hold herself in that position and slowly lifted up to ease the throbbing in her thighs. The movement caused pleasant friction against her pussy lips and she couldn't stop herself from sliding down the bottle neck again. She started to fuck herself over the bottle, reaching her hand down to stroke her clitoris and rub the thick juice into her skin. A few moments later she felt hot streams of come splashing the back of her hand and she gasped her delight. Two more men replaced those spent as Mia raised her hand to her lips and licked it clean. Her thighs were aching terribly and she lifted herself off the bottle before lowering herself to her knees and glancing over her shoulder. It was Paul's eyes that met hers and he nodded as he moved towards her. He lifted the juice covered bottle and she expected it to slide once more into her pussy but instead he slowly screwed it into her arse. Mia cried out as her tight arse was filled and suddenly her open mouth was filled with come as one of the men climaxed. She tipped her head back to swallow his juice and felt hot splashes against her neck and breasts. A moment later she felt Paul's fingers sliding into her cunt and suddenly, unbelievably, she was coming. She screamed her climax, tossing her head as her body beaded with sweat. She cried out again as the bottle was pulled from her arse and then a thick cock was sliding into her cunt. Fingers found her clitoris and she screamed in desire just as a cock pushed between her lips. Invaded at both ends, without her consent being sought, it was too much and she came again moments later. The man fucking her cunt buried himself deeply in her, riding the quivers of her orgasm. Both men came quickly and were promptly replaced. By the time five men had enjoyed her cunt, her pussy was burning but still eager for more pleasure. Lost in a delirium of arousal and lust, she cried out as she was flipped onto her back. A tongue stroked lovingly along her pussy lips and she lifted her head to stare at the female eyes that looked up at her from between her spread thighs. Her hips bucked and she came in the unknown woman's mouth. Suddenly she was swamped by women and from the depths of her arousal she heard male voices commanding them and urging them on – ordering them to pleasure her. Female hands and mouths touched her everywhere, in ways that a man could not and she screamed over and over, begging them to stop but wanting the unbearable pleasure to go on. She became swamped by it all and fell into a faint, mumbling nonsensically as they continued to enjoy her body.

She had no idea how much time had passed. She was vaguely aware of people talking and of gentle hands moving her but she could not respond or react. The pleasure had been too much for her to handle. After everything that Kent and his colleagues had done to her, to be on the receiving end of such power and pleasure had robbed her of her senses.

*

She awoke with a start, her eyes snapping open and her hands gripping for anything that she could hold on to. Her hand brushed material and she managed to focus enough to realise that she was lying on a beautifully upholstered sofa. She heard the clink of ice against a glass and turned her head towards the sound. The man that she saw stole her breath. Perhaps it was the residue of the lust that had consumed her but he was so handsome he was beautiful. His blue eyes were ice, his lips thin and harsh, everything about him screamed cruelly and Mia had never seen a man that had aroused her as much. He smiled and she felt her heart hammer against her ribs.

'How are you feeling?'

She managed to pull herself into a sitting position and was grateful to realise that someone had put her dress back on. As she moved she realised that her panties were missing and she squeezed her thighs together. She remembered, vaguely, how many men had used her pussy and wondered why she wasn't as sticky or as dirty as she should have been – but then she remembered the female submissives who had worked so diligently. She felt a flush rise up her neck and cheeks at the memory of what she had done. She looked again at the handsome man and remembered that he had asked her a question. She cleared her throat and licked her lips, 'Yes, I'm … fine, thank you.'

'Would you like a drink?'

'Water … please.'

Laughing, he gave her a glass, 'There's water in this.'

She took the glass and smelt the strong scotch. Her hands were trembling as she lifted the glass to her lips and gulped it down in one go. Her hands trembled less as she gave the glass back. He took it, smiling.

'What?' she asked.

'Nothing,' he laughed, 'I'm just impressed, not many women can toss back thirty year old scotch like that.'

'I had a mis-spent youth,' she replied and stared around the room. 'Where am I?'

'My office.'

She looked up at him, 'Who are you?'

'Gary Marshall, I own this place.'

Sergeant Kent's face swam before her vision – it was a sobering effect. Despite the pleasure that she had, very much, enjoyed – thoughts of what Kent would do to her if she didn't succeed in her task quickly came to the fore. Okay, so she had made an impression and had got herself into his office – what next?

'You put on a good show tonight – perhaps I should hire you.'

Mia smiled at him, 'No thanks – I only do it for fun.'

He moved to sit beside her, his hand moving to his fly to unzip his trousers. She felt his fingers on her shoulder as he gently pushed her off the sofa, 'Come and have fun then.'

She saw no alternative but to do as he wanted. His cock was huge and she struggled to get her sore mouth around its girth and only managed to slide a few inches down is length. Thankfully that seemed enough for him and he relaxed as she licked and sucked his twitching cock. After a few minutes her lifted her up and spun her round. She sat on his lap, his cock rubbing against her clitoris and igniting her passions once more. His hand on her back pushed her forward until her hands were resting on the floor between their legs. She gasped as his fingers ran over each of the welts in turn.

'I was sitting at the bar when you talked to that guy about these,' he announced as he slowly slipped two fingers into her cunt and his thumb into her arse. She groaned and pushed back against him. 'I heard what you said and how you said it ... you didn't get these willingly and you didn't enjoy getting these as much as you claimed ...' his fingers continued to stroke in and out of her, '... but you did enjoy it.' She gasped suddenly, her pussy gripping his fingers as she climaxed. He smeared her juice over his cock and then pulled her back onto him, sliding his thickness into her arse. She cried out and struggled, lifting herself into a sitting position. His cock was too big for her and she gasped and sobbed in pain. His arm encircled her neck, pulling her back against his broad chest and holding her while he fucked her bruised anus. Tears coursed down her cheeks and he licked them from her skin, tasting her pain as he heard and felt it. 'Cry all you like, my little whore, but we both know that you're going to come any minute.' His other hand found her breast and he twisted the nipple, making her buck against him.

'Oh God ... please stop!' she cried in pain as he drove into her, his fingers twisting her nipple again, 'Please ...

please ... oh God!' Her climax came so unexpectedly that she was unprepared and her scream was shattering. Amidst the depths of her pleasure and pain she felt his come pumping into her. He groaned his pleasure into her neck as his cock twitched. When he was done he slowly lifted her off and left her, gasping on the floor. He walked into an adjoining room and a moment later she heard a shower running. Despair at what had happened suddenly consumed her and her head fell onto the sofa as she sobbed loudly.

No! She told herself, she had to do what Kent had instructed – she could deal with everything else later. Climbing to her feet, her knees shaking, she moved as fast as she could towards the desk. What was it Kent had told her to find? A file. She remembered that but what file? She searched through a pile on the corner of the desk, hoping to jog her memory. A blue file appeared under her searching fingers and she snatched it from the pile. Yes! A blue file with a picture of a ... a ... camera. She searched the front, the back, even the inside but there was no sign of a camera. Trying not to sob with desperation, she slipped the folder back where she had found it and moved for the drawers. There were three drawers in the desk, all unlocked and none of them contained the file. She moved round the desk, searching the rest of the room. The only other furniture was the sofa that they had just fucked on. The file wasn't there and that could only mean one thing. Her heart hammered against her chest as she tried to work out what to do.

She heard the shower stop and moved quickly to the desk, sitting on the edge and spreading her legs invitingly.

'You still here?' Marshall queried as he stepped back into his office, a towel around his waist.

'I was hoping we could have some more fun.'

He was momentarily surprised and then shrugged before using another towel to dry his hair. 'I have things to attend to.'

'You gotta get home … to her?' she waved at the photo on the desk that she had noticed previously, 'She's pretty.'

'You think so?' Marshall's eyes glinted with interest.

'Does she ever come here?'

The interest grew brighter in his eyes and was quickly turning to arousal, 'No, she doesn't play in public.'

'But she does play.'

'Yes, she does,' he replied thoughtfully and then said, 'It's our anniversary tomorrow.'

'Were you thinking of getting her flowers?' Mia asked as she slipped off the desk and walked slowly towards him, 'Because you can call me Rose, if you want.'

An hour later and with a second lot of Marshall's come drying on her inner thighs, she collected her coat and walked wearily from the club. She was just walking past an alley that ran up the side of the building when hands grabbed her and dragged her into the darkness. She was thrust harshly against the wall and her skirt lifted. She would have cried out if she hadn't recognised his smell and the sound of his breathing but she did cry out as he drove into her aching pussy. He crushed her against the wall as he fucked her, hissing in her ear, 'You look a little empty handed.'

'The file wasn't there,' she replied and then cried out as he drove angrily into her, 'but I'm going to his house tomorrow night!'

'Make sure you get it,' Kent told her, 'or I'll have you banged up for wasting police time … and you know how long I've been dreaming of getting you into one of our cells for a couple of nights.'

She groaned as he pumped his semen into her before pulling put and slapping her bare arse as he walked away.

*

The next night she was sitting quietly in Marshall's car as they approached a large house, shrouded in the suburbs of London. Marshall spun the wheel and manoeuvred the car into the driveway. His finger pressed a switch on the dashboard and the garage door ahead of them slowly opened. There was something ominous about the way that the garage loomed ahead of them ... waiting for them to drive in. Mia felt her shoulders tense but forced herself to relax. She knew that if Marshall picked up on more than just nervous anticipation, there was a chance that he would guess that something wasn't right. They drove into the garage and the door slid closed behind them.

Marshall climbed from the car without saying anything and she followed him, shutting the passenger door behind her. He came to her side, his hands on her shoulders, his breath hot on her neck. She leant against him for a moment, enjoying the broad strength of his chest. She jumped as something slipped over her eyes but forced herself to remain calm as the blindfold was tied around her head. She felt rough rope binding her wrists and her body quivered with the desire to escape and the desire to stay – it was a potent mix that settled in her groin.

He led her through the house, moving with the easy grace of someone who could both see and knew their way. Mia stumbled after him and he seemed to enjoy her blindness. Seconds seemed to take hours and every step was like a mile. She was breathing heavily by the time she heard a door opening and then she sensed that she was moving into a room. The door closed and Marshall walked her forward a few more steps and then pushed her to her knees. She was wearing the same dress that she had been wearing the night before – quickly washed and dried during the nervous hours that she had counted down to seeing him again at the club. She felt his hands at her breasts and she gasped as he pushed the material down, sliding it beneath her naked breasts and exposing her upper half. She bit her lower lip nervously, her hands clenching and unclenching behind her.

'Happy anniversary, darling,' she heard him say and then the unmistakeable sound of a whip striking his palm echoed around her. She tensed, awaiting the blow that would surely flatten her breasts. Turning her head slightly to the side, she held her breath. The sound of the whip striking flesh came a moment later and Mia gasped in surprise when her breasts remained untouched. Another blow and she listened carefully to the aftermath and the unmistakeable sound of a muffled gasp of pain … and desire. Further blows were followed by female gasps and groans. With every blow Mia felt her own arousal growing as strongly as if she were on the receiving end. She was so lost in her growing lust that she gasped in surprise when the blindfold was suddenly yanked from her eyes. She blinked within the harsh light and forced her eyes to adjust. Another gasp escaped her lips as she stared up at Marshall. He was standing over her, naked and aroused. His toned body was as handsome as she had imagined and his cock even larger than she remembered. She had the sudden desire to take that cock in her mouth and show him what she could do … what she had learnt to do to ensure that Sergeant Kent was done with her as quickly as possible. She forced thoughts of the policeman and the real reason she was here aside and let her arousal shine in her eyes.

Using the end of the crop, Marshall turned her head to the right and her eyes widened at the sight that greeted her. An attractive blonde woman was tied to an upright x-shaped frame. She was blindfolded and gagged, her chest heaving as she fought to regain her breath. Her breasts and the front of her thighs were lined with red where the crop had struck. He gave a nod in his wife's direction and Mia slowly crawled over until she was positioned between her widely spread legs. She stared at the swollen pussy before her and breathed heavily as her own passions rose in response to the arousal that she could see before her.

She leant forward, her tongue flicking between the labia lips and seeking out the hardened clitoris. The woman jumped, her groan muffled as her cries had been and tiny quivers ran down her thighs. The woman's reaction had an instant effect on Mia and she immediately started to feast on the pussy before her. The groans grew louder and once he had removed the gag, they became tiny cries. Mia worked even harder at her pussy, determined to make her scream. She had only ever pleasured one woman before – Harper's slave, Kelly – but that had always been under orders and she rarely enjoyed it. But this, this was so different and she could feel herself getting aroused at the same time. She knew that Marshall was watching her and that, as much as anything, caused the aching wetness between her own legs. She imagined how aroused he must be by now. He had beaten his wife and was now watching another woman licking her out. She squeezed her thighs together and worked even harder, suddenly eager for Marshall to share his arousal with her. She lifted her hands and when he didn't stop her, she slipped three fingers into the gaping cunt and smeared the woman's juice around her anus before sliding her thumb in. She couldn't help but wonder if Marshall recognised that she was doing the same to his wife as he had done to her the night before – but with one main difference. Her tongue lashed the woman's clitoris and a high pitched scream suddenly echoed around them as juice gushed over Mia's hand. She lapped at the thick, musky cunt juice and had never tasted anything so wonderful.

Mia sensed Marshall standing next to her and turned, instinctively opening her mouth to take the cock that waited for her. She swallowed him to his root, making him gasp in surprise that she had taken his entire length. She gagged but managed to hold him for a few more moments before slowly, deliberately sliding her mouth back along his shaft. She heard the woman groan and she looked sideways, her eyebrows flicking up when she realised that Marshall had also removed her blindfold. His wife had lifted her head so that she could watch what Mia was doing. Keeping their eyes locked, Mia swallowed his cock once more and his wife groaned loudly, shuddering with rapidly growing passion. He let her suck him for several minutes before he suddenly pulled free and hauled her to her feet. She gasped as she was thrown against his wife. Mia stared up into the woman's eyes as he lifted her skirt and pulled her panties down to her knees. Mia closed her eyes and waited for the first touch of his thick cock against her pussy lips.

Smack!

Mia cried out as the paddle flattened her bruised buttocks, the pain made all the worse because she had expected pleasure.

Smack! Smack! Smack!

The blows came rhythmically. The paddle flattening her buttocks and pausing for a moment before lifting, pausing and then falling again.

Smack! Smack!

Mia knew that the woman was watching her and enjoying the sight and sound of her pain as much as Mia had enjoyed hers. She wondered if she would enjoy watching her husband fucking her as much – because Mia had no doubt that that was what he had planned next.

Smack! Smack! Smack! Smack!

The sound of the paddle hitting the floor was quickly followed by a loud cry of passion from Mia as Marshall stepped forward to sink his cock between her pussy lips. Even as aroused as she was, his girth still stretched her and she savoured the feeling of being completely filled, closing her eyes and groaning loudly. She looked at the woman as she heard her gasp and felt a quiver run down her spine at the sight of her pleasure-filled face. The sight was too much for her and she came instantly, tossing her head as her orgasm racked her body. Marshall continued to fuck her, drawing her pleasure out like a string. He suddenly pushed into her as deeply as he could, pushing against her wounded buttocks and making her cry out. She felt his thickness quiver and then hot spunk filled her pussy, making her come again.

Marshall made Mia move back while he freed his wife from the frame and then adjusted the frame so that it was horizontal. He didn't speak but just nodded and Mia knew what he wanted. She lay on the frame, spreading her legs and arms and quivering as the leather straps fastened around her ankles, wrists, thighs and upper arms. She had never been in a frame and her passions rose quickly, her nipples swelling to hard buds to welcome the clamps that Marshall moved towards them. The clamps bit painfully into the sensitive flesh, the weights that he hung from them made her grit her teeth and his wife's tongue on her breasts made her groan as he took pictures. She quivered in her bonds, her pussy leaking his semen onto the floor. Ten lashes across the breasts was the punishment and she loved every single one – screaming her pain and pleasure in equal measure. Then suddenly his wife's mouth was at her pussy and she was tonguing her better than anyone ever had. Mia's head swam with pleasure and she lifted her head to watch, groaning when she saw Marshall lifting a harsh crop. It landed with a snap across his wife's shoulder blades and for a moment the glorious mouth was gone from her pussy. She groaned her disappointment and received a lash across her thighs for the indiscretion. Another blow to the woman's shoulder blades and her tongue quickly returned to Mia's pussy. She came loudly and with a spray of juice that splattered the floor and brought more punishment down on her tenderised breasts. Then Marshall's wife rested her hands against Mia's leg and presented her arse to her husband. He lifted the crop and seared her flesh with several blows before moving in to spread her juice around her anus and then quickly forced himself into her tighter passage. Mia knew all too well how painful and how good his huge cock felt in that tighter entrance and she longed to feel it again herself. She watched, jealousy making her passions rise again, as Marshall brutally fucked his wife's arse. They came together, gasping their passions and sinking to their knees in a shattering embrace.

'I have to go to the toilet.' Mia said softly, several minutes later as Marshall released her from the frame.

He helped her to stand and waved towards the door, 'Up the stairs, second on the right.'

'Thank you.' She headed for the door, her legs quivering and barely able to support her. She climbed the stairs wearily and by the time she reached the top she had forgotten what he said. She turned to the first door on the right and pushed it open – freezing when she saw what was beyond. The study was tastefully decorated and clearly the domain of a man. She didn't think about what she was doing, she just entered the room and approached the desk. Her heart hammered against her chest when she saw the blue file on the side of the desk. Her shaking hand reached out for it and she flipped it over, staring at the picture of a camera. This was the file that Harper wanted, the one that Kent had ordered her to get. She looked quickly over her shoulder, listening for any sound on the stairs – all was quiet but they would come looking for her soon and there was no way that she could sneak that file out of the house. She quickly left the study and went into the bathroom. After peeing she stared at herself in the mirror and wondered who was looking back.

*

It was two o' clock in the morning and, although exhausted, Mia knew that she had to try and think straight. Kent would be looking for her in the morning and he knew the places where she stayed. She couldn't go anywhere – she just hoped that he wouldn't be too hard on the girls if he found her absent. She walked aimlessly, trying to decide what to do. As she turned into a residential road she looked around, hope making her heart flutter when she realised that she recognised a house further down the street. She hurried towards it. It was dark, naturally, but she had to get in. She hammered on the door with her fist and called through the letter box when she heard movement within.

'Mia?'

She smiled with relief at the female voice that hissed back at her, 'Yeah, it's me.'

The door opened and a pretty dark-haired girl, stared out at her. She had obviously dressed in a hurry and was very much alert. 'For fuck's sake,' she gasped and moved aside so that Mia could come in, 'what are you doing?'

'I'm calling in a favour.' Mia replied. Six months ago she had stood as an alibi for Alex when Kent had been trying to pin several burglaries on her. The one piece of evidence that Kent had was a witness who placed Alex at one of the scenes of crime. That witness happened to be a shit of an ex-boyfriend who was very much aware of how Alex made her living. Mia knew that Alex had committed the other burglaries but not that particular one, since they had been having a drink at the time. She had given the alibi, Alex had been released without charge and her ex-boyfriend had a friendly visit from Kent. Since the ex-boyfriend was the one who had encouraged Alex to steal from houses in order to fund his drug habit, neither of them had felt particularly guilty about what happened. But Alex owed Mia a favour and now she was calling it in. Originally Mia had only meant to stay with Alex until she could figure out what to do. But now that she remembered what Alex's particular talents were, she had a better idea.

*

Alex had used her charms on one of the bouncers at the club and found out where Marshall lived and now, at approaching ten in the evening, Mia and Alex were huddled in the shadow of some trees opposite, studying the house. There were lights on inside so they had no option but to wait. They had expected to have to wait until the Marshalls went to bed but Mia couldn't believe her luck when she saw the garage door sliding open and the car reversing out.

Ten minutes later and they were at the back of the house, Alex working at the lock. A few moments later and the door popped open. Grinning in the darkness, Alex slapped Mia on the shoulder, 'After you.'

Mia shook her head, 'No, we agreed, just me.'

'Come on,' Alex sighed, 'in for a penny, in for a –'

'No.' Mia snapped. The last thing she needed was Alex taking a look around the house. There was a chance that she might come across the photos that Marshall had taken the night before and that was more than Mia could handle. She was having enough trouble understanding what had happened without that. 'Look, I don't want you getting into trouble. You've done me a favour now ... piss off.'

'Right,' Alex growled and disappeared into the darkness.

Mia hated upsetting her friend but had no choice. Sighing, she went into the house.

Having not been in this part of the house, it took Mia some time to navigate her way to the stairs. On the way she passed a locked door which she guessed led into the playroom. Her pussy warmed as her gut twisted at the thought of what lay beyond that door. Forcing herself to walk past, she climbed the stairs as quickly as she could. The sooner she found the file, the sooner she could get it to Kent and put this all behind her. She would have to put up with Kent for a bit longer but recent events had made her more determined than ever to get away from him.

She went into the study, cursing that she didn't think to bring a flashlight. There was just enough light coming through the window for her to see the desk and that the file was not where it had been. She cursed again, moving to the desk and flicking the lamp on. She searched the top of the desk and then moved round to try the drawers. They were all locked. She had no choice. She used the paperknife to force open the top drawer and searched through the contents. Nothing. The second drawer held files but not the one she was looking for. Slamming the drawer shut she pulled the bottom one open and her heart leapt into her mouth when she saw the blue file that she was looking for. She yanked it from the draw. And froze. Beneath the file was a huge pile of money. She lifted the money from the darkness of the draw and stared at it. It was a bundle of fifty pound notes, at least three inches thick. She had no idea how much money was there but she knew, beyond a shadow of a doubt, that it was enough money to get her away from Kent. But not just Kent, it was enough money to get her away from everything that had happened these last few days. She could start again. Become someone new. Someone better. She dropped back on her haunches, slipping the file back into the draw and closing it.

Click!

The room was suddenly filled with light, blinding her. She threw an arm across her eyes to shield her vision and felt fingers closing around her wrist. She was hauled to her feet and, squinting, stared into Marshall's angry eyes. He took the money from her and dropped it onto the desk. 'Now then,' he said quietly, his voice vibrating with anger, 'what am I going to do with you?'

She stared at him, remembering all too well, the night before when he had whipped and fucked her as a present for his wife. His wife had also felt the whip and the pleasure of his cock and Mia had enjoyed herself as much. But now that she stared at him, his anger rolling off him in waves, she suddenly had a horrible inkling of what he would do if he used the whip with fury rather than desire. 'I'm sorry,' she said quickly, knowing how ineffectual it sounded, 'but you don't understand ... I need to get away ... I ... I'm in trouble.'

'You certainly are,' he responded and reached inside his jacket for his phone. He flipped it open, his thumb hovering over the '9'.

Mia thought of Kent. He was on duty tonight. Would he respond to the call? The thought of what Kent would do to her was more terrifying than anything Marshall could do. Fear sapped her strength and she fell to her knees. 'Oh God, please, don't call the police.'

'You're in trouble with the law then?'

'You could say that.'

He didn't seem interested in details and snapped the phone shut. 'You got family? Friends?'

Mia shook her head but then added, 'No family, a few ... friends ... I guess.' She thought about Alex who had helped her to break in and was grateful that she had told her to leave.

'Anyone who would miss you?'

'No.' Mia answered his question before she had really considered it and as the word hung in the air between them, she suddenly regretted her response.

He laughed at the fear in her eyes, 'It's not what you think. I'd like to make you an offer.'

'What offer?'

'The kind that you will agree to or I call the police right here and now and let them have you.'

'I need more details,' Mia replied, although anything that he offered had to be better than the alternative.

'A year, working for me.'

'Working?'

'Do you agree?'

'What would I be doing?'

'Do you agree?' he asked and then flicked his phone open when she didn't respond fast enough.

'Okay … okay,' she half cried, holding her hands up, 'I'll work for you.'

'For a year … twelve months is all I want from you and then you will be free to go. Agreed?'

Mia took a deep breath, 'Okay.'

He studied her for a moment before reaching into his pocket and retrieving a roll of money. He lifted a few notes and held them out. 'Go to the station tomorrow and buy a one way ticket to Glenhassen.'

'Where's that?'

'Scotland.'

'But … I thought I would be working for you.'

He smiled nastily, 'You will be … you'll be working very hard, trust me.'

She stared at him, wanting to tell him to forget it but what could she do? Go back to Kent empty handed? She swallowed and held her hand out for the money.

'Be at the station,' he told her, still holding the notes, 'or you'll regret it.' He let go and she stared at them, there wasn't enough there to get very far even if she had considered taking his money and running. As it was, the thought had never even entered her mind.

Chapter three: ... into the fire

She stared at the station name, Glenhassen. She looked around. Desolate was probably the best description of the filthy station. Sunk between grey houses and greyer shops. But beyond those buildings that seemed to hunker over her threateningly, she could see rugged moorland that called to her. She had lived in the city all her life but there was something incredibly appealing about that open space ... freedom. She closed her eyes and sighed. Freedom ... she could no more define what that meant to her than she could lift her arms and fly to that distant beauty.

Pulling her battered leather jacket tighter around her as the biting Scottish wind whipped at her hair and clothes, she walked towards the exit.

The battered minibus matched the desolate surroundings; the two men who stood beside it looked equally at home. They saw her approaching and flicked their cigarettes away. She stood in front of them and let them study her in silence. When neither of them spoke she took a deep breath, 'I'm Mia,' she announced.

The older of the two ... brothers? ... looked at her through narrowed eyes, 'And that's the last time that you'll say anything without being spoken to first.'

Mia could feel her anger rising but said nothing.

The man waited for a few more moments before he nodded at the bus, 'Get on.'

Mia walked past him and a pile of luggage at his feet. She climbed the steps, moving between the seats careful not to touch the filthy upholstery. As she moved as far back as she could, she felt eyes on her and for the first time she noticed the three other girls already on the bus. The oldest was no older than thirty, the youngest, perhaps Mia's age. The youngest looked terrified and her tear-filled eyes seemed to plead with Mia as she approached. Mia couldn't help but wonder what the young girl expected her to do and the scared-rabbit look annoyed her almost as much as the man had. Her anger must have shown in her eyes because the girl's lip quivered and she shrank back against the window.

Mia took her seat without looking at the two other girls. She stared out of the window, squinting for a glimpse of moorland between the buildings. The bus shifted and she looked up to see the two men climbing aboard. As they pulled away, Mia looked out at the pile of luggage that had been left behind and felt grateful that she had had nothing to bring anyway.

She was surprised when the houses started to thin out as they drove out of the town and into the country, the moorland that had seemed so distant drawing nearer. They reached the moors a few minutes later and she rested her forehead against the cold window, staring out and wondering if she had ever seen anything so beautiful. The scenery changed to woodland and Mia became lost in her thoughts for several minutes until the trees parted and they drove along a long gravel driveway. A few moments later and she was looking out of the window at a beautiful, old manor house. It had been added to at various intervals and had become a mismatch of buildings but somehow had managed to retain its charm. It was huge and as they drew nearer, Mia realised that it was set in a large area of land with cultivated fields on one side and dense woodland on the other. There were also a number of outbuildings of various sizes and, she guessed, various uses. The mini-bus was guided round the back of the house and parked beside two equally battered cars. The two men led them inside the building, neither of them looking back to check that they were being followed. Once inside they were led through a series of narrow corridors before being ordered to line up against the wall of a corridor that looked no different to any of the others that they had walked down. The older of the men walked off, leaving the younger to lean against the wall and light a cigarette.

Chapter four: Thomas

They seemed to be left standing in the corridor for ages and Mia counted three cigarettes smoked by the young man.

'Alright,' the man's voice was loud in the corridor, making them all jump. 'You are new here but you are expected to learn the rules quickly. You will become familiar with the rules and the structure of this house. You will be able to recognise the five House Masters on sight and will, always, afford them the proper respect. Never look a House Master in the eyes and only look any other man in the eyes if you are given permission to do so. Do not speak unless given permission to speak.' He stopped and looked at Mia, his eyes boring into hers as she stared back at him, 'As you have learnt, punishment for breaking these rules is given swiftly … this helps you to remember them. Turn around.'

It took her a moment to realise that he had given her an order. His lips twitched with anger and she turned quickly. She felt his hands at the waistband of her jeans, moving round to undo the belt and clasp. The material scratched her flesh as it was forced down to her knees. She flinched as his fingers traced the darkening bruises. She heard the swish of leather slicing the air before the strap connected with her tortured buttocks. She cried out, flattening herself against the wall. Another quickly followed but the third was held back as a new voice called, 'That's enough!'

'I'll decide when it's enough,' he responded angrily and the belt struck her again with the force of his anger, making her cry out.

'Give her to me,' the newcomer said calmly, 'unless you would care to explain to the Third why we are off schedule.'

'You've got fifty slave whores at your disposal, why the fuck do you want this newcomer?'

'I don't have to explain myself to you.'

Mia felt a hand on her arm and a hand tugging at her jeans and pants. When they had been pulled up, she held the jeans at her waist with shaking hands and glanced at her saviour. He was younger than the other men she had seen, no more than thirty, handsome and strong.

'Bring her to the dormitory when you're done with her,' the man who had beaten her ordered, anger still deepening his voice, 'and Thomas, don't have any fun yourself, you know the rules.'

The man glanced over his shoulder but said nothing as he led Mia away.

'Thank you,' Mia said once they were far enough away from the others.

Thomas paused and glanced at her, his eyebrows raised in puzzlement and then he laughed loudly, shaking his head as they neared a door at the end of the corridor. He pushed it open and Mia gasped as she found herself stepping into a brightly lit film studio. It was small but a film studio none the less. Three huge cameras mounted on moveable platforms were arranged in front of a large wall of white tiles. As Mia was led closer, she realised that it was the mock up of a shower room, complete with tiled floor and six shower heads. Thomas guided her towards two women who appraised her quickly before undressing her – working in silence. Neither commented at the fresh marks across her buttocks and once she was naked she squirmed under their appraisal. One of the women reached forward and Mia gasped as her nipples were tweaked into hardness. They led her to the shower set and left her with a heavyset man who looked as bored as she was nervous. He took her wrist in his huge hand and pulled her onto the set, forcing her over to the wall and pushing her hand above her head. Her breasts were crushed against the cold tile as her wrist was fixed to a link above her head. The other hand was forced up and she was secured tightly against the wall. She gasped as his foot pushed between hers and kicked her legs apart. Satisfied with her position, he moved to the side and turned the dial. Mia gasped loudly as freezing water jetted from the shower head above her, soaking her instantly. The water was like needles digging at her flesh and she could hardly catch her breath. She forced herself to relax and slowly became accustomed to the feel of the icy water on her skin. As her breath quietened, she became aware of someone behind her. She glanced over her shoulder. Thomas was there with another man, neither of them were looking at her and Mia studied the naked man who was nodding as Thomas spoke. Her eyes drifted down his firm torso before coming to rest on the thick, hard cock that pressed against his abdomen. Even as she stared at him, she heard Thomas saying, 'Just fuck her, nothing fancy, this is just a fill-in scene before the big stuff.'

'Okay,' the man responded as Thomas walked off.

A few moments later she heard Thomas shout something and then the man's hands gripped her shoulders as he moved in on her. He lowered his hips, pushing the head of his penis beneath her, searching for her labia and cunt. When his thick helmet found her opening, he suddenly drove upwards, lifting her feet from the floor and making her gasp. He pushed down on her shoulders, making sure that he filled her as much as he could. She gasped, his invasion made all the more painful by his thickness and she felt herself being stretched to the very limits, far beyond what she was used to. But as she had found herself getting used to the freezing water, so she found herself getting used to his invading cock. Her breasts rubbed against the freezing tile, the water cascaded between her legs and made her clitoris burn with the cold. His cock was hot inside her, a pleasurable accompaniment to the freezing water. She could feel her own pussy heating up as he fucked her, could feel her own warmth battling with the cold as blood filled her hardening clitoris.

'Right ... ease off a sec ... let's see some slow and deep, okay?'

The man's only response was to pull back, his cock almost slipping free. Mia squeezed her thighs together, desperate to hold onto him. His gasp of surprise was hot in her ear as he slowly moved back into her constricted vagina. She gasped with him, her clitoris humming with pleasure as she squeezed her thighs as tightly as she could. After a few moments she was ready to come but his slow movements were never going to be enough. She wanted to scream for him to fuck her, to pleasure her, but she knew better. Whenever she had felt like this with Kent or any of his friends, she had always been careful to disguise her pleasure and hold off until they climaxed themselves and were too busy to notice hers. She felt sure that he would fuck her harder soon, desperately hoping that these movements, although wonderfully pleasurable, would not be enough for him either.

'Okay ... change holes ... do her arse and then that will do.'

Mia wanted to scream with disappointment as his cock slipped from her cunt but then she suddenly realised what Thomas had said and her heart thumped against her ribs.

'Let's hear her with this one, eh?'

The man positioned his cock, his hands moving to her hips. He slammed forward, crushing her against the wall. The only lubrication was the water from the shower and her own juice and the sudden painful invasion of his cock arched her lower back and thrust her breasts forward, crushing her hardening nipples against the cold tile. Her head fell back, her lips pulled back from her gritted teeth and her arms quivering as she strained against the bonds that held her. Water cascaded over her face but she barely noticed as he slipped free and then drove into her again, harder this time, trying again to make her scream. When he failed he lifted his hands to her breasts, ready to scratch and pinch the flesh – but the director told him no and, instead, he raked his nails down her sides to grip her hips. He fucked her hard, using his grip on her flesh to pull her back onto him. At the director's hoarse command, he slipped his hand round to her front to search out her cunt. When he found her clitoris she quivered uncontrollably. He continued to fuck her, playing with her cunt the whole time. And then, slowly, unbelievably, she lifted her thigh to give him deeper access to her arse. The director waved for him to continue and he pinched her clitoris, finally making her scream as she climaxed over his hand.

Chapter five: Initiation

The first thing that Mia was aware of was the sound of sex. Male and female grunts and cries echoed all around her and she half expected to see a carpet of naked, thrusting bodies. She had been led from the studio, through the grounds and the back of the house until they reached the dormitory area. She had been pushed through the door, which had been slammed shut behind her, leaving her to try and adjust to the sudden gloom and the sound of sex. She stepped further into the dimly lit room, the flickering light making her squint in an attempt to adjust to the gloom. She stopped and stared ahead, the source of the noise and the flickering light becoming clear. At one time it would have probably been a barn but now the large open space had been given over to twenty or more television sets, dotted around the walls with a bank of five or six shining out from the middle of the room. On each of the TV screens, men and women were carrying out varied sexual activities. There was a palpable atmosphere in the room, an almost expectant muskiness that Mia found almost overwhelming. In the shadows cast by the TVs, Mia noticed that the floor was moving and writhing. Disorientated, she stepped back and felt the cold of the door pressing against her back. Naked bodies glistened in the flickering light, the screens causing a strange silvery glow across each one. Mia blinked and looked again as the shapes gradually dissolved and separated so that she could identify different people among the mass. She quickly realised that they were all female and that some of them were dressed the same way as her, in leather waistcoats and small thongs. There were more of the naked women and they took up most of the floor space in the centre of the room, lounging in a circle around the bank of TVs in the centre. There must have been thirty or more women in the room and they were all staring at her.

'Another fucking newbie,' a harsh female voice snarled and the mass of bodies before her shifted to reveal a lounging redhead. She was leaning against a mound of pillows, her arms draped loosely over the shoulders of two other women who rested their heads against her breasts. Other women were lying on her thighs and legs, all of them staring at Mia. The woman clicked her fingers and the women around her slowly moved back, giving her space.

'Well, I suppose I should enjoy you too ... it is our custom after all.' She turned slightly and Mia looked in that direction. Kneeling amongst a group of naked women were the three girls that had arrived on the bus with her. They were dressed in waistcoats which made them House Slaves, but what did that make the naked women? Cooper had mentioned Slaves ... but the distinction was lost on Mia.

'I said, come here,' the woman said, her tone indignant.

Mia stared at her, 'Why?'

'Because it is time to pay your respects to me.'

"Who are you?'

A ripple of laughter ran round the room, although Mia noticed that it was only the naked women who seemed to find anything amusing.

'Roxanne,' she responded, 'I'm what you might call Top Bitch around here.'

Mia frowned, 'I don't understand.'

'Then come here and I'll explain.'

Hands suddenly grabbed Mia's arms and she was propelled towards the older woman and forced to her knees at her feet. Roxanne spread her legs and hands pushed on the back of Mia's head, forcing her face towards the glistening cunt before her. She kept her lips closed, refusing to comply with the obvious demands but Roxanne only laughed, 'Lick or suffocate … it's up to you.'

Mia slowly parted her lips and at the gasp that her first touch caused, the pressure on the back of her head was released. She moved back a little so that she could draw her tongue up between the swollen labia lips. The woman's clitoris pulsed against her tongue and Mia felt herself quiver in response to the woman's onrush of pleasure. A heat seemed to fill the air around her, strangely intoxicating, it made her work harder at the pussy before her. She slipped her tongue into the vagina that welcomed her by quivering and contracting as she forced her tongue as far as she could go.

'Oh God, you're fucking good,' the woman sighed, her thighs quivering and hips lifting to force Mia's tongue deeper, 'Oh … fucking … yeah …' Fingers stroked her hair, urging her on and Mia couldn't stop her own hand from sliding between her thighs and stroking herself through the material of her thong. She could feel her own climax building in time with the woman's and at the first onrush of juice she felt the material dampen at her fingertips. She gasped her pleasure and then in surprise as a foot was planted against her shoulder and she was shoved backwards.

'Okay, that's enough.'

Gasping with unspent lust, Mia stared at Roxanne as she wiped her mouth with the back of her hand. 'What the fu-'

'Hmm … spirit as well as finesse,' Roxanne laughed, 'they're going to have fun with you here … we all are.' Another ripple of laughter followed her words, dying to silence as she started talking again, 'That was the best cunt licking I've had in quite a while so I'll return the favour with some advice about how things work here.' She leant back, opening her arms and stretching her legs to allow the naked women to drape themselves over her again. 'Have you ever heard of a Slave House?'

Mia shook her head.

'There are several in this country alone, each run by either five Masters or five Mistresses. Each house has its own speciality. There's the Games House in Wales and the Whore House in London. Tell me, can you guess what this house is?' She didn't wait for an answer and just continued, 'Each house has House Slaves, sluts like you who are worth little, if anything. In this house, your job is to keep us Slaves happy and, how shall I say ... hot.' Another ripple of laughter died away before she continued, 'We slaves are here to perform for the cameras and to ensure that we perform well, we are not allowed any pleasurable release unless it happens in front of the camera. We must be able to come on command and to help us do that ...' she waved at the TVs, '... do you get the gist?' Mia nodded slowly and moved to sit up but Roxanne shook her head, 'Why don't you finish what you started?' Frowning, Mia just stared back, causing Roxanne to sigh angrily, 'I want to see you come, you stupid slut.'

'I don't think so,' Mia responded, 'I'll take orders from those bastards out there but that's as far as I'm going to go.'

Roxanne's eyes darkened with anger, 'I said that I want to see you come.'

Hands grabbed Mia and she struggled as she was held down. Unknown hands found her breasts and tore at her thong, pulling it up between her buttocks. She cried out as the material rubbed against her sore anus. Her legs were held apart and Mia cried out again as a tongue slid along the groove of her sex and teeth found her clitoris. She tipped her head back and groaned, quivering as fingers were slipped into her cunt. A thumb rubbed against her clitoris and then, unbelievably, she was coming. She cried out in disbelief, the pleasure so intense that she could barely stand it. Her whole body convulsed and then went limp.

Satisfied with the show, Roxanne lay back against the pillows and the naked women who had pleasured her melted away into the flickering shadows, leaving Mia to curl onto her side and shudder with the last throes of her climax.

*

'I am here to serve the Masters as they wish ... without question ... without hesitation.' Mia heard herself saying the words, but that was all they were – words, they had no meaning. 'I will do as I am asked, as I am told. I am a whore, a slut, a tool to be used and I will be used as needed and as wanted.' Mia half glanced sideways towards the young girl beside her as her companion's voice broke half way through the sentence. The other two women, on Mia's other side, seemed convinced and almost resigned to what they were saying but the young girl was almost in tears. Mia turned back and found herself meeting the gaze of one of the five men seated opposite them. She quickly lowered her gaze but not before she had seen the half smirk that he afforded her. Her stomach lurched with the sudden realisation that she had just met the gaze of one of the five House Masters. She felt the eyes of the Second Master burning into her flesh as he studied her body, the curve of her breasts half hidden beneath the waistcoat, made all the more prominent by the position of her arms behind her back. Like the others, she was kneeling on her haunches, her knuckles resting against the soles of her feet. The position was uncomfortable and caused the waistcoat to gape without revealing everything, but Mia sensed that that was the point. 'A House Slave, that is all I am. I serve the house, that is all I live for.' Mia continued to repeat the words that were given to her but she was used to saying what was expected. Sergeant Kent occasionally gave her things to say and on one occasion, he had told her something and ordered her to keep it secret before letting three of his friends loose on her for interrogation. She had not repeated any of what he had told her, despite what they had done. In the finish the men had been furious and Kent had punished her mercilessly for shaming him. As was so often the case, Mia suffered his punishment without even knowing what she had done wrong. She told herself that a year in this house would be no different, if anything it would be better. At least here she knew what they wanted and they would ensure that she met their expectations.

'You.'

She looked up and quickly dropped her gaze again, the third was beckoning her. She stayed on her knees and crawled towards him, the waistcoat slapping her breasts as she moved. As she neared him his hand waved at his crotch and she lifted her hands to his fly.

'I don't think so,' he laughed, slapping her hand away, 'if I wanted your filthy hands to touch me I would have told you.'

Swallowing, she moved her face closer and gripped the zipper between her teeth. She managed to pull it down and used her tongue to probe between the folds. She heard him groan and the more she licked at the hidden organ, the more he hardened beneath her attentions. Within a few minutes she had managed to tease him to full hardness and eased from within the confines of his clothes. Once he was free her job became much easier and she swallowed the length of his cock, fighting the gag reflex to take him as deep as she could, satisfied when she heard his groan deepen with pleasure. She felt his cock twitch at the back of her throat and sensed him tensing as he fought the urge to hold back his climax. She sucked his length as hard as she could, dragging her teeth along his foreskin and drawing the folds of flesh into her mouth before plunging down again. She gasped as her hair was harshly twisted in his fist and her mouth was yanked free of his cock. He threw her away from him, laughing as she sprawled across the floor. 'All in good time,' he laughed and stood up, 'bring the frames.'

Mia was hauled to her feet by two men dressed in black leather trousers and nothing else. She had seen them dressed the same way when the four of them had been brought into this huge ballroom to be introduced to the five masters. Thomas was there as well, along with many other men, dressed in smart tuxedoes and drinking from crystal glasses. The smell of cigar smoke was heavy in the air, mingled with expensive aftershave. To Mia the smells did little to mask the all too familiar smell of male anticipation.

As she was dragged back to her three companions, she looked up in time to see four wooden, triangular frames being wheeled into the centre of the room. The purpose of these frames was made all too clear by the links and straps that were positioned at various heights along the supporting legs. Mia was the first in the frames and was thrown over the top bar, her ankles secured to the base on one side and her wrists to the base on the other. Thick straps bound her upper arms and thighs, forearms and calves while the thickest strap of all secured her lower back. Another strap rested across her middle back, pulling her downwards at an uncomfortable and well restrained angle. She was very much aware that her buttocks were prominent, her cunt well exposed by the sharp spread of her legs. The other girls were secured identically. The young girl had been gagged to stop her constant whimpering. With her head down, Mia could see through her legs to where the five masters were sitting in their place of prominence. As she watched, four of the masters stood to take the thin crops that were offered to them by four other house slaves. As soon as the crops were taken from their trembling hands, each house slave fell to her knees, quickly shedding her waistcoat. Mia watched, fascinated, as all four of them reached their hands back to grip their ankles, unbidden, they presented their breasts to their masters. In turn, each master raised his crop and delivered two swift blows to each breast, forehand then back, forehand then back. With the blows delivered, the slaves quickly turned so that they were on all fours, their faces pressed to the floor to raise their buttocks to the harsh crops. Four more slices, two to each buttock, followed for each slave. The Masters studied the marks that the crops had made and, satisfied, they approached the new slaves and their, now trembling, buttocks. Mia had known that the Second would choose her and he approached slowly, bending the crop between his large hands. He must have known that she was watching him but he said nothing.

'Gentlemen, please begin,' the oldest of the Masters, who had remained seated, said loudly so that all of the room could hear. 'Ten each, if you please.'

Mia gritted her teeth as the crop sliced first her right and then her left buttock, searing the flesh with a line of fire, the like of which she had never felt. After the following two blows she realised that two things were contributing to the increased discomfort. The first was the whip itself. It cut the air with such a fine whine that she could barely hear its approach at all. Had she known more, she would have recognised a craftsman's piece but for all she had suffered at Kent's hands, she could only sense the difference and not understand it fully. The second factor that brought stinging tears to her eyes were the bonds that so cruelly secured her in the frame. More than just a restraint, they were positioned and tightened sufficiently to draw the flesh taut, stretching the nerve endings and allowing no cushioning of the fatty layer beneath the skin. Like the crop, Mia had a sense of things being done better, with a sort of finesse that had always been lacking from every other beating that she had suffered. Even at the hands of Gary Marshall, as she had suffered for his pleasure and his wife's, the whipping had never been so ... perfect. The stinging tears spilled from her eyes as the pairs of blows continued to fall and she felt strangely honoured to be on the receiving end of such a punishment. It all felt so right. She thought of the house slaves who had presented first the whips and then their breasts to their masters, how must it feel to know your place so well as to not require instruction but just to give yourself over, unquestioningly? She had never imagined herself being like that, had always fought against submitting to Kent but here, in this house, she wondered if submission was not weakness as she had believed, but a strength that she couldn't imagine. She wept long after the blows had stopped, her mind in a turmoil of emotions and new thoughts, too much to deal with, not here, not now, not in front of all those hungry male eyes.

A cock slid between the folds of her tight pussy and she gasped with relief as she was penetrated and filled. The feel of the invading cock drew her from her thoughts. The stinging pain of the male thighs pressing against her wounded buttocks brought her back to her senses. The rhythmic pounding of her pussy made her gasp over and over as his long cock penetrated her to his hilt, the penetration deepened by the angle of her body. She was far from climax, far from real pleasure and she was grateful for that. She didn't dare think what would happen if she were to give into her pleasure in front of the Masters, without their permission. She felt his cock swell and suddenly the heat of his climax filled her belly, making her groan. He pulled from her, his wet cock sliding across her welt smothered cheek, the salty fluid stinging the flesh. She was left empty and strangely alone ... but not for long. Another cock, shorter yet thicker than the first, found its way easily into her and began to pound her restrained body. The tautness of her flesh added to the fucking just as it had added to the beating. The frame rocked with the violence of his thrusts and Mia feared that she would be toppled forward but the man fucking her clearly knew the limits of the frame and fucked her as harshly as he could. He groaned once and then pulled free to spray his come across her buttocks. She was still feeling the sensation of him inside her as another cock filled her. She gasped at the bizarre sensation, as if two cocks were filling her and working in tandem to force her body to respond. And respond it did. Her nipples had hardened painfully and she knew that her labia lips had swollen around this man's cock, her clitoris pushing back its hood to seek the sweet friction of his slapping balls. She sensed his approaching climax and gasped loudly when he pulled free and spread her buttocks, resting his helmet against her opening and gushing his spunk. He squeezed her buttocks against his cock and then stepped back, leaving his hot spunk to run down her cunt and thighs. She half cried out when another man placed his hands on her flesh and spread her buttocks to allow his entry. That cry became louder as she felt him nudging at her anus, forcing entry into her tighter passage. She swooned, her head hanging limply as the sudden pain of his invasion mixed with unbelievable pleasure. She came round as she felt his spunk blossoming in her anus, heating her passageway. More men followed, too many to count. They took her arse or cunt as they saw fit. Neither was denied them and Mia took them all with little more than a desperate, wordless cry. She was oblivious to the other women who were suffering the same fate as her. She had no idea if they had swooned as she had, only to come too and swoon again or whether they had shuddered in climax or screamed in agony. If any of them had screamed in either pleasure or pain, Mia had not heard them – she was too caught up in her own world of penetration and salty pleasure.

'Lift your heads.'

Mia did as she was told, barely able to but fighting to obey. Her shoulders shook with the effort and she gasped as she fought to keep her head up. A moment before her strength gave out and she dropped her head, she saw the First standing before her, studying them all ... selecting. A moment later, as she felt his cock slide into her cunt, she felt her climax build, swelling with the sense of pride that he had chosen her. She couldn't have known that he had only chosen her because, out of the four, she was the only one still conscious and responsive. On the edges of her senses she heard men talking, one of the voices she recognised as the young man, Thomas, who had filmed her beneath the shower earlier that day.

'You're sure?'

'I know she can do it.'

'But what about what has been filmed so far?'

'I can edit it ... the scene she did earlier -'

'I've seen it, I agree, she's perfect.'

'It will take perhaps two weeks to set up.'

'Then she will stay as a House Slave until then?'

'No, she will be damaged and unusable.'

'Then she cannot do the film, I want to enjoy her some more.'

'There are three others for you to enjoy, have them all at once, you'll soon forget this one.'

'And besides, if you miss her, you can always watch her while you fuck the others.'

The first stayed silent for several moments, fucking her slowly and nearly driving her mad as her climax hung on the very edges of her senses, desperate to break over her. 'Let me think about it,' he said softly, his palm circling her bruised buttock, 'I will give you my answer soon.'

'With respect, don't take too long – she will be sought after as a House Slave and I wouldn't want to miss the opportunity.'

His fingers drew patterns on her flesh, 'I will make my decision and let you know as soon as I am ready. I respect your abilities, Thomas, but do not forget your place.'

'My apologies, sir, I only want what is best for business and this house.'

The first laughed but it was a strange, disbelieving sound, 'Goodnight, Thomas.'

Mia had the sense of someone moving away and then suddenly the First Master was driving into her, pounding her flesh and rocking the frame that held her so completely. Her body seemed to swell within the binds, reminding her of her submissive position and the sheer vulnerability of it all. Suddenly her body finally submitted to the intensity of it all and she cried out as her climax seized her, shaking her in the frame with the force of it. She felt him pull free of her cunt and slide quickly into her arse, groaning as his cock spasmed and filled her with his hot spunk. 'Wonderful.' he sighed as he wiped his cock across her buttock.

Mia closed her eyes, breathing heavily as she tried to regain what little composure she had left. Her eyes snapped open again when she sensed someone approaching. 'Please, no more,' she whispered as she felt the first touch at her pussy lips, 'I beg you, no more.' She gasped in surprise as she felt a tongue gently caressing the bruised folds of her cunt and stared at the young house slave who was gently cleaning the spent semen from her flesh. Mia quivered as her eyes alighted on the four purple stripes that lined the slave's breasts. She gasped once before her vision blurred as a final, shattering climax, finally robbed her of her senses.

Chapter six: Opportunity

She had been a house slave for three days and along with the other new slaves, she was fucked regularly. It seemed that every man in the house wanted to try her out and she seemed to receive more attention than the others – a fact that wasn't missed by Roxanne who seemed to be keeping a close eye on her also. An hour of the day did not go by without a cock being slid into her tight cunt or between her unresisting lips. They left her alone at night, choosing the other house slaves to entertain them but Mia had the feeling that that wouldn't last. She was proved right in this respect when, at the end of the third day, while clearing away the dining room, she was suddenly grabbed from behind. She expected to be tipped over the table and roughly taken, as had happened twice before, but instead her hands were fastened behind her back and a hood thrown over her head before she was led out of the room. She gasped within the darkness, a fear that had grown worse during the time that she had spent with Kent. He hadn't blindfolded her very often but enough for her to know that she hated not seeing what was going on. She had always been of the opinion that if she could see it, she could fight it. While that had been proved wrong time and time again since Kent had first abused her and during everything that had happened since, it was still impossible for her to not fear the darkness.

By the time they reached their destination, Mia's chest was heaving and she was beginning to feel light-headed with fear. Disorientated and afraid, cold sweat stood out in beads along her forehead, dripping down her face. Her sweat and breath made the material cling to her face, making the sensations inside the cloying darkness all the worse. She was pulled to a stop and her hands released from the cuffs that held them behind her back. In near panic, she reached for the hood but a swift blow from a crop across the backs of her hands made her drop them to her sides. The waistcoat and shorts were stripped from her body and then her hands were lifted and forced into cuffs above her head. She gasped as she felt her arms being stretched and then again as her feet were lifted off the floor. Her shoulders began to burn after a few moments but the continued darkness and claustrophobia inside the hood reduced the burn to a dull ache.

The hood was suddenly snatched from her head but any relief that she felt was quickly shredded when she saw the man standing before her. He was middle-aged, short and portly but he had the same aura of power as all the other House Masters. She vaguely recognised him from the first night and remembered that he had sat beside the First Master – he must be the Second. Mia felt none of the pride that she had when the First had chosen her on that first night, all she felt was fear. There was sadism in this man's eyes, he had a cold, calculating stare and Mia couldn't help but think that it was cunning rather than strength that had allowed him to achieve such high standing within the house. Mia was a good judge of character and it had served her well in the past – it did not fail her here either. Her judgement of him was as accurate as it could be, she just couldn't have known exactly what he was capable of and would never have guessed in her worst nightmares. She took an instant dislike to him and despite her fear, that dislike must have shown in her eyes because his lips thinned with distaste as he stared at her. He lifted his hand and stroked her breast, making her quiver with revulsion. Cursing quietly to himself, his fingers slid down her body until he was pushing between her legs. She tried to pull away from him but he slapped her buttock with the other hand and held her still. His thick tongue licked his lips as he probed between her labia lips, pinching her clitoris and making her gasp. He pulled his fingers free and held them up to the light, his fingers glistened.

'Did you just come without permission?' he asked her.

'No, Master,' Mia gasped, 'I swear.'

He suddenly thrust his fingers between her lips, rolling them over her tongue so that she could taste herself, 'What do you call that then?'

Unable to answer, Mia just shook her head and when he removed his fingers she gasped, 'I did not come, Master, I promise.'

'A double punishment then – first for coming without permission and second for lying about it.'

Mia opened her mouth to protest but stopped herself at the last minute – damn it, she would not give him the pleasure of hearing her beg. Her resolve nearly faltered when she saw his assistant hand him a long bull-whip. She had never been beaten with such a whip before and she had a fearful sense of how painful it would be. She gritted her teeth, desperate to keep her plea silent. She stared at him as he raised the whip, unable to close her eyes and await the blow – she had to see it coming.

'Do not deliver that blow, Jeffrey.' a vaguely familiar voice boomed across the room. Mia looked towards him and then quickly lowered her gaze when she recognised the First Master.

His arm trembling with the urge to set the whip free, the second master slowly curled the whip, 'May I ask why?'

The First glanced at the man on his right and Mia recognised the director, Thomas, 'She is to become a movie slave.'

'So soon?' his voice was incredulous, 'Why?'

The First stepped forward, his stance challenging, 'I don't have to explain myself to anyone!'

The second bowed his head, 'Of course, Jacob, I'm sorry.'

The First nodded and waved for Thomas to release Mia, 'We shall send a replacement, no one expects you to go without.'

'I appreciate that.'

Thomas led Mia from the room, he was saying something to the First who then went in the other direction. As Mia followed Thomas down the corridor she thought of the second Master and the horrifying whip that had almost found her flesh. 'Thank you.' she heard herself say.

Thomas stopped and turned towards her, amusement shining in his eyes, 'Don't thank me yet. You may well beg me to return you to him before too long.'

Mia stared back, 'I will beg no one.'

Again that damned amusement, this time pulling at the corners of his mouth, 'I'll remember that.'

Chapter seven: Dungeon

The rough sacking that covered her naked frame scratched her skin as she moved, her fear and apprehension heightening everything until it was almost unbearable. She wondered, if the feel of the rough sacking on her skin felt so intolerable, how was she going to cope when the whipping started? They had only told her what she needed to know and she was prepared to give the answers as they had been given to her. They had told her nothing beyond that – they hadn't needed to – the post in the centre of the dungeon was evidence enough of the fate that awaited her. The dungeon set was much like the prison shower set – in that the three walls had been carefully crafted to allow the illusion of a dark and fearful dungeon. The entire front was open and two large cameras were positioned to capture every moment as events unfolded.

The sudden silence made her look up and she knew that the cameras had started to roll. A large hand grabbed her arm and she was dragged onto the set and thrown at the feet of a heavy-set man, naked from the waist up, the muscles in his arms bulging as he flexed the handle of the stock whip. She stared at him fearfully, her mouth suddenly dry and her nipples pressing against the sacking.

'Why are you here?'

Her apprehension almost robbed her of her senses but she managed to remember what she was to say a moment before it was too late, 'I was caught stealing food from my Master's table,' she told him, her voice quivering.

'And should you be punished for this?'

There was no way that she could forget what she was expected to say next – and perhaps, deep down, she was eager to say it for as the words slipped from her lips she felt a familiar tingle around her nipples that slowly moved downwards. 'Yes, sir, I should be punished.'

Without another word he took her arm and marched her to the post. Her hands were yanked over her head as she was forced to face the pole. The thin leather straps cut into her wrists and she stared up at his large hands as they tied the bonds as tight as possible – he would spare her no discomfort. The power with which he ripped the sacking open made her knees go weak as she imagined how that strength would cast the whip across her skin. She shuddered as the sudden cool air blasted the naked skin of her back, lifting Goosebumps across her spine. She closed her eyes and awaited the first blow. It wasn't long in coming.

Snap.

Her gritted teeth squeaked together as the whip landed again, slicing across her shoulder blades, forcing blood to the surface to form a harsh welt that spanned the width of her back. Sweat beaded across her forehead as she shivered with cold and pain. The whip fell again and again. Her back was soon ablaze and her cries became louder, soft whimpers escaping her lips between each terrible blow. She hated the sounds she was making, wished she could close her ears to them but they were as much a part of the punishment as the braided leather that scored her flesh. She had been told to cry out – that they wanted to hear her scream.

When he had finished he untied her hands and let her stay where she fell. He at least let her catch her breath before asking, 'Have you learnt your lesson?'

'Yes, Master,' she managed to respond, biting back her sobs.

He grabbed her upper arm, making her gasp as he dragged her to a thin layer of straw in the corner. 'Then show me your gratitude,' he demanded as he threw her to the ground and unfastened the lace at the front of his trousers. Behind him another slave was being tied to the whipping post and the sound of her punishment would accompany Mia's efforts to pleasure the man. She ran her teeth along his cock, tentatively reaching beneath him to cup his bollocks in her hand. She tensed, waiting for the admonishment. When it didn't come she squeezed the hot sacs and was satisfied to hear him groan. She used the last of her strength to force her head forward and take him as deep as she could. She used her tongue along his length and squeezed his bollocks harder. She was rewarded quickly with a sudden groan and then he pulled free of her mouth. He snarled loudly as his fist clamped around his length and Mia turned her head to the side as the first hot splashes hit her breasts. More splashes followed and she winced with disgust as a large drop struck her lips. He snarled again, this time with anger when he noticed her reaction. His open hand found her cheek and she cried out as she fell sideways onto the straw. Too weak to move or to care, she closed her eyes and drifted into darkness.

The groan started deep in her throat, her eyes squeezing tightly shut as the wave of pleasure rolled up her chest. She had no desire to leave the darkness but the pleasure was dragging her from the peace. The tongue slid across the flesh of her breasts, cleaning the man's come from her skin. The memory of him and his pleasure suddenly dragged her to full consciousness and she tried to pull away, suddenly remembering the threat of what would happen if she took pleasure without being permitted. Her eyes slowly cleared and she saw past the slave to the camera and crew who stood silently watching her. She couldn't make out faces behind the harsh lights, just silhouettes and lots of them. Her pussy tightened at the sight of all of them watching and her body shuddered. She gave a half cry as her back scratched across the harsh straw but the tongue at her breasts quickly turned that pain to something very different.

'Lick harshly ... make her squirm.'

The sound of his voice made her shudder with both hatred and revulsion. His harsh commands and filthy words made her want to scream but she couldn't disobey. Her legs seemed to move of their own accord as she slowly slipped her thighs apart to welcome the attentions of the pretty young slave. As she dipped her head between Mia's thighs, Mia raised her head and gasped. The blonde was wearing the same type of sacking, ripped down the back to expose her skin that was smothered in angry welts. Mia knew that her own back must have been a mirror of the slave's, the thought made her push her hips up, as if presenting herself to those beautiful lips.

The slave's tongue lapped at her clitoris and her body shuddered in response. The gasp turned into a hiss of pleasure as teeth closed gently over her sensitive bud and then the slave's tongue was sliding inside her and Mia was gasping loudly.

'Fingers ... start with two and go from there.'

Mia's hips bucked involuntarily as two fingers slid easily into her. The mind-numbing pleasure was almost too much and Mia shook her head as her climax crested. She felt her body tense and then suddenly the slave pulled her fingers free before sliding four back in and stretching Mia wonderfully. She gasped and held her breath, sensing that moment when everything would explode. The cry escaped her as a whimper as she succumbed to the pleasure. The slave between her legs gasped in surprise as the first jet of juice squirted from Mia.

'Keep her going.'

She continued to punch her fingers into Mia, groaning with lust as she watched Mia convulse as she ejaculated in a great spray that covered them both.

'What a filthy couple of whores.'

Mia looked up through half open eyes to see the man who had whipped her. His erection glistened as he moved behind the slave, his huge hands gripping her hips. The slave lifted her head and gasped as he slid into her. His hand found the back of her head and pushed her face down, holding her firmly against Mia's soaking pussy as he fucked her. Unbelievably Mia could feel another climax building rapidly as the slave gasped her own climax into Mia's cunt. The two slaves came at the same time, the sight of their quivering bodies too much for the man who thrust harshly and held himself deep inside her as he shuddered.

Chapter eight: Witness to submission

The candle flickered, the heat from it warming her breasts and nipples. She hardly noticed the heat or the wax that dripped onto her fingers as she watched the slave crawl into the room. Her eyes followed the slave's every move – fascinated by the way she moved so easily on her hands and knees. The slave's head was lifted slightly and there was a quiet dignity in her posture that enflamed Mia's dark passions. The chain around the slave's neck, although pulled tight and held firmly in the fist of her Master, did nothing to lower her dignity and it was almost a badge of honour that she wore around her neck. Mia, standing at the edge of the room with her candle, one of ten human lights that offered the only illumination in the room, was nothing to this slave or the men that dominated her.

Shadows shifted and then slid away as the large arc lamps above slowly brought more light to the set. For a moment Mia had forgotten that she was standing in front of the cameras – yet again – at least this time it was not her that they were focusing on. When the light reached its desired level, she heard Thomas's voice but not the words. It didn't matter, for once his commands were not meant for her.

The slave had assumed a kneeling position in the centre of the room, the five men surrounded her on all sides but left enough of a gap so that the camera could see her. Her Master lifted the chain, bringing her chin up so that he could look into her eyes. 'What will you do?'

'Anything you ask, Master,' she responded easily and with no hint of acting – she meant every word.

Mia then watched as the men dominated the slave.

Mia had thought that the slave had seemed dignified as she had crawled into the room but now she felt that that had been the act. The men did anything they wanted and it seemed that their sole source of pleasure was to strip the slave of every dignity, every ounce of pride – and she let them without a murmur or hint of defence. It sickened Mia to watch the slave as she opened her arse to each in turn and then swallowed their cocks without pause. She opened her mouth to their jets of urine and swallowed their come without spilling a drop. She held her thighs open so they could whip the swollen folds of her pussy and took each blow with a whimpered, 'Thank you, Master.' They made her clamp her own breasts and clitoris and she made no complaint as they told her to turn the closing screws as tight as was possible. She masturbated for them and stopped the moment she was told to – despite the quivers of impending climax that rippled her widely spread thighs. Mia couldn't help but think of everything that had been done to her, everything she had suffered. All the times she had screamed and begged them to stop but Kent and his colleagues had continued without mercy. She had done everything they had asked but had done it for survival. She had never done it willingly - and made sure that they knew it. She had never submitted to their will, they had just imposed their will upon her and she had stood defenceless. Now to see this slave so willingly give herself to these men was enough to make Mia tremble with rage. How dare she? How dare she submit so easily and with no fight?

'You!'

Mia jumped as one of the men beckoned her angrily.

'Sorry, Master,' she gasped as she realised that he had already called her once. Someone took the candle from her and she hurried to him, falling to her knees at his feet.

'Present breasts,' he snarled.

Wincing with apprehension, Mia lifted herself and then leant back to grab her ankles, presenting her breasts to his open palm. He slapped her several times, reddening the flesh and reminding her to keep her attention on the men who would punish her if she again became lost in her thoughts.

When he was satisfied that she had learnt her lesson, he waved at the quivering slave who knelt in the centre of the room. 'We are finished with her,' he announced as he turned away, 'see to her needs.'

'Yes, Master,' she responded and crawled to the slave. As she approached she could smell the Masters on her. The submissive slave glistened with sweat, semen, piss and saliva and as Mia drew nearer she saw flecks of blood along the harshest welts that striped her buttocks and breasts. The slave watched her approach through heavily-lidded eyes, her lips slightly parted to allow her shallow breaths. She twisted to lie on her back, opening her legs and waiting for Mia to do as she had been ordered. Mia's lip curled slightly. Did the slave think she had earned the pleasure that Mia had been ordered to give? Was that why she had done all of those things, to earn a few moments of climax? Mia dipped her head between her thighs. The first taste was of the men and she cleaned the soft pussy quickly, eager to remove their taste. The slave quivered and gasped and Mia remembered the beating that this pussy had received. She pressed her tongue against the bruised flesh and the slave bucked her hips, suddenly flooding Mia's mouth with juice. The scent of her was intoxicating and made Mia's own cunt moisten. Mia sucked at her clitoris, drawing the bud out from its protective hood. She drove her tongue between the swollen labia and cleaned the semen filled passage. Intoxicated by the taste and smell, Mia dipped lower to clean the slave's arse before returning to the sweet taste of her quivering pussy.

The slave suddenly tensed, 'Master,' she gasped, 'may I come?'

'Not yet.'

The soft whimper that rippled from the slave was the first show of defence that she had given but that was all as she quivered, desperate to hold back her climax. After everything that they had done to her to now continue to hold back her desires ... Mia felt pity for the slave for the first time.

Mia gasped as a whip suddenly sliced the middle of her buttocks.

'Don't even think of slacking off.'

Mia continued to work at the slave's cunt, amazed to feel the throb of impending climax and the quiver of restraint. As she had watched the slave submit to her Masters and do everything they had demanded of her, Mia had despised her weakness. But now, as she witnessed that unquestioning obedience first hand, she realised the strength needed for such submission and her fevered tongue delved deeper, her own lust driving her on.

'Oh, God! Master, I beg you ... may I come?'

'No.'

The slave groaned and cried out, thrashing uncontrollably as she fought to restrain herself. Mia gasped into the pussy lips as the whip found her arse again – the message was clear. She licked and sucked, felt the slave's juice oozing from her and knew that when the tide broke it would gush.

'Master, please!' the slave cried pitifully, her nails scratching at Mia's shoulders. No answer came and tears rolled from her eyes as the terrible arousal just kept growing. Seconds dragged into minutes, each a lifetime of torturous pleasure with no end.

Suddenly the slave's back arched and her juice flooded into Mia's mouth, almost choking her. The slave screamed – first with release and then with fear.

Mia gasped as her head was suddenly yanked back. The slave's juices glistened on her lips and chin.

'You fucking whore! What have you done?'

Mia whimpered, not knowing what to say.

'You have broken my slave! She is worthless now!' She heard the slave sob as she was hauled to her feet.

'Punish her for a week!' the Master yelled, ignoring her cries for mercy as she was dragged away.

The men who had enjoyed the slave slowly circled Mia as she knelt, shivering with fear. A whip cut the air, catching her shoulder blades and pitching her forward onto her hands. A harsh blow to her buttocks sent her onto her front, squashing her breasts beneath her. She lifted herself up and a blow to her side, aimed at her breast, spun her onto her back. Her arms were wrenched over her head and held as more blows fell on her breasts. She gasped and cried, twisted in their grip but hands grabbed her ankles and held her steady as the whips found her breasts, stomach and thighs. When she was glowing and lined, they rolled her over and started on her back. By the time they were finished she was sobbing pitifully. In the moment of respite, after the whips fell silent, she dared to hope that they had finished with her. But suddenly she was forced onto all fours and a thick cock was sliding into her arse. She gasped and then cried out as she was pulled backwards, forced to lie on top of the man who was buried so deep in her anus. A shadow fell over her as a second man lowered himself and slid into her cunt. She cried out as the two cocks worked simultaneously and her open mouth was quickly filled by a third.

This was what she could handle – what she was used to. Kent and his companions had taught her that she was a tool for pleasure – to be used and discarded. She had never understood the way they treated Harper's slave, Kelly, the way they spoke to her, they way they teased her. Mia understood cruelty – it was easier to suffer than to submit and she was comfortable with that. As angry as it had made her, it had also been fascinating to watch the slave submit to the masters who now fucked her so viciously. The slave had submitted so completely – Mia could never see herself in such a position. It was the fear of losing what little she had left that forced her to make such a promise to herself. She would not submit as the slave had – she could not. As the man's cock twitched in her mouth, she looked sideways and suddenly he pulled free. She saw the director, Thomas, watching her intently, studying her every reaction. She realised then that it didn't matter what she promised herself – what happened to her, her fate was in the hands of the enigmatic young man.

She closed her eyes as hot liquid splashed her face. In the darkness she saw Thomas. Suddenly she felt that it was him pounding her cunt. She saw him looming over her, driving into her. She screamed as her climax tore through her, gasping and choking as her mouth was filled with semen. Her eyes snapped open and she stared up at three men who were aiming their twitching cocks at her open mouth. She coughed and spluttered, swallowed as much as she could. The cocks in her arse and cunt twitched simultaneously and then both holes were filled with yet more hot spunk. The man in her cunt pulled free, his fingers suddenly rubbing her clitoris. She screamed again as his other hand slid thick fingers into her. She cried out, lifting her head in time to see the spray of juice arcing from between his fingers. The pleasure was too much and she fell back again, her vision spinning.

Chapter nine: Vicki

The braided leather sliced across her breasts, distorted and stretched by the weights that were clamped to her nipples and which now rested on the floor at her sides. She had been chained, spread-eagled, to the floor and the clamps and weights attached. The whip had been used on her breasts and thighs mercilessly and her hair was soaked with sweat and tears. But now she was whimpering for another reason as the submissive slave's head bobbed between her legs. Mia looked up and met the blue eyes of the slave – she had learned that her name was Vicki, but that was all she knew and had yet to speak to her directly. They locked stares as Vicki slipped her tongue into the soaking crevice.

'Just ask and you may come.'

'Fuck you,' Mia responded angrily, tossing her head to stare at the master who bent the crop between his hands. At any other time Mia would have been terrified at the punishment that was to follow but she had been instructed carefully on how she was to react. It seemed that Thomas was looking to balance the 'submission' of Vicki with someone stronger.

'You have been kidnapped and he wants you to submit,' Thomas had told her as they walked through the house, 'Do not submit to him ... can you do that?'

'It's what I have been doing,' she had responded and he had laughed at that. His mocking of her only made her angrier and that was perhaps the point because she had turned that anger on the actor who had been told to make her submit.

The crop sliced her breasts just above her crushed nipples and she cried out, her hips thrusting upwards and knocking Vicki off balance. The man advanced on Vicki and lashed her buttocks, forcing her flat to the floor. She suffered each blow, her face turned to the side to stare at Mia.

'Get back to it,' he demanded angrily, 'or I'll have you down there next.'

The look that flashed across Vicki's face suggested that she had been hoping for as much and as she stared at the clamps and weights she licked her lips. Mia curled her lip as she stared at her, 'You fucking enjoying yourself?' It hadn't been part of her brief to interact with the slave but Mia was sickened by her.

If Vicki was surprised by Mia's words then she didn't show it. She smiled as her eyes roved over Mia's stretched body, 'Not as much as you're about to.'

'You think you can make me come?'

'I can make you squirt.'

Mia snorted and then cried out as the crop sliced her thighs.

'Make her squirt and I'll fuck you senseless,' the man told Vicki.

'Yes, Master,' Vicki breathed, 'Master, could you untie her ankles?'

He glared at her and raised the crop until he realised her intention and he smiled. He still delivered a blow across her shoulder blades but then released Mia's ankles and allowed Vicki to chain them to the rings that held her wrists. Mia groaned as she was bent double, her glistening pussy pointing upwards and exposed. She screamed as the crop found her swollen lips.

'Master, please,' Vicki gasped and then winced as he turned the crop on her, slicing her breasts in punishment. 'Master, if I am to make her squirt ...'

He lashed Mia's pussy again and laughed loudly, 'What's the matter, slut, don't you like a challenge?'

Four more terrible blows found her cunt and Mia was on the verge of crying for mercy when Vicki's tongue suddenly slid along the groove of her sex. She sucked at

Mia's clitoris and the bruised bud hardened between her lips. As she sucked at the sensitive bud she slid three fingers into Mia's pussy, making her shudder uncontrollably.

'Oh, god!' Mia gasped, half with pain and half with pleasure. She cried out again as Vicki slid a finger from her other hand into her arse. She moved her fingers simultaneously while her lips continued to suck at her clitoris. Mia cried out, 'Please ... stop.'

The crop landed across her breasts, 'The only sound I want to hear from you is the cries of pleasure as you soak that whore!'

Vicki thrust her fingers firmly and Mia quivered, twisting against the binds as her body reacted to the attentions. Vicki slid her fingers from her arse and sat up so that she could drive her fingers into Mia's pussy, crushing her bruised flesh and making her scream. But then suddenly she could feel the walls of her cunt constrict and spasm. At that very moment Vicki yanked her fingers free and Mia screamed pitifully as she ejaculated across Vicki's breasts.

She had barely stopped climaxing when Vicki was pushed over her. The slave held Mia's wrists to support herself as the man slid into her. Mia's body was rocked beneath them and somehow she managed to keep her balance as Vicki was violently fucked. Yet again she found herself staring into the slave's eyes and she could feel her arousal growing again as the slave rubbed against her pussy. The slave tossed her head, showering Mia with sweat as she neared a shattering climax. She threw her head back and groaned but moments before she climaxed, the man yanked himself free of her and pushed her to the side. He squatted over Mia and forced his cock into her arse, groaning loudly as he forced his way into her tight passage.

'Master,' Vicki gasped and crawled over to him, 'please.'

He looked down at her and grinned nastily, 'Open your fucking mouth.'

She did as she was ordered, whimpering with unspent lust as he pulled free of Mia's arse and jetted his come into her mouth. He groaned as he watched her swallowing his come and wiped himself across her cheeks.

'Thank you, Master,' she whispered.

Ignoring her, he bent to release Mia and nudged her with his boot when she fell onto her side, quivering. 'I'm not done with you yet.'

Mia looked up at him, using every last ounce of strength she had to show defiance, she had no doubt that this would be her last opportunity to be herself for a while and she wanted it to last – despite the pain. 'Haven't you had enough fun?'

'Oh yeah,' he sighed and looked at Vicki, 'but she hasn't.'

'Master, thank you,' she gasped and crawled to him, kissing his feet.

He laughed at the sight of her and then smiled at Mia, 'This will be you soon.'

'The fuck it will.'

Laughing angrily, he turned and walked away. When he returned he dropped something beside Mia and she stared first at him and then down at the thick strap-on dildo. He bent the crop between his large hands, his meaning clear. Slowly, she reached for the dildo.

'Stop.'

Mia froze at the sound of Thomas' voice.

'Don't give in so easily.'

She turned in the direction of his voice but couldn't make him out amongst the other silhouettes and settled for glaring in his general direction.

'Make him force you to fuck that slave!' There was laughter in his voice as he spoke and she hated him all the more for it.

She turned her venom on the man with the crop, using her newfound strength to lift herself into a sitting position, 'You want your slave fucked? Then do it yourself.'

The crop found her breasts, cutting across the top of her nipples and making her sag. She stifled a cry and continued to stare at him, anger making her tremble. Another blow, this time slightly higher and then another to the same spot. Several terrible blows fell against the same line of flesh and soon blood had beaded on the surface. She cried out as he struck her again, smearing the blood across her chest. Sweat ran in rivulets down her skin, beading on her forehead and soaking her hair. Tears welled in the corners of her eyes as she watched him raise the crop once more.

'Alright,' she whispered. The crop landed anyway and she cried out, falling sideways to grab the dildo before he struck her again. It made no difference and he continued to lash her with the crop every few seconds until she had fastened it around her waist.

'Tighter,' he ordered as she fastened a strap between her legs.

Mia winced as she tightened the strap over her bruised pussy lips.

The crop continued to find her flesh as she crawled to Vicki who had lifted herself onto all fours. She stared over her shoulder at Mia, her breaths coming in short, painful gasps, desperate to feel the rubber cock sliding into her. As Mia positioned the dome at the glistening lips, the crop suddenly sliced between them, catching Mia's nipples and then falling further to slice the outer lips of Vicki's pussy. Both slaves gasped and then both cried out together as the crop found Mia's buttocks with a shuddering blow that slammed her forward, driving the dildo into the other slave. A blow to the breasts made Mia arch back and then a blow to the buttocks sent her forward again. She gripped Vicki's hips to steady herself as her body was rocked by blow after blow to front and back. Her thighs slammed the other slave's buttocks as Vicki tossed her head, screaming her pleasure. She fucked her as hard as she could, desperately hoping that once the slave had come he would stop striking her. He increased the tempo of his blows and Vicki was fucked faster and harder.

'Hold onto it,' Thomas' voice echoed around them and they all knew that he was talking to Vicki, 'Just hold onto your climax ... it will be worth every moment.'

Vicki tossed her head, eyes squeezed tightly shut, teeth gritted as she desperately tried to obey the command.

'Just ten more lashes front and back,' Thomas announced, ignoring Mia's shuddering cry in response, 'Just ten more and then you can explode.'

The lashes fell, slower than before as he built Vicki's arousal all the more. After the tenth blow had landed he bent to Mia's ear, 'Now, make that whore come.'

Mia's fingernails dug into Vicki's flesh, making the slave cry out and look over her shoulder as Mia dragged her back onto the invading dildo. She held the quivering slave steady as they locked stares. Slowly, she pulled back and then slammed forward. Vicki's orgasm started immediately and she screamed over and over again as her body was slammed by wave after wave of pleasure, the dildo a constant, thrusting accompaniment to her spent desires.

Suddenly Mia cried out as she felt a thick cock sliding into her. Her head fell back against his chest as his hands gripped her wounded breasts. She screamed in pain and pleasure, pulling Vicki back onto her and making her cry out as she climaxed again. He fucked her harshly, tossing her violently and making sure that each movement was mirrored by the dildo in Vicki's pussy. His fingers found her clitoris and Mia sobbed as she sprayed across Vicki's arse. Still in the throes of her climax, she hardly noticed when he repositioned the dildo. Vicki's pitiful cry made Mia look down as he thrust into her pussy, in turn forcing the thick dildo into Vicki's arse. He grunted in her ear and then she felt the heat of him filling her. She came again as Vicki collapsed beneath her. When he let her go, she had no strength left and she fell across the prone slave, her chest heaving as sobs of pleasure and exhaustion racked them both.

Chapter ten: The special project

Mia awoke to the sight of four house slaves enjoying each other for the pleasure of Roxanne. She rolled over to turn her back on the scene. The sounds were harder to block out as four enthusiastic slaves rapidly reached they crescendo. Mia groaned with them, her lower stomach cramping painfully as she squeezed her thighs together. She could feel her swollen, soaking pussy lips and ached desperately to slide her fingers between the smooth folds. But, despite her desire to keep from submitting completely, she wasn't stupid and certainly wouldn't risk a punishment just because she was unable to control her own desires. Sighing angrily, she sat up and rubbed her eyes with the palms of her hands.

'Feeling a little tense?' Roxanne asked from the other side of the room and laughed, 'How I'd love to taste that desire right now ...' She continued to speak but Mia managed to tune out her words before the desire to pleasure herself was overwhelmed by the desire to strike the other slave – something that would undoubtedly lead to a similar punishment. It took Mia a few moments to realise that someone else was speaking and that Roxanne was responding angrily, 'What did you say?'

Mia looked at the slave who was the recipient of Roxanne's fury, 'I said ... leave her alone, go find someone else to play with.'

'How about I play with you?'

Vicki smiled and then laughed, 'You couldn't keep up!'

Roxanne snarled but seemed unable to come up with a suitable response. Instead she cursed harshly and turned her fury on an unfortunate house slave who was close at hand. Mia turned back to Vicki who smiled but then quickly fell to her knees when the door to the slave room was thrown open. Each slave quickly mirrored her actions, each turning towards the door, heads bowed and hands behind their backs. Mia was closest to the door and she was the first to feel a sharp snap of a crop on her shoulder, 'On your feet!'

She did as she was told, keeping her eyes down.

'That one.'

Mia recognised Thomas' voice as the man who had told her to stand approached another slave and gave the same order. Three more slaves were selected and led from the room. Once lined up outside, Mia half lifted her head to see who else had been chosen. A mixture of feelings settled in the pit of her stomach when she saw that both Roxanne and Vicki stood with her.

'Follow me,' Thomas ordered and led them through the house. He took them on a familiar route which would take them to the main studios but as they neared the usual doors they didn't slow but just kept on straight past. Mia squinted as they were led outside into brilliant sunshine. They were led across a courtyard to a narrow corridor between two out-buildings. Ahead of them a door was opened and they were ushered inside. The room was empty and devoid of windows.

'Against the wall,' Thomas ordered and then moved towards the door at the other end of the room. He stepped through before turning to beckon the first slave. Nervously, she followed him and the door closed behind them. It was several minutes before the door opened and Thomas beckoned the next slave – the first slave was nowhere to be seen. Roxanne was the next to be called in, leaving Mia and Vicki standing side by side. Mia risked studying her more carefully. She really was stunning. She was a little shorter than Mia's own below average height with mid-length blonde hair that hung in a simple, straight cut around her neck. Her eyes had an interesting shape, hinting at an oriental background at some point in her family's past – they were a vibrant blue and almost cat-like. Mia's gaze travelled down. When she had witnessed the slave's submission, she hadn't noticed how strong she was but as she breathed Mia could see her muscles rippling beneath the skin. Toned and tanned with gorgeous, full breasts that still bore the marks of heavy abuse.

'You like what you see?'

Mia jumped, guiltily looking away.

'It's alright,' the slave laughed, 'I'm quite used to being studied.' There was nothing egotistical in her voice, just a simple fact that made Mia look at her again. Vicki smiled, 'I like what I see too.'

Mia couldn't help but smile when she realised that the slave had been studying her while she had been doing the same.

'I'm Vicki,' she announced, a hint of an Australian accent creeping into her voice.

Mia swallowed past the dryness in her throat and nodded, 'Mia.'

'A pretty name ... it suits you.'

She didn't know how to respond and eventually just said, 'Thank you.'

Vicki smiled again, her full lips curling up with genuine amusement. Before either of them could say anymore the door opened and Thomas beckoned Vicki, leaving Mia on her own.

The minutes seemed to stretch forever as Mia's anxiety grew. She remembered that the masters had mentioned a special project and assumed that this was it. Suddenly the door opened and Thomas beckoned her over. She went through the door and into a small anteroom with an identical door on the other side. Thomas closed the door and then turned to her, his grey eyes studying her.

'You have been chosen to take part in a special project.'

'Why me?'

Amusement flickered in his eyes as he answered,

'That's why.'

Mia frowned.

He didn't explain any further, instead he told her, 'I am going to push you to the very limits of what you can bear. I expect you to take it without question. I expect you to do as you are told. I expect you to suffer ... do you understand?'

Mia swallowed painfully, 'Yes.' It wasn't what she wanted to say and they both knew it – it was just the only thing she could say.

He studied her carefully, 'I will give you no further instruction – I expect you to react to what I have done to you in a suitable manner ... I expect you to be strong and I will not tolerate weakness. You I expect to be stronger than the others, which is why I will push you harder than them.'

She stared at him and felt her anger rise. At that moment she hated him more than she had ever hated anyone. At least Kent fucked her himself, he didn't just sit back and order others to do his work so that he could sell the result. 'Why me? Why are you doing this to me?'

Her question made him smile, 'Because I can.'

Her palm had struck his cheek before she had realised what she was doing. She gasped and lowered her hand as he rubbed the side of his face. She had expected him to strike her back but he didn't. Instead he leant close to her and whispered, 'There is no camera in here – be thankful for that because if anyone else had seen you do that ...' he left the sentence unfinished.

'Am I supposed to be grateful?'

He gave a tiny shrug that only infuriated her more.

'I'm sure you'll find a way to punish me.'

'Count on it.' his voice was low, sultry almost and Mia felt herself sinking into his eyes as her pussy moistened. He must have noticed her reaction because his hand moved forward and he slipped a finger between the folds of her pussy, gently sliding over her clitoris. She gasped and her knees weakened, she fell back against the wall her back arching. Chuckling softly, Thomas lifted his finger to his lips and gently licked her juice from his skin before grabbing her shoulder and pushing her towards the door, 'Time to play,' he whispered in her ear, 'You ready?'

Mia glared at him as she was pushed into line with the other four slaves. Thomas turned without saying another word and left via the same door, closing and locking it behind him. For the first time Mia looked around and felt her breath catch in her throat.

They were in a prison.

Built on just one level, the white walls and painted metal doors were more than an illusion, more than just a set. This was as real as it could be and Mia was suddenly very afraid. If she had learnt anything in the short time she had been here it was that those in charge could do whatever they wanted, for as long as they wanted. Mia swallowed, for the first time since arriving at the house she was truly afraid of what was going to happen and her ability to survive it.

A metal door clanged open somewhere behind them and then clanged shut again. Three sets of heavy footsteps approached and Mia trembled along with the slaves on either side of her. The men who stood in front of them were large and dressed in the harsh uniforms of prison wardens. Their hair was shaved close to their heads and their eyes were hidden behind mirrored sunglasses. Two of the men stood slightly back while the tallest and broadest addressed the slaves.

'You have all been found guilty of various crimes for which you have been sentenced to various lengths of imprisonment.' He approached the line, starting from the first slave and slowly walking past each in turn. 'Your crimes, your length of stay here means fuck all to me.' He reached the end of the line, turned smartly and started to walk back again, 'Your obedience to the rules, to me and my officers is all that matters. Punishments will be given swiftly and without mercy. Every punishment will serve as an example to all of you.' He stopped at the head of the line. 'You will address me as Warden, my men are to be addressed as Officer or Sir. You will not be reminded of this again.' He started to walk along the line again, this time stopping at each slave in turn. 'Six,' he said to the first slave and then moved on to Mia. She kept her head bowed as he said harshly, 'Seven.' He moved on, 'Eight, Nine, Ten.' Mia knew from their position in the line that Roxanne was Nine and Vicki Ten. He took a few steps backward until he was standing in front of the slave standing between Mia and Roxanne, 'Who are you?'

'Master?'

The sound of his hand striking her face echoed loudly in the large room, 'Who are you?'

The slave gave a confused sob, tears welling in her eyes, 'Master, I do not -'

Her words were cut off by another blow, this one sent her to her knees. 'Would anyone like to answer for this stupid slut?'

'Warden,' Roxanne said smugly, 'she is Eight.'

He moved to stand in front of her, 'And you are?'

'Nine, Warden.'

He nodded, 'Then that is the number of lashes that you shall both have.'

Roxanne gasped, 'Warden, I -'

'Eighteen lashes.' he announced as his two colleagues stepped forward and dragged the slaves out of the line to force them onto all fours, their backs presented for punishment. The beating began as the warden turned back to the line, 'Every time I or my men have to punish you, another will suffer the same fate to ensure that the lesson is learned by all.' He turned back to the prone slaves and his officers to watch the rest of the punishment being carried out. When they were done, the slaves were dragged to their feet and pushed back in line. Roxanne glared at the other slave who sobbed softly, her harsh gaze spoke of trouble ahead for the younger slave. Mia noticed the look but ignored it – she had enough to worry about without provoking Roxanne any further.

'Seven!'

Mia jumped as the warden bellowed at her, 'Yes, Warden?'

'Your cell.'

She looked where he was pointing towards an open door. The small room beyond held a bunk bed and a bucket. Mia swallowed and stepped forward.

'Ten! You're with her.'

Mia half glanced over her shoulder as Vicki moved to stand beside her, saying softly, 'Yes, Warden.'

'Well – get fucking in there then!'

Both slaves moved quickly and Mia heard Vicki gasp as the warden's crop snapped across her buttocks. They entered the cell and the door was slammed and locked behind them.

'Top or bottom?' Vicki asked from behind Mia.

Mia rested her hands on the top bunk and sighed, 'Which bed do you want?'

Vicki's slim fingers stroked Mia's hips and slowly spun her round, 'I didn't mean the beds.' She announced with a smile and suddenly her lips were smothering Mia's, her tongue searching between them. Mia was too stunned to respond to the kiss but then Vicki's hands found her breasts and she quickly pushed the other slave away.

'What are you doing?'

'I thought that was obvious,' Vicki stepped closer, her fingers twisting Mia's nipples gently, making her gasp. Her fingers traced lines down her skin as Vicki slowly dropped to her knees, her hot breath making Mia quiver as the slave's tongue traced a line across her pelvic bone and then lower.

'Stop it,' Mia sighed half-heatedly and then groaned

with frustration when Vicki pulled back. She looked down and Vicki smiled up at her, 'What?' Mia asked, her voice hoarse.

The slave's smile widened, 'I do what I'm told,' she announced, 'I thought you realised that.'

Mia swallowed, unable to take her eyes off the kneeling slave.

'Do you want me to stop?'

'No,' the word was out of her mouth before the thought had formed in her mind.

'Then ... you know what to say.'

The pause was almost unbearable as Mia's lust raged inside her, fighting with her common sense. They would both be punished if they were caught – but, this wasn't the movie house anymore, did the same rules still apply? The Warden hadn't said that they couldn't. A cry of pleasure suddenly echoed from the cell next door and Mia froze – waiting for the sound of the cell door to be opened and the slaves to be punished for their indiscretion. When it didn't come Mia slipped her hands sideways to grip the edges of the top bunk. She licked her lips, forced saliva to moisten her dry throat and half gasped, 'Make me come.'

Vicki's tongue was in her almost instantly and she threw her head back, crying out with delight and abandon. She started to climax almost instantly and the mind numbing pleasure didn't stop. Vicki's fingers found her clitoris and her thumb pushed hard at the sensitive bud, teasing climax after climax from her quivering body. When Mia could stand no more she sank to her knees. With surprising strength, Vicki lifted her up and spread her on the lower bunk. Holding one of her legs up, Vicki slipped her own leg beneath Mia's buttocks and moved her pussy forward. Mia cried out again as she felt Vicki's pelvis pushing against her own, her swollen, soaking labia pressing against its mate. Vicki quivered and groaned as she rubbed her pussy firmly against Mia's. Both became lost in the sheer filthy pleasure of it and climaxed over and over again before they both fell breathless onto the thin mattress.

'On your feet!'

Mia's eyes snapped open and she quickly disengaged her legs from Vicki's as the two slaves scrambled to their feet.

'Turn and face the bunk.'

'Yes, sir,' they replied in unison as they turned, automatically reaching up to grip the metal frame.

'Did you enjoy yourselves?'

'Yes, sir.' they said together.

'Did you both come?'

'Yes, sir.'

'Prepare for punishment.'

Mia quivered, unsure what was expected. She felt Vicki nudge her and she looked over to see that the slave had taken a step backwards so that she could bend forward and present her buttocks to the guard. Mia quickly followed suit, staring down at her breasts that quivered as her whole body shook with the last of her pleasure. Vicki received the first five blows, her breath hissing through her teeth as the thin crop sliced her buttocks. As the guard moved to give Mia the same, they heard a cry from the next cell. Mia gasped as the crop found her flesh, her buttocks quivering beneath the first of the five blows. Sweat sprang out along her forehead and her fingers gripped the bar as the crop sliced her flesh again and again. Mia dared to hope that that was all but the guard moved to Vicki and rested the crop against the back of her thighs. It took six blows with the crop before, with a cry, Vicki sank to her knees. That had clearly been the intention because the guard immediately moved to Mia.

'She'll take more than six.'

Mia jumped as the voice echoed around the cell. It was Thomas' voice but it was tinny, as if coming over a loud speaker. Mia felt anger blossom in her chest and heat her cheeks. That anger only deepened as the crop found the back of her thighs, making her hiss. After nine such blows she felt her knees buckle but with a clever flick of his wrist, the guard sliced the crop up and under her buttocks, lifting her onto her toes. She gasped but refused to cry out, squeezing her eyes tightly shut and gritting her teeth. Seven more blows found her thighs before Mia was about to surrender and sink to her knees but the guard stepped back. She gave a tiny sob and let her head hang between her arms, her legs quivering with the effort of keeping her upright. She stayed like that for a long time after the cell door had been closed and locked once more. Slowly, Mia opened her eyes and realised that Vicki was no longer kneeling beside her. She looked quickly over her should and saw the slave leaning against the opposite wall, breathing heavily. Her eyes were dark and heavy with arousal.

'Are you okay?' Mia whispered.

She took a deep, shaking breath and blinked, as if a spell had been broken. Her eyes lifted to Mia's face, 'You're beautiful.'

It was then that Mia realised that the other slave had been staring at the lines that smothered her buttocks and thighs. Mia didn't know what to say and so instead she carefully lifted herself onto the top bunk and lay on her stomach. She suddenly cursed and flinched as she felt Vicki's fingernail tracing a line across the five lines on her buttocks.

'Does that hurt?'

'Yes,' Mia responded but the other slave's smile suggested that she had seen the half-truth for what it was.

'God, I'd love to flip you over and fuck you again.'

Mia closed her eyes, squeezing her thighs together. 'Please, stop.'

'Why?' Vicki's fingers moved to the backs of her thighs and traced each one in turn, 'Don't you want to?'

Mia's eyes snapped open, 'I'd rather not feel the crop again, thank you.'

Vicki seemed surprised by the response, 'Really?'

Mia moved away from her touch by rolling her back

towards the wall, 'Do you?'

The other slave sighed longingly, 'I prefer the feel of a good stock-whip or lash but ...' she sighed again, '... the crop did its job.' She studied Mia and then gave a small laugh, 'You thought it was pain that drove me to my knees?'

'Yes ... I mean ... I ... what was it?'

Vicki's smile was indulgent, 'After what we did ... that crop just fired up my lust all over again, it was just what I needed.'

'You came?'

'Didn't you?'

The two slaves stared at each other – both unable to understand the other. Mia saw her own confusion mirrored in Vicki's eyes.

Any further discussion was cut off by a harsh bang on the door, 'Silence!' a voice bellowed. Still frowning, Vicki dropped onto the lower bunk. Lost in her own thoughts, Mia drifted off to sleep.

*

It was raining heavily when they were marched out into the exercise yard – a square of concrete, each side about ten metres and bordered by thick wooden fencing with curled barbed wire running along the top. Two yellow lines had been painted just inside the fence and it was between these lines that the slaves were ordered to walk in single file. There were ten slaves in all and Mia had realised that five of them must have already been in the cells when they arrived. They had been walking for about five minutes when the Warden appeared and stood in the centre of the square. He stood beneath a huge umbrella, watching the slaves intently. After a few minutes he pointed and beckoned. Mia felt movement behind her and realised that he had beckoned Vicki. Mia watched from the corner of her eye as Vicki knelt before him, presenting her open mouth to his swollen cock. She didn't move, hands behind her back, as he rhythmically fucked her mouth. After several minutes he grunted and forced himself deeply, making her gag as he gushed his semen into her throat. Barely giving her time to recover, he suddenly pushed her head down until her cheek was pressed against the harsh concrete, her buttocks in the air.

'Peters!' he called and one of the guards approached, unfastening his fly. The Warden placed his booted foot on Vicki's head, keeping her face pressed against the concrete as the guard squatted behind her. The guard seemed unconcerned by the driving rain as he thrust into her unresisting cunt. He came quickly, slapping Vicki's bruised buttocks as he groaned his climax. As the guard left the exercise yard, another appeared, already undoing his trousers and belt. He slipped the belt from his trousers and delivered several harsh blows to her raised buttocks before sinking his cock into her arse. He rode her harshly, his fingers scouring harsh lines across her hips before he groaned loudly and then pulled back to splash his come across her rain soaked buttocks. The guard rearranged his clothing and then returned to the building.

'Stay as you are,' the Warden told her as he moved his foot and then studied the line of walking slaves. His gaze fell upon Mia. 'Exercise is over – back inside.' His finger stabbed at Mia, 'Not you!'

Mia stopped walking and stood, waiting for further instruction.

'Come and slide your hand into this whore's cunt.'

'Yes, Warden.'

'Thank you, Warden,' Vicki gasped as she watched Mia approach.

The Warden sliced her back with his crop, 'Silence!'

Mia knelt behind Vicki's raised buttocks and slowly slipped two fingers into the soaking cunt. Vicki groaned with delight, squeezing her eyes tightly shut. Mia thrust her fingers firmly back and forth, feeling her own arousal growing. She gasped as the Warden's crop found her shoulder, 'Did I say to finger the slut?' he demanded, 'I told you to slide your hand in there – fucking do it or it will be my hand sliding into your cunt!'

'Yes, Warden,' Mia whispered quickly and then withdrew her fingers. She closed her fingers tightly together and slowly slipped the tips into the unresisting pussy. Vicki wriggled her hips as four of Mia's fingers sank into her. She continued to push, forcing her hand and thumb into the slave.

Suddenly Vicki tossed her head back and screamed in delight, 'Thank you, Sir!'

Her shout brought the crop slicing down across her shoulder blades. That had perhaps been her intention because her whole body shuddered under the onslaught of her climax. Mia continued to thrust her hand into the spasming pussy, desperate to draw every last ounce of pleasure from the slave. A few moments later, both slaves received the bite of the crop as they were ordered back to their cell. Mia supported Vicki as they were led back and when they reached their cell Mia managed to get her inside and lay her on the bunk. She was about to stand up when Vicki suddenly grabbed her and pulled her down, rolling so that Mia's was back was pressed against the wall. Vicki's hand dipped between Mia's legs, making her gasp, 'Don't, they'll discover us.'

'Then keep quiet,' Vicki whispered as she slid her fingers into Mia.

Mia hissed and clamped her lips down on Vicki's shoulder to gag herself. Lost in the delicious feel of Vicki's fingers, Mia sucked at gorgeous flesh and bit gently at her shoulder.

Later, during cell inspection, the livid purple bruise on Vicki's shoulder was enough to earn them both ten lashes each.

*

They became lost in the routine of the prison as three days passed – at least, they had the impression that it was three days. With no clocks and no record of time passing, they had only the routine to guide them. They were exercised twice a day, always in daylight, fed three times a day and allowed time out of their cells. At the end of the day they were given fifteen minutes of light after their cells were locked and then they were left in silent darkness. How long the nights lasted was impossible to gauge and it mattered little. They were left alone at night – despite Mia's original fears that the Warden or guards would seek their night time pleasures. As it turned out, they didn't need to. The Warden and the guards took their pleasures during the exercise time. If the mood took them they would also enjoy a prisoner after a punishment had been handed out – usually at the end of their ever-present crops. The crimes for which the punishments were received were varied. Not cleaning their cell correctly. Answering back or not saying Warden or Sir when speaking to the guards. Mia had been punished three times with harsh blows to both breasts and buttocks. Twice had been to share the punishment of another prisoner and the third time because she had been distracted by the sight of Vicki on her hands and knees, scrubbing the floor of their cell. She had stood, mesmerised in the doorway and hadn't heard the guard come up behind her, so had failed to greet him correctly – by dropping to her knees with her hands behind her back. Vicki had shared her punishment and Vicki had then risked further punishment for them both by masturbating with the handle of the brush that she had been using. Mia hadn't joined her nor had she tried to stop her and the sounds of the other slave's pleasure had made Mia spread her legs and gently stroke her swollen pussy lips. She hadn't dared fully pleasure herself and envied Vicki's abandon. For Vicki it was a no lose situation – if she was caught and punished then she would no doubt climax under the whip. Later that day, it had been Mia's turn to be enjoyed by the guards in the exercise yard and she had surrendered to a powerful climax as the Warden fucked her mouth while the two guards had her arse and cunt. They had whipped her for her pleasure, delivering harsh blows to her pussy lips that, later in the darkened cell, Vicki had kissed and gently eased.

In the corner of the cell, the camera lens turned as it focused in on Vicki's gently attentions to Mia's quivering pussy. If the slaves knew that the camera was watching, they paid no heed. By now, each slave must have known that there were cameras everywhere, filming constantly. Occasionally they heard Thomas' voice but mostly they were left to play out their roles as they saw fit – or as the Warden and the guards allowed them. Mia had not heard Thomas' voice for several hours, if he had given any direction than she had been too lost in whatever was happening to notice. Vicki's sweet, gentle licks to her pussy lips were arousing her so wonderfully that she became lost in a delirium of peaceful pleasure and she didn't hear his voice then either. But a moment after he had spoken, Vicki's finger slipped into Mia's cunt, making her back arch off the bunk. Vicki moved with her, sliding her thumb into Mia's anus and another into her vagina, her tongue found Mia's clitoris and she sucked firmly before using her shoulders to push Mia's legs up. She drove her fingers into Mia's bruised cunt, the welts shining beneath the glistening juice. Mia groaned, biting her lip against the cry that was both pleasure and pain. Another command, unheard by Mia, and Vicki's other hand pressed at the bruises, making the slave gasp and quiver.

'Please, stop,' Mia gasped but Vicki didn't stop and soon she was driving four fingers into the open, swollen pussy. Her finger nails dug into Mia's breast, scratching the skin and causing tiny pin-pricks of blood to appear just beneath the surface. 'Oh god, please stop!' Mia cried, trying to pull away from Vicki but the slave went with her, driving her fingers even harder into her sore pussy. Mia's back arch, her buttocks quivering and then Vicki pulled her fingers free, her other hand rubbing firmly over her pelvic bone and clitoris. Mia cried out as she ejaculated in a great jet that soaked Vicki's face and breasts. Groaning, Vicki opened her mouth and closed her eyes, rubbing Mia's juice into her skin before leaning forward to lick her clean and making her climax once more.

Suddenly both slaves were blinded as the harsh light came on and the cell door was thrown open. They scrambled quickly off the bunk, falling to their knees with heads bowed and hands behind their back. It quickly became clear that the guards were not about to punish them for their indiscretion – instead they pushed them to the other side of the cell and made them sit against the wall. The Warden entered a few moments later and then nodded at the guards, 'Begin the search.'

There was nothing in the cell to search except the mattresses on the bed. The guards ripped the covers from them, tearing the material between them and pulling the filthy stuffing out.

'Warden,' one of the guards said, 'we've found something.'

Glaring at the two slaves the warden approached the bunk and sighed angrily, 'Bag all that contraband and take them to the Governor's office – he should deal with this.'

Ten minutes later and the two slaves were standing in front of a large oak desk. Lined up in front of them and looking very much out of place, were eight dildos of various shapes and sizes – the contraband that had supposedly been found in their mattresses.

'Would either of you two care to explain these to me?'

They both kept their heads down, not looking at the portly governor who was polishing his glasses on the tail of his shirt. He slipped his glasses back on and studied the line of phalluses spread out on his desk. He sighed loudly, 'Have you used all of these?' Neither of the slaves answered, making him sigh again. 'Very well,' he leant forward and pressed a button on a small box on his desk, 'Warden.'

A few moments later there was a knock at the office door and the Warden entered, nodding at the governor, 'Yes, sir?'

'Put these two in solitary confinement, perhaps some time apart will encourage them to answer my questions.'

'Yes, sir.'

Mia glanced at Vicki as the Warden grabbed their arms and dragged them towards the office door. The submissive returned her gaze and Mia saw the excitement flickering like electricity through her vibrant blue eyes. For the first time ever, Mia wished that she could feel as Vicki did – anything was better than the cold knot of fear that settled in the pit of her stomach. She remembered the interrogation games that Kent had played and feared that the sadistic sergeant had only been playing, and these men weren't going to be.

The cell into which she was thrown was the same size as the cell she shared with Vicki – but was completely empty without even a window. The cell door slammed shut and she retreated to the far corner, standing with her hands crossed over her breasts. It was the first time that she had been alone for almost three weeks, as far as she could tell, and it was a strange, frightening experience. She shivered, telling herself that it was the cold of the cell and not her fear that made her quiver. She listened, hoping to hear Vicki in the next cell but the lack of sound only heightened her fear and loneliness. She was almost grateful when the cell door opened but that feeling quickly fled as she saw the looks on the faces of the governor and the Warden.

'We'll start with her.' the governor announced, never taking his eyes off Mia, 'She's the weakest and easiest to break – the other will enjoy it too much before she breaks.'

'Not that that isn't fun,' the Warden smiled.

'Indeed,' the governor laughed, still staring at Mia, 'so we shall get the weak, boring one out of the way first?'

His words stung Mia in a way that she wasn't prepared for – his words hurt her pride. After everything that had happened, everything that had been done to her – she still had her pride? A smile tugged at the corners of her mouth, small enough that neither man noticed. Let them think what they liked – she would not be broken. After all, she had no knowledge of the contraband that had been found in her cell so she had nothing to say anyway. She stared back at the governor, locking his eyes with hers and he seemed surprised by the challenge that he saw there.

'Let's begin,' he announced and raised his hand to beckon her. She stepped forward, kneeling at his feet when he motioned for her to do so. 'I shall give you this warning – the punishment for smuggling in those objects will be severe – consider that before you confess too easily.'

She remained kneeling in the centre of the cell, her hands on her head, as the two men slowly circled her. It was several minutes before the governor spoke again, 'If your hands leave your head, I shall take that as an admission of guilt, do you understand?'

'Yes, Sir.'

The crop found her breasts and she sank beneath the blow, gasping.

'Who smuggled the contraband into your cell?'

She remained silent and the crop fell again, this time catching the curve of her buttocks.

'Who hid the contraband?'

Further silence was followed by several more blows to her front and back.

'Who used the contraband first?'

The questions kept coming, each one followed by a greater succession of blows.

'Who use the contraband on you? ... Who made you come? ... Where did you hide the contraband during cell search?'

Her only responses were gasps and small cries as the blows became progressively harder. The warden paused on his next circle around her to squat down and stare into her eyes, 'You think you're protecting your cell mate?'

She stared back at him, trying to hold back the tears that prickled at the corners of her eyes.

'We know that one of you smuggled it all in ... probably both of you. But the Governor, well he likes things nice and tidy, see?' He stood, resting the crop against his shoulder, 'The Governor believes in justice and for justice to be served ... well we need a confession or someone to blame.' The crop sliced her nipples and she cried out, quickly biting her bottom lip to stop any further sound. He squatted down again in front of her, 'We know it was her – just tell us that it was and this will all be over.'

'No,' Mia whispered.

Sighing sadly and shaking his head, the warden stood up and grabbed her arms, forcing her to the back of the cell. He crushed her against the wall, squashing her breasts as her hands were hauled over her head. The governor clicked a pair of handcuffs around her wrists and then looped the chain over a metal hook above Mia. She had to stand on tip-toe to stop her arms being stretched too painfully and struggled to keep her balance as the two men left the cell.

When they returned they both stood on her right and lifted the harsh looking floggers that they both carried.

'Last chance,' the governor announced and when she made no response he sighed angrily.

Mia closed her eyes as the men moved to stand either side of her. Her hands clenched into fists as she held her breath and waited for the first blow. It was soon in coming and quickly followed by another as the men beat her in turn. The strands of each flogger had barely fallen from her skin before the next took its place. They delivered the blows in a line travelling down from her shoulders to the backs of her thighs and then back up again. They had completed four such revolutions before they both stopped to catch their breath and study her glowing red skin. Barely an inch of the target area was left unmarked and to Mia it felt as if her whole back had been flayed. She sobbed openly, all pretence at hiding how much it hurt was forgotten. When no further blows fell she dared to hope that they respected her strength and would leave her alone. That thought was followed by the guilty realisation that once they finished with her they would move onto Vicki. The moment of relief when she realised that they had far from finished was fleeting as they turned her round and began again – this time starting at her breasts and ending at her thighs.

*

Mia's legs had long since given out and, despite the pain that seared her shoulders and wrists, she hung limply from the cuffs. At some point they had finished the interrogation and had left. Mia had been vaguely aware of a man fucking her but had not had the strength to acknowledge what he was doing. Eventually she had been left alone and had drifted in and out of darkness since then. Voices drifted to her and she felt herself crying as she heard, 'The other one broke ... confessed ... no surprise ... can't wait for the punishment.'

It was sometime later that Mia was practically carried from her cell and into the exercise yard where she was dropped beside the other slaves.

'Kneel,' the guard ordered, flicking her shoulder with the crop.

She managed to lift herself onto her knees and put her hands behind her back as was expected. As she lifted her head the breath caught in her throat at the sight that greeted her.

In the centre of the exercise yard was a leather bench

– lying on her back, tied to the bench with her knees bent and her ankles fixed to her wrists, was Vicki. Her pussy was open and exposed, swollen and aroused. She fought for breath, her chest constricted by the harsh straps that made her breasts swell painfully. The clamps that cruelly squeezed her nipples were pulled to the side by heavy chains and weights that hung just above the ground. Her inner thighs were striped with red and purple welts, evidence of the interrogation that she had led to her confession and current position.

The Warden stepped forward, a heavy multi-stranded whip gripped in his large fist. He raised the whip to shoulder height, took a breath and then delivered a blow with all his strength, lashing not just with the wrist but his whole arm. The leather strands sliced down between her legs, smothering her pussy lips and making her body shudder. The assembled slaves all flinched at the sight of such a vicious blow – Vicki made no sound, her only reaction was a tear that slid from the corner of her eye and rolled down to become lost in her sweat-soaked hair. Stunned by what had just happened, Mia stared at the Warden as he turned to the governor, 'She's ready, sir.'

Nodding, the governor stepped forward and stood at Vicki's head, staring down at her but speaking loud enough for all of the slaves to hear, 'You have confessed to smuggling in and hiding illegal items in your cell. Do you accept your punishment?'

Vicki swallowed a sob, 'Yes, sir.'

'Very well – begin!'

A trolley was wheeled across the yard and Mia's eye widened when she saw the array of dildos lined up on it. She realised quickly that these were the items of contraband that had been 'found' in their cell.

'Since you were the only one to confess the crime, you shall be the only one to suffer the punishment,' the governor announced and turned to look pointedly at Mia. She stared back, despite herself, feeling a flush of heat rise up her neck and face. A part of her wanted to step forward, to confess and share Vicki's punishment but she knew that if she did, their punishment would only be worse – the look on the governor's face had made that quite clear. He had clearly intended Mia to confess beneath the whip but her strength had saved her ... and condemned Vicki. The governor turned to watch as a guard slid a dildo into Vicki's exposed pussy. It was followed a few moments later by another. 'Make sure they are all inserted before the anaesthetic wears off,' he announced, 'Maybe then she will fully appreciate the crime she has committed.'

Mia felt her throat dry as the realisation of what he had just said slowly sank in. So that was why she had barely reacted when he had struck her with the whip. Two more dildos were inserted and Mia averted her eyes, she couldn't bear to watch. A slice of a crop across her shoulders made her fall forwards. Another blow and she struggled to her knees, turning her eyes back to the awful spectacle before her – the meaning behind the blows clear.

'How many is that?' the governor asked.

'Four so far.'

'Hmmm ... put that large one with the others and then the remaining ones in her arse.'

Vicki whimpered, tears rolling down the sides of her face.

It was several minutes before all of the dildos had been inserted. Bending to study the guards work, the governor nodded with satisfaction. 'The prisoners are to remain there. I have paperwork to attend to. Call me when the anaesthetic is wearing off.'

'Yes, sir,' the guard nodded, 'of course.'

It was perhaps twenty minutes before Vicki whimpered and groaned. One of the slaves had passed out as she had watched the guard shoving the phalluses into Vicki and as the anaesthetic started to wear off, the sound of Vicki's groans drove another to her knees. She was hauled out of the line by a guard and dragged back into the building. When the guard returned a few minutes later, he was rearranging his uniform, evidence that he too had been affected by the sight of Vicki's punishment and had taken the opportunity to relieve himself.

'Sir?' the prisoner beside Mia asked nervously as he passed.

'What is it?' he demanded.

'I need to pee, sir.'

The guard glanced at the warden who waved towards Vicki, 'Pee over her.'

The slave glanced over and gave a tiny shake of her head, 'Actually, sir, I'm okay, sir.'

The warden's eyes narrowed dangerously, 'Get over there and piss on that whore.'

'Yes, Warden,' the slave whispered as she walked slowly to the centre of the yard. She climbed onto the bench, standing with her feet either side of Vicki's chest. Closing her eyes, a tentative splash of urine splattered Vicki's breasts followed by a stream. Gasping, Vicki stared up at the slave, her breath heavy with submissive arousal. When the slave had finished she jumped off and returned to her space in the line.

'Warden, sir.'

Mia glanced sideways, realising that it was Roxanne who had spoken.

'What?'

'I need to pee too.'

'Go on then.'

Smiling, Roxanne went quickly to the centre of the yard and climbed onto the bench, squatting over the prone slave. She had to press her stomach for a moment before she was able to jet a stream of piss at Vicki's face and neck, smiling sadistically as she watched Vicki turn her head to the side. When she was done she jumped off and grinned as she returned to the line, pausing in front of Mia to whisper, 'I think she enjoyed that almost as much as I did.'

As Roxanne turned, Mia couldn't stop herself and launched at the slave. The rough concrete grazed their skin as they rolled across it, clawing at each other's flesh.

'That's enough!' the Warden bellowed as the guards dragged them to their feet, 'Get back in line – we'll deal with you two later.'

Mia glared at Roxanne as they were pushed back to their places.

'Go get the governor,' the warden told one of the guards as Vicki suddenly moaned loudly, 'the anaesthetic is wearing off.'

A few moments later the governor strolled into the yard. He paused by the warden who said something quietly to him. Both men stared at Mia and Roxanne before the governor shook his head angrily and continued to the centre of the yard. He stood over the whimpering slave, staring down at her filthy, quivering body.

'Have you learnt your lesson?'

'Yes, Master,' Vicki croaked through dry lips, 'I mean ... sir ... I –' she couldn't finish the sentence as her words turned into a cry. She tossed her head, groaning and sobbing. 'Please, sir ... I beg you ... I'm sorry.'

The governor laughed, 'I'm sure you are.' He studied her quivering body as the pain grew worse. Nodding to himself he crossed his arms, waiting, 'Yes, I think another fifteen minutes should do it.'

'Please, sir!' Vicki cried, 'Have mercy!'

The governor waved his hand dismissively, 'Gag the whore.'

Within five minutes the anaesthetic had worn off completely and, despite the gag, Vicki's groans echoed around the yard.

It was another few minutes before Vicki's quivering body suddenly went limp and her head fell to the side.

Sighing angrily, the governor glanced at his watch, 'Leave her five minutes and then remove the contraband. When she comes round, string her up and beat her for five minutes - she'll not escape a full punishment by fainting.' He turned to walk back towards the prison, pointing at Mia and Roxanne, 'Bring them to my office.'

The governor stared at Mia, his fury clear in his dark eyes. 'This is the second time that you have been brought before me,' he announced, ignoring Roxanne, 'that is unacceptable. A severe punishment is being arranged and you will be kept in solitary confinement until the electric chair is ready.'

Mia swallowed painfully, trying not to give in to the fear that was coursing through her veins – could they really do anything worse to her than they had to Vicki? The thought of what they had done to her cellmate was almost too much to bear – but the electric chair – thoughts of what that could mean made her stomach knot.

The governor turned his attention on Roxanne, 'A punishment for your part, you will spend the next two days serving me as I see fit.'

'Yes, sir,' she replied.

'Well, come on then,' the governor said angrily and pushed his chair back from the desk. Roxanne went to him quickly and dropped to her knees between his legs, undoing his fly and freeing his penis which she quickly swallowed. The door to the office opened and the Warden entered. As he led Mia out she glanced over her shoulder to see the governor lighting a cigar. The cry that echoed from the office a few moments later suggested that the governor was doing more than just smoking it and Mia couldn't help but smile as she envisioned what was happening to Roxanne.

*

Mia screamed – she couldn't help herself. The electricity coursed through her breasts, shooting like needles through her nipples and making her flesh contract. The guard released the switch and Mia's body sank back down. She groaned as the metal phalluses pressed deeply into her arse and pussy. The guard had yet to use the switch that would send a bolt of electricity through those – he had been enjoying himself with the copper coils that had been wrapped tightly around her nipples. Similar coils encircled her breasts and thighs and the chair itself had various metal plates that pressed against her skin.

Her body convulsed again as he flicked another switch, the muscles in her legs quivered uncontrollably. She tossed her head, sending droplets of tears and sweat in all directions. He held the switch for longer and then with his other hand flicked the switch for her nipples. She screamed loudly as her whole body was slammed with electricity.

The door to the cell opened and Mia sagged as he released the switches.

'I could hear her in the corridor,' the governor announced and smiled as Mia slowly lifted her head. She realised now why the guard had not turned the dial that controlled the flow to the phalluses – he had been waiting for a suitable audience.

'Start her slow,' the governor said and crossed his arms to study Mia as the dial was turned.

She jumped – the leather straps around her thighs, chest and arms the only thing to stop her from flying out the chair. The use of the dial meant that the guard could keep the electricity flowing through her most sensitive areas while playing with the other switches.

'Very good ... I like it,' he told her as he leant closer, 'Tell me, why did you attack that other prisoner?'

Mia swallowed and shook her head. The governor glanced sideways and Mia cried out as the dial was turned up. She hissed through her teeth until the dial was turned down slightly. 'Well?'

Breathing heavily, Mia whispered, 'Because of what she said about ... Vicki ... I mean ... number ... number Ten.'

He frowned, 'Why should that bother you?'

When she was slow to answer the dial was turned up and held for several seconds. As it was turned down her head fell forward.

'Well?'

'I ... I ... I care about her.'

He laughed harshly, 'Really? Yet you stood there and let her take your punishment?'

Mia slowed raised her head, her eyes filled with tears, 'I didn't know.'

'Ignorance is never a defence.' He flicked his hand and the guard turned the dial to full. Mia's body convulsed, her eyes wide and her body quivering. For a moment she was too stunned to scream but as the pain burned through her she found her voice. Her body strained against the straps for several seconds before it was turned off.

As she slumped forward, she heard Thomas' voice echoing around the cell, 'Keep going until she blacks out.'

Showing no acknowledgement to the command, the governor bent to look at her, 'Well then, since you are so keen to share your cellmate's punishment ...'

Mia looked up sharply, making him laugh, 'Oh, don't worry, my little whore, I didn't mean that you would share the same punishment – merely the same outcome.' He turned to the guard, 'Keep going until she passes out.' He leant forward to whisper in her ear, 'Fake it and you will share the same punishment as your friend.'

She glared at his back as he turned to leave and he perhaps felt her eyes on him because he turned to glance over his shoulder. He opened his mouth to speak but stopped when Thomas's voice echoed around them, 'Such insolence should be punished.'

Moving to Mia's side, the governor took control of the switches and dials for several minutes – punishing her but not enough to make her lose her senses. He stepped away when Thomas' voice announced, 'Perfect – nicely done. Now, finish her off.'

The governor handed the controls back to the guard who flicked all of the switches and turned the dial to full. Mia couldn't even scream as her body convulsed and shook. When he let her go she groaned but remained conscious.

'Hold it for ten seconds this time,' Thomas ordered.

'You sure?' the guard asked.

'She can take it.'

Once again the pain slammed through her body and in the depths of her mind Mia found herself counting. She reached ten and sobbed but the electricity continued to course through her and she realised that Thomas had demanded more. When the current was finally cut, Mia slumped and didn't move as the darkness took her.

She came to as she was dragged back to her cell. Her eyes were blurry and her entire body ached terribly. Her throat felt red raw and she could barely support herself. When they reached her cell they stopped at the entrance and Mia lifted her head, aware that they had stopped outside. She blinked and tried to clear her vision and then wished she hadn't. The warden was kneeling on the top bunk, he held Vicki by the thighs as he thrust into her. Her body hung backwards, over the edge of the bunk to where the governor stood, thrusting his cock between her lips. Mia sank against the guards that held her and closed her eyes. She didn't have the strength to watch the men as they neared climax but the look of rapture on Vicki's face was even harder to face.

*

Punishments came more frequently in the coming days and all the slaves suffered at the hands of the guards. They sought what little pleasure they could from each other, fearing that a punishment would be their reward but having no other avenue to vent their arousal. At least while filming in the house they were forced to come for the camera, in this place they were afforded no such luxury. So each of the slaves sought pleasure from their cellmate or what they could give themselves. Sometimes they were caught and sometimes they were left to groan and sigh with no interruption. Sometimes the guards would stand and watch – ensuring that the prisoners knew they were there and that they knew what to expect once they were finished. Other times they would join in.

Mia had been leaning against the top bunk, her head buried between Vicki's widely spread legs, when unknown to her a guard had entered the cell. The first she had been aware of him was as he slid his thick cock between the folds of her pussy. He had gripped the bunk in front of him and rammed himself into her, making her scream against the soaking pussy before her. Vicki had climaxed quickly at the sight and had moved from the bed to fall beneath them both, her hands and tongue working at the joined sexes to bring them both to a shattering climax.

'And now ... your punishment,' the guard breathed as he rearranged himself.

Mia sobbed as she presented her bruised buttocks to the crop. She had been beaten less than an hour before and the fear of more made her quiver. Vicki stood beside her and laid her hand over hers where she gripped the bed. Mia glanced sideways, tears misting her vision. The guard landed a devastating blow that mad Mia howl. Three more blows and Mia sank to her knees, begging the guard for mercy. She was exhausted and pained, the feel of the crop so much more intense following her climax. The guard sighed and turned his attentions to Vicki but Thomas' voice echoed around the cell, 'She can take more.'

The guard lifted Mia to her feet and ordered Vicki to sit on the bed and hold her hands, keeping her upright.

'Five more,' the cold voice said and Mia felt her chest

tighten. She rested her head against the top bunk, her tears soaking the rough blanket. The guard studied her for a moment as he raised the crop. His hesitation must have been noticed because Thomas said, 'She can take it.'

She stiffened as she heard again the words that had echoed around her as she suffered within the electric chair. Since that day, his voice had become a constant accompaniment to her pain. He had spoken more and more – not to her, but to the men that abused and tortured her. Every time she begged them to stop, when she could bear no more – he would always say those awful words and she knew that her torment was far from over. He constantly pushed her beyond the limit of what she could bear. It became that, no matter what other sounds or noises were present, she always heard him. She heard his directions and his voice haunted her dreams – driving her to the point where it was hard to tell reality from dreams. The only way that she knew for sure that she was dreaming was that in her dreams she submitted wholly and completely – something that she vowed never to do in real life. In her dreams she was like Vicki and often they shared torment and abuse, degradation and pleasure. In reality they did the same but Mia refused to allow herself to succumb to the desires that plagued her sleeping hours. She couldn't. Wouldn't. To give in would be to lose and Mia couldn't lose, not while she still had the strength to fight. Let Thomas push her and drive her to the limit. Let him force her to scream and sob – he would not make her submit, for that was surely his plan.

*

The ten prisoners were eating breakfast when one of the women announced excitedly that she had overheard the governor and the warden discussing their plans for a finale. She didn't know when – but surely it must be soon. Looking around the table, it became clear that Mia wasn't the only one who had forgotten that they were on an impressive film set and not an actual prison.

It was to be two more days before the finale. All of the slaves knew that something big was going to happen because the punishments had all but stopped and none of the cells had received a visit from the warden or the guards. However – none of them enjoyed the brief reprieve because every passing moment built the tension and fearful apprehension of what was to come.

On the morning of the final day the prisoners were taken to a shower room and ordered to wash in pairs. As Mia waited beside Vicki she couldn't help but think back to her first outing in front of the cameras and how much had happened since then. She wondered what she would be doing now if Thomas hadn't picked her at random from the line and she couldn't help but wonder why he had chosen her to become a Movie Slave after that. She had seen how the House Slaves were treated but couldn't help but feel some sense of relief that she was a Movie Slave. Even when she was pushed to the very limits, she managed to retain a sense of self-worth. The House Slaves were nothing, no one, and their sense of self was beaten out of them until they became unquestioning servants to their Masters. Mia couldn't imagine being like that, even Vicki was more than that.

'Seven and Ten – get in there!'
The two prisoners stepped forward and washed thoroughly. The water was lukewarm but Mia didn't care as she scrubbed herself clean, enjoying the feeling of the water cascading over her skin. All too soon they were ordered out from under the showers and made to stand off to the side while the last pair took their turn under the shower.

When they were done they were marched out into

the courtyard and into whatever final scene Thomas had planned.

The governor appeared, the warden at his side. As he entered the yard all the prisoners watched him expectantly. 'A competition has been arranged for the amusement of the guards.' He let his words sink in before he continued, 'To win, you must simply beat the other prisoners in an endurance contest. ' He reached into his pocket and retrieved a stopwatch before nodding at the warden, 'Let's begin.'

'One!' the warden yelled. The prisoner stepped forward and was made to stand in the centre of the yard with her hands on her head. As Mia watched two guards stepped forward, each carrying a flogger, Mia was suddenly reminded of her interrogation at the hands of the governor and the warden. She swallowed as the floggers were raised and the governor started the stopwatch. The floggers fell simultaneously front and back. Mia didn't need to watch to know that the leather strands would work their way down the slave's back and front before travelling back up again. When the prisoner could take no more and collapsed to her knees with a sob, the stopwatch was stopped and the time recorded. As she was dragged back to the line, the next slave was brought forward.

It was impossible to tell for sure but Mia was quite sure that both Vicki and Roxanne had posted impressive times. Roxanne had certainly lasted longer than Vicki – but Mia suspected that Vicki's fall to her knees had as much to do with the sudden wetness between her thighs as the floggers. Mia was called from the line and made to stand as the others had. She lifted her hands to her head and closed her eyes. She had no desire to win this stupid competition but she knew what Thomas expected of her and she was in no doubt that if she didn't perform, things would get far worse. Time lost all meaning as she quivered beneath the blows and soon nothing existed but the floggers and the burning of her flesh. She felt her knees weaken and almost fell but was stopped by a voice that echoed around her mind – She can take more. She was aware that no one else had heard him – his damn voice was in her head! With every blow that fell she just said over and over again – one more, just one more. When she did finally fall to her knees it was several seconds before she realised that the beating had stopped.

Breathing heavily, she didn't hear the results as they were announced and was only vaguely aware that some of the slaves in the line had taken a step backwards. Slowly she looked to the side to see Roxanne and Vicki standing beside her.

'These three shall go through to the next round.'

The three of them were given water to drink as a frame was wheeled into the yard. Impressive looking – made of expensive wood and metal – it had fixings for three people to stand vertically within it. When it was decided that they had had enough time to recover, the three slaves were fixed into the frame – their hands above their head, ankles spread and a thick band placed around their waist. The need for the band around the waist was made clear when locks were opened and the frame was turned until the slaves were held horizontally – facing the ground. By means of a winch, the inner frame that held the slaves was then lifted further off the ground until they were at chest height. Three guards then stepped forwards and attached tight clamps to each of the slave's nipples. With the clamps attached, chains were added and then the guards stepped back to await further instruction.

'A simple test,' the governor announced, 'just say Mercy when you have had enough.'

The guards stepped forward again, this time to add large weights to each of the hanging chains. All three slaves gasped in unison as their breasts were cruelly stretched. The frame was then lowered to give each guard access to the slaves. They fucked them harshly, rocking the frame with the power of their thrusts and sending the chains swinging. Vicki was the first to climax, her juices splattering the ground beneath her. Mia groaned at the sound of Vicki's pleasure and, despite the agony at her breasts, felt her own climax quickly building. Suddenly the guard who was fucking her reached his hand down to rub her clitoris and Mia's juice joined the growing dark stain beneath them.

When the guards had finished, three more guards appeared to add more weights to the chains. Then they too enjoyed the slaves. It was during the next cycle of guards, as Vicki climaxed for the third time, that she screamed for mercy. The governor immediately ordered the guards who were fucking Mia and Roxanne to stop. The two slaves groaned with unspent arousal as the men pulled free. They then had to wait until they had both pleasured themselves in Vicki's soaking pussy before all three of them were released from the frame.

The weights had been removed but the clamps and chains remained – no doubt to serve for the third and final round. After being given a few minutes' respite, Mia and Roxanne were ordered to the centre of the yard. Made to stand facing each other, the chains at their breasts were lifted and joined together. The slaves were then forced to step back until their breasts were at full, painful stretch.

'Twenty lashes,' the governor announced, nodding to two guards who approached with thin, braided whips, 'unless one goes down. Begin.'

Mia stared into Roxanne's eyes as the first of the twenty blows snapped across their breasts. Both slaves winced but neither made a sound. By the tenth blow they were both hissing through their teeth and although they were gasping by the last strike, neither had fallen. With neither slave surrendering, two guards stepped forward and slid their thick cocks into their welcoming cunts. They were made to stand with their hands on their heads as they were fucked – the movement causing their joined breasts to stretch and pull apart. Both slaves stayed standing following noisy climaxes from the two guards. A fresh pair appeared and this time whipped their buttocks before sliding their cocks between them. The guards each held a vibrator and – turned to full – they moved it round to slide it between the slaves' throbbing cunt lips. Roxanne suddenly threw her head back and screamed in abandon as she climaxed. The sheer pleasure sent her to her knees and Mia screamed as the action yanked the clamps from her nipples. Seeing what had happened sent Roxanne senseless with desire and she rolled onto her back, begging a nearby guard to fill her. He snatched the vibrator from his colleague and slammed it into her wide pussy before sliding his cock in alongside. He rode her violently as she writhed beneath him. When he was done, she was rolled over and beaten for her insolence while Mia was taken to the governor's office to be enjoyed by him for the final time.

Chapter eleven: seduction and betrayal

The ten slaves were lined up outside their cells, just as they had been when they had first arrived. No one spoke, not even the guards or the warden. The warden clicked his fingers and the slaves turned to walk towards the door through which they had entered an unknown number of days ago – for most of them it seemed like months. Mia glanced over her shoulder at Vicki. Despite the time they had spent together, they hadn't spoken much since that first day – most of the time had been spent pleasuring each other or falling into exhausted sleep.

They were taken directly to the main hall where the House Masters were waiting for them. Lined up in front of them the Masters studied them carefully, perhaps searching for damage or loss of value. When they saw none they nodded their approval and offered their congratulations to the warden, the guards and Thomas who smiled at their praise.

Mia tensed as the second Master approached her, running his fingers over her welt smothered breasts. 'How did this one perform?' he asked.

'As expected,' Thomas responded.

'Hmm ...' he sighed and stroked her other breast, '... have her taken to my room, I've wanted to play with this one for some time and I think it's time to have my fun.'

'No.'

The second master turned furiously to Thomas, 'What did you say?'

Before Thomas could answer the First Master stepped forward, power wrapping around him like a cloak. His voice was rich and smooth and made goosebumps prickle along Mia's exposed skin. 'He is right to deny you, Jeffrey, she is a Movie Slave and the rules of the house state that a Movie Slave can only be enjoyed by a Master once a month.'

His lip curled, 'Yes, and I missed the last opportunity.'

'You shall miss the next as well,' the first responded, 'I intend to enjoy her again.'

'But ..!' Jeffrey began to protest but a glare from the first cut him off.

'Yes? You have something to say?'

The second backed away, dipping his head with respect, 'No, First Master, my apologies.'

The First waved him away before his fingers gripped Mia's nipple and twisted it painfully. She hissed air through her teeth but that was her only reaction. Smiling with anticipation, he turned to Thomas, 'I shall enjoy watching the first edit of the movie at this month's showing ...' he turned back to Mia, '... before I enjoy this whore.'

Mia swallowed, with no idea how long they had spent in the mock-prison, she had no idea how long it would be until she once again fell into the hands of the First – she had no idea that he would not have her this month but by the end she would surely wish that he had.

*

They were allowed to shower before being led back to the dormitory. At some point Mia lost sight of Vicki and by the time she found a set of cushions to fall upon, exhaustion took her.

She was awoken by a hand stroking the side of her breast and she opened her eyes to see Vicki staring at her, smiling. Now that she was awake, Vicki allowed her hand to travel further. When her fingertips reached Mia's groin, Mia grabbed her wrist, 'What are you doing?'

'We've been given two days off,' Vicki replied, 'do you know what that means?'

'No, what?'

'The usual rules do not apply.'

Mia frowned and then slowly the words sank in.

Vicki leant closer and whispered in her ear, 'I want to kiss you and hold you and ... make love to you.'

Mia swallowed and, fearing that she couldn't trust her voice, she stood and led Vicki to a shadowed corner where they wouldn't be disturbed. They knelt and stared into each other's eyes – saying nothing, just staring as if seeing each other for the first time. Vicki gave the smallest of smiles, so sweet and genuine that Mia felt her heart flutter. No one had ever looked at her like that and she couldn't help but smile back. Everything that had happened in the past year melted away until nothing existed but her and Vicki. Slowly, tenderly, Vicki cupped her face in both hands and leant forward to kiss her. They had rarely kissed in the past and even then it had been frantic and crushing with desire. Now their kiss was tender and warm, it spoke of shared desires and pain and the need to escape for just a short while. Mia lost herself in the kiss, closed her eyes and let herself go. She submitted to Vicki completely and the experienced submissive, for a time, became the dominant. She laid Mia on her back and stroked her breasts, gently squeezing the nipples and making her back arch as she slipped her lips over the bud. She cupped the other breasts, kneaded the flesh gently and then wet the other nipple with her tongue. Mia groaned, lifting herself to find Vicki's lips once more. When they met and Vicki's tongue darted forward to find its mate, she was pushed back down again. Still kissing her deeply, Vicki's hand stroked down Mia's stomach and fluttered at her pelvis. Reflexively, Mia slid her legs apart and Vicki stroked her inner thigh, gently teasing the flesh with her nails. Her hand moved on, stroking her calf and the back of her knee. Mia shuddered at the new sensations and gasped, tipping her head back and closing her eyes as Vicki's lips moved from hers to find her neck. She kissed and nibbled the flesh of her neck and shoulder and Mia quivered, laughing gently. Vicki laughed in response and continued with the teasing. Her fingers traced patterns on the inside of her other thigh, making Mia sigh. Vicki's lips found her breast once more as she moved slowly down her body. Quivering with anticipation, Mia lifted her head to watch as Vicki's lips finally reached her pelvis. She held her breath, waited for that first delicious touch. But then she groaned softly with disappointment as Vicki bypassed her pussy and kissed her thighs. A soft laugh rolled across Mia's flesh, 'Patience.'

Mia fell back, desperate for Vicki to place her beautiful tongue inside her – but at the same time never wanting the gentle build up to end. Vicki kissed and stroked her way back up Mia's body to smother her lips with her own once more. By then Mia was hungry with desire and Vicki smiled at her, her eyes twinkling with passion. They kissed again before Vicki's lips and hands began the now torturously slow journey down her body. Mia lifted her hips to meet Vicki's mouth and that gentle laugh stirred the hair as she dipped her tongue between the wet folds. Mia half cried out, biting her lip to stifle the cry as her hands went to her own breasts and squeezed them, rolling her nipples between thumb and forefinger. Vicki's tongue slipped lower, darting into her pussy to be met with a rush of juice. She lapped at it and then moved to kiss Mia, sharing the musky taste of her as her fingers gently stroked where her tongue had left clean. She slipped her fingers inside and Mia's hips rose, driving the fingers deeper as she groaned against her mouth. Gently stroking her inner walls, Vicki moved so that she could tease her clitoris, sucking the bud between her lips and engorging the flesh. Mia shuddered and gasped as Vicki pressed her lips against the swollen bud and hummed. The delicious vibration was almost too much to bear and Mia quivered uncontrollably. Her fingers went deeper, seeking that innermost sweet spot and then suddenly Mia was gasping and crying out as her climax slammed through her. Tears squeezed from the corners of her eyes as she gasped and moaned, Vicki's expert fingers drawing every last ounce of pleasure that she could from her. Lost on the tide of pleasure, Mia closed her eyes as the climax ebbed. Temporarily sated, she stretched and sighed, keeping her eyes shut to languish in the sweet after glow. Time passed – she had no idea how long – and then she felt Vicki's slim fingers stroking her hips. Her fingers pressed gently into Mia's flesh and, sighing softly, she rolled over as the fingers guided her and lifted her onto her knees. Mia gasped as she felt a thickness pressing against her opening and she moaned as she glanced over her shoulder to see Vicki kneeling behind her. Still holding her hips, Vicki gently pulled her back onto the thick phallus, smiling as she watched a ripple of desire run up Mia's spine. She pressed gently between Mia's shoulder blades, pushing her chest to the floor and increasing the depth and angle of the penetration. Mia turned her head to the side, pressing her cheek against a cushion and sighing as Vicki slowly withdrew the phallus until only the very tip remained inside her. Then slowly she pushed forward, ensuring that Mia felt every wonderful inch of the phallus as it slid into her sensitive flesh. She buried it deeply, crushing Mia's swollen lips and clitoris with the base of the phallus and leaning forward to squeeze her breasts against Mia's back. Mia stretched her hands out so she could take both their weights. She never wanted this moment, or the sensation of having Vicki so close, to end. All too soon Vicki lifted herself and slid the phallus back. She held it at her entrance for a moment before pushing forward, harder and faster this time. Mia gasped, pushing her hips back to meet the thrusting, fake cock. Her desire made clear, Vicki gripped her hips and quickly slid back before slamming forward again. She hesitated for a moment, perhaps fearing that she had been too rough but Mia's hissed, 'Yes!' made her smile and she repeated the action. She held the phallus inside Mia for several seconds after each thrust, in turn pausing as she slid out before slamming forward again. After several minutes, Mia wriggled her hips, her meaning clear. Gently stroking her fingers down Mia's spine before gripping her hips again, Vicki increased the tempo and strength of her thrusts. Mia cried out, a part of her wishing that Vicki would be gentle again, she wanted to believe that she could orgasm through gentler means. But as Vicki's thrusts became stronger and stronger and her body was rocked violently beneath her, she knew beyond any doubt that this was what her body wanted – whether her mind had yet to accept it was of no consequence. She succumbed to the thrusts, felt her thighs bruise where Vicki's legs met hers. The tiny pin pricks of pain where the bruises on her buttocks were crushed between them only added to her desire. She let herself cry out, let herself give vent to her pleasure and as the wave of climax built to unbearable levels she moaned uncontrollably and then screamed in abandon.

She collapsed forward, shivering and sobbing. Vicki slowly stroked her hair and whispered gentle words. A part of her wanted to stay awake, to show Vicki her gratitude, but she continued to soothe her until she fell into a deep sleep.

*

When she awoke it was to the sound of someone being fucked and judging by the sound they were making, she was enjoying it. Yet another House Slave performing for Roxanne no doubt. She reached her hand out, searching for Vicki, it was time to repay the compliment. When her hand found only a disarray of cushions, she opened her eyes. Vicki was gone. The sound of the woman being fucked grew louder, whoever she was she was clearly on the point of climax – her rising moans suddenly turned to a scream and Mia stiffened, her eyes widening. She turned slowly to stare up at the huge screens – to stare at herself.

'Oh, God,' she whispered. It wasn't the sight of herself that had her trembling with fear – they had played movies that she had made before – it was the sight of Vicki fucking her so vigorously, their thighs slamming together and Mia's juice soaking the floor beneath her – the very floor where she now sat.

A shadow fell over her and she looked up, 'Vicki – what the hell -?' she stopped, realising that it was Roxanne and not Vicki who now stood over her.

'You're in trouble now,' she laughed and then looked over her shoulder as the door to the dormitory opened, 'Ah, right on time.'

'Please,' Mia whispered.

Roxanne laughed again and then turned to the men who had entered, 'She's over here!'

Without saying a word, they reached down and grabbed her arms, hauling her to her feet and dragging her away.

*

Mia knelt, head bowed, before the five masters, her hands cuffed behind her back and a leather strap fastened over her mouth.

'I told you that it was wrong to make her a Movie Slave - she clearly cannot restrain herself,' the Second Master announced.

'I fear he is right,' another of the Masters agreed, 'her films have been ... mediocre ... to say the least.'

Another Master sighed, 'I have enjoyed watching her greatly – but I must agree that a crime has been committed. Regardless of her talents. She clearly was unaware that the security cameras were watching, but she did know that what she was doing was wrong – why else would she seek to find a shadowed corner?'

Mia looked up, Thomas must have known that the slaves had been granted some time off –he would defend her. After everything that he had put her through, surely she deserved that much. When she didn't see him she hung her head again – she was lost. She just hoped that Vicki was too valuable to share the same fate – whatever that might be.

'Before we make any decision – I want to know what happened,' the First Master announced.

Mia looked up, relief flooding through her. Yes - perhaps she could make them see that it had been a mistake ... a foolish, stupid mistake. If they would just let her speak. A few moments later it seemed that fortune had smiled on her and her heart swelled as Vicki was presented to the five masters.

'You are the slave that fucked that whore?' the First asked.

'Yes, Master.'

'I expected more from you,' he responded angrily, 'Of all your abundant skills, restraint is one of your strongest.'

Vicki bowed her head, 'This slave is grateful for your words, Master. I have always served this house to the best of my ability.'

'And it has been noticed,' he replied, the anger growing with each word. 'Perhaps then you could explain to me why you saw fit to fuck that slave when you knew that it is forbidden.'

Slowly, Vicki raised her head, 'Master, please ...' her voice broke, '... this Slave made a mistake. One that I shall not make again.'

'What happened to cause this mistake.'

'Master, I ...' she paused and then lowered her head, '... I was commanded to fuck her.'

The First leant forward, anger vibrating along his arms as he gripped the arms of the chair, 'By who?'

Vicki swallowed and glanced over her shoulder to stare at Mia, 'By her.'

Mia stared back in shock – frozen by Vicki's words. Surely she had misheard, surely she had misunderstood. Her eyes slowly moved back to the First and she shrank from his furious gaze.

'She ordered you to fuck her?'

'Yes,' Vicki whispered and then louder, 'She knows

what I am and she knew how to make me obey. I had no choice, Master ...' she fell onto her front, sobbing, '... please, Master, forgive me.'

Mia shook her head and struggled against the cuffs, desperate to make herself understood. At the same time a voice screamed in her mind – How could she? What has she done? How could she do this to me? She cried against the gag as three swift blows from a crop made her keep still.

'I will punish you myself,' the First announced. Mia's head shot up and she was granted a moment of relief when she realised that the First was talking to Vicki.

'Thank you, Master.'

'And as for you ...' his angry gaze fell on Mia once more, 'twenty-five lashes every day for the next week.'

Mia sobbed as he announced her punishment but knew that he had more to add.

'And you are to return to the role of House Slave,' he sighed angrily, 'and I suspect that that is how you will remain until the end of your contract.' He stroked his chin, 'With that in mind, for every misdemeanour or need for punishment from now on, I shall add a week to your contract. Is that understood?'

Mia nodded slowly, tears coursing down her cheeks.

'Very well,' he turned to the Fifth Master. 'Deliver her punishment, enjoy her if you think she's worthy and then put her to work.'

'As you command, First Master.'

'Then this concludes our business.' He stood and beckoned to Vicki, 'With me.' She scrambled to her feet but the look on his face sent her to her hands and knees. 'You forget your place.' He turned to one of his assistants, 'Put her in collar and cuffs and then bring her by her leash to my room ... I feel that this one needs a reminder of how fucking shit worthy she really is.' He turned and left, two of the other Masters following him. The Fifth Master waved for two assistants to prepare Mia and as she was made to stand, the Second approached. He studied her quivering body, a terrible smile creasing his lips, 'See you soon.'

A few minutes later and Mia was hanging a few inches from the floor, her wrists encased in harsh metal cuffs hanging from the ceiling. Everyone but the Fifth Master had left the room and he seemed almost bored as he approached her, a heavy flogger held in his large fist. He didn't speak, just raised the whip and sent it swinging towards her back. Her cry was muffled by the gag as the second blow caught her across the hip and sent her spinning. He cared not where the whip landed and each blow was worse than the previous. Her body, still marked and bruised, suffered yet more abuse and she wondered how much more she could truly take. She didn't even try to count the blows – knowing full well that it would only make it worse. The whipping lasted an eternity. When it finally ended, Mia sobbed and hung her head, expecting him to move in and take her. She was surprised when the chains were lowered and she slumped to the floor as soon as her hands were released.

He bent to remove her gag. 'Get up and get to work.'

'Master?'

Curling his lip angrily, the Fifth waved at a bucket of water that had been placed just inside the door. 'This floor needs scrubbing – get to it.'

'Yes, Master,' she whispered and crawled over to the bucket. As she lifted the brush and started to scrub the floor, she realised that she was alone. Clearly thinking her unworthy, the Master had left to find another to share his passions. Sobbing, Mia tended to her work, wondering why the Fifth's decision not to fuck her seemed to hurt more than the whip he wielded. But no matter what he had done, nothing hurt more than the echo of Vicki's words in her ears.

*

Following her daily punishment the next morning, she was sent to scrub the floor of one of the movie sets. As she worked she hoped that Thomas would see her. He had treated her differently to the others, had he seen her as special in some way? If he saw her now, just a common House Slave, surely he would want her back – he would save her.

By the end of the fourth day, with her body raw from the beatings, she realised that Thomas wasn't going to help her. She felt a strange sense of betrayal that seemed to hurt even more than Vicki's. Why had he forced her to endure so much in the prison only to leave her like this? Strangely, looking back, she realised that he had made her feel special and now ... now she was nothing. She wept as she scrubbed the floor, only the thoughts of the punishment that she would receive if she didn't complete her work properly, kept her moving. She felt lost and alone – betrayed and isolated. Her only consolation was that things could not get any worse – she had no idea how much worse they would soon get.

She was so lost in her melancholy thoughts that she didn't sense someone approaching. She was only aware of another when a hood was suddenly forced over her head. Pushed to her front, she struggled as her hands were yanked behind her back and forced into cold, metal cuffs.

Without any real conscious effort, she struggled blindly. The hood smothered her and she neared panic as the darkness robbed her of sensible thought.

'Stop struggling,' a harsh male voice commanded in her ear. 'Remember your fucking place.'

Mia's chest constricted and she stopped fighting. He was right. Sickened by her own reaction that halted her struggles, but having no choice, she let him lead her to whatever awaited.

By the time they reached their destination, Mia's anger had grown. Damn it – let them add days to her contract, if she didn't start fighting back there would be nothing left of her when the contract did end.

Her hands were released from the cuffs and she quickly snatched the hood from her head, turning to glare at the man who had brought her here. She succeeded only in staring at his back as he left the room. Frowning, she moved to turn round but froze when a horribly familiar voice said, 'As fucking defiant as ever, I see.'

She continued to turn, slowly, and lifted her eyes to the Second Master, quickly looking down again when their eyes met.

'There really is no end to your disobedience, is there?'

'This slave apologises, Master,' Mia whispered.

Jeffrey snorted, 'Like fuck you do. You speak the words but there is no meaning behind them.' She sensed him approach and tensed. He clearly noticed because there was sadistic humour in his voice when he said, 'You should be fucking afraid.'

'Master, what have I done?'

His hand struck her cheek, snapping her head to the side. 'You draw breath!' His fury was all encompassing and Mia flinched as he lifted his hand again. He stroked the livid red mark that his fingers had raised on her skin. If anything his gentle touch was worse than the blow. 'You have no respect for my position. You have no respect for your place in this house. I have seen slaves like you come and go ... serve your contract and be gone.' He shook his head, 'I have never agreed with such a business and have elevated myself to this position with the aim of changing such things.' He struck her again, sending her to knees, 'This is a House of Slaves! Yet it is run as a whore house! Bitches like you need to learn respect. You are no slave ...' he squatted down beside her and hissed in her ear, '... but you will be!'

She turned to look at him, she couldn't stop herself. He allowed her a few moments to stare into his eyes before his hand snatched her hair and forced her head down. Bent forward, her buttocks raised, he held her down as his other hand smacked against the rounded flesh. He spanked her harshly, making her cry out with the strange sensation of his flesh upon hers. Her buttocks were soon red and glowing, quivering and glistening with sweat. He pushed her away from him and she stayed where she landed.

'Vicki!' he bellowed.

The door opened and the submissive entered, immediately falling to her knees at his feet. 'Master?'

'What will you do for me?'

'Whatever you desire, Master.' There was no hesitation but at the same time it wasn't an automatic response – she meant every word.

Slowly, he lowered his fly. She needed no further instruction and lifted herself up to free his semi-erect cock. Taking it between her lips she swallowed his length. Only half aroused, it was easy enough for Vicki to take his entire length, and her chin pressed against his balls.

'Hold it there.'

She stopped and waited, her hands resting on his hips. Jeffrey closed his eyes as his arousal grew and with it his cock. Even as it swelled in her mouth and slowly stretched down her throat, Vicki didn't move. She gagged, her eyes watering, but made no attempt to pull back. He waited until he was fully erect before he slowly slid back and then thrust forward making her swallow his length.

'This is a true slave,' he announced as he pulled his cock free and wiped it across her cheeks, then turned his attention on Vicki, 'Make yourself come.'

'Thank you, Master.'

Both Jeffrey and Mia watched as Vicki lay on her back and spread her thighs, her slim fingers rubbing at the bud of her clitoris before sliding inside.

'Such a filthy whore ... where else could she go?' Jeffrey watched her as he continued. 'Spoilt little rich brat, so bored of spending mummy and daddy's money that one day she stumbled into a sex club and found somewhere where she really belonged.' He glanced at Mia and then back at Vicki, 'But just playing wasn't enough ... she wanted to live the life of a slave. A year's contract, that's what she paid for.' He knelt beside her, 'You tried to beg your way out of that contract so many times during that first year,' he laughed, 'but once the contract had been signed, you were mine.' He sighed, 'Of course, after a year I let her go. Within two months she was back with another pile of daddy's money and a healed arse so desperate to be marked.'

Vicki sighed as her arousal grew. Mia had no idea if Vicki was listening to what he was saying. She wished that she didn't have to – the thought that Vicki had paid to lead this life made her feel sick.

'Another year and this time – not once did she beg to be released. She served her year and returned to mummy and daddy.' He laughed harshly, 'Only mummy and daddy had found out what she had been up to and they refused to see her. The butler gave her a note and sent her on her way.'

Mia stared at Vicki, emotions warring inside her.

'Where else could she go? She came to me, begged me to take her in. But what did I want with a penniless whore? I sent her here and with her arrival I secured my place as Fifth Master. A year as a House Slave and I don't think she even remembered mummy and daddy. But such talents ... as soon as she went before a camera we saw the potential.'

Vicki groaned and sighed, her fingers a blur as she drove them into herself, her legs raised and knees resting on her chest.

'Enough!' he commanded and Vicki stopped, slowly slipping her fingers free. She kept her gaze averted as she panted with unspent lust. 'Do you think you even compare to her?'

Mia stared from him to Vicki and then back again. 'Do you think I really want to?' She knew she shouldn't have said it but she had spoken the words before she could stop herself. And once she had given her feelings voice, there was no taking them back.

He moved to her and bent at the waist, 'And what makes you think you have a choice?' He spoke quietly but Mia had learned that when the Masters were quiet, then she should be afraid. Jeffrey was no different. She wanted to meet his eyes again, she wanted to be defiant but her fear won out and she stared at Vicki who lay prone behind him. 'Keep fighting me and you'll only make it worse.' He stood and returned to Vicki, glancing over his shoulder, 'Come here.'

She went to stand but he shook his head and directed for her to kneel. Sighing softly, she crawled towards him. He motioned for her to kneel beside Vicki who now knelt with her hands behind her back. He undressed and then moved to lie across a bench at the side of the room, resting one foot on the seat. He stroked his cock and then beckoned them both. 'Suck me,' he ordered Vicki and then, as her lips slid down his cock, he crooked his finger to beckon Mia closer. 'Suck my bollocks.'

Mia swallowed as she crawled closer and then knelt beside Vicki, leaning forward to bury her head. She sucked at the fleshy sacs, drawing the flesh between her teeth. He hissed with pleasure, his hand stroking the back of her head. She rode him as he started to thrust his hips up, forcing himself harder into Vicki's mouth. Suddenly he tensed and grabbed a handful of her hair, forcing her mouth to his anus and holding her there as he thrust upwards. She struggled for breath but he just laughed and held onto her until the last quivers of his climax had eased. 'Don't swallow,' he hissed at Vicki who fell back, waiting for further instructions. Sighing with satisfaction, he let go of Mia's hair and sat up, turning to Vicki, 'Open your mouth.' She did so, revealing his come smothering her tongue. Jeffrey beckoned Mia, 'Clean her mouth.'

She moved towards the slave and they locked stares as Mia bent to smother Vicki's mouth with her own. Her stomach lurched but she forced herself to push her tongue forward, licking and sucking, cleaning her out. Vicki groaned with arousal and Mia remembered that she had been on the point of climax when Jeffrey had stopped her. When she was done she fell back and hung her head, forcing down the nausea.

'You make such a beautiful couple,' Jeffrey announced, 'I still watch that video of you two in the dormitory and very much enjoy it.' He leant forward. 'Do it again.'

Vicki needed no further instruction and fell upon Mia, sucking at her breasts and forcing her hand between her thighs. Mia wanted to push her away but with one sudden thrust of her fingers Mia was gasping for air as her climax smashed through her.

Jeffrey laughed in surprise, 'Well, that was fucking quick!'

Shuddering, Mia rolled away from Vicki, squeezing her thighs together and quivering with the last throes of climax.

'Master,' Vicki gasped, 'Please.'

Jeffrey stared at her, smiling as he moved his foot forward, 'Help yourself.'

Mia turned away as Vicki straddled his foot, sliding over his toes and pleasuring herself. It was easy enough to block out the sight but the sound of Vicki's pleasure was harder to ignore. The slave cried out in climax, her cry drowning out the sound of the door opening.

'Master?'

Jeffrey sighed and glanced towards the slave who had appeared, 'What?'

'Her presence has been requested.'

'Very well.' He waved Vicki away and then ordered Mia to clean Vicki's juices from his foot. When she was done he grabbed her by the hair and threw her over the bench. 'Stay there.'

He returned a few moments later, a thin crop held in his hand. He kicked her feet apart and stood between them, the crop resting against his shoulder. 'You will count the lashes and thank me for each one, do you understand?'

'Yes, Master,' Mia whispered.

The crop sliced her shoulder blades.

'One! Thank you, Master. ... Two! Thank you, Master ...' Five blows fell upon her shoulders and then he shifted slightly so that he could deliver the next blows to her buttocks. She counted them and thanked him for each one, her voice breaking as she reached ten.

'Roll over.'

She did as he commanded, groaning as her wounded back pressed against the bench. He moved round to her head and pulled her back until her back was arched off the bench, causing her breasts to thrust upwards.

'Start counting.'

The crop found her breasts and she screamed, 'One! Thank you, Master.' He continued to whip her until she begged him to stop.

'Pathetic!' he snarled as he sank between her legs and thrust into her, 'If you come, you will receive ten more lashes to your breasts.'

The thought of another beating made her sob but at the same time her hips thrust up to meet him. He rode her hard, crushing her beneath him and making her scream in a mixture of both pleasure and pain. She struggled beneath him, desperate to get away but at the same time desperate for the climax that ticked away in her loins. Suddenly he pulled free and splashed his come across her bruised breasts. When he had finished, he bent to pick up the crop.

'Master, please,' Mia cried, 'I didn't -'

He delivered the first of ten blows before responding, 'Do you think I care if you climaxed? You have a lot to learn, my little whore.' The crop fell again and Mia wept as she suffered beneath him.

Chapter twelve: a true Master

Mia knew what was going to happen as soon as she saw the Second Master's assistant approaching her. She had to fight down the urge to drop her cleaning materials and run for the door. Only the certain knowledge that she would never make it kept her where she was. The brush and pan fell from her loose fingers but the assistant seemed unconcerned. As before, he slipped a hood over her head and she was seized by the cloying darkness that seemed to constrict her chest and make her breath heave in her throat. She was led through the house and this time she didn't try to snatch the hood from her head when the hands were freed from behind her back. She tried to breathe normally as her hands were hauled above her head and then her feet were lifted from the floor. The hood was snatched from her head and although she wasn't surprised to the second Master standing there, she couldn't help but tremble with fear at the sight of the bullwhip. He noticed her reaction and the smile that creased his lips only worsened her opinion of him – he was a sadistic, manipulative bastard. She was now sure that he was the one who had forced Vicki to seduce her so that she would be demoted to House Slave. She had to tell herself that he had forced Vicki because the only other possibility was that she had willingly betrayed her and Mia wasn't ready to believe that.

As if reading her thoughts, Jeffrey said, 'Would you prefer it if a certain ... very submissive ... slave was hanging in your place right now?'

Mia had no doubt that Vicki would have preferred it, she just didn't want to be there to see it. She stared back – her only way to fight him now was with defiance and she surprised herself that she still had some left.

'Very well then,' he announced and stepped back,

locking her gaze with his as he let the curls of the whip fall to the floor. He watched her eyes widen as she studied the long, thick whip. 'You haven't felt the bite of a real whip before, have you?'

She swallowed, unable to answer even if she had words to say.

'Oh, that is wonderful,' he laughed and lifted the whip. Her body convulsed as the long whip curled around her torso. The thick leather felt as if it was crushing her in a burning vice. He was an expert with the whip, with each cast it gripped her, tightened around her flesh and constricted her body. She gasped, stunned by the sheer power of the whip and the way that the blows seemed to last forever. Every whip blow that she had ever felt before – whether crop, strap, cane, flogger or belt – after the initial sting the blow throbbed or burned but slowly faded. The blow from this whip and the constricting hold that remained was terrible and she felt her chest heave – it was like nothing she had ever felt before. He allowed her time to appreciate the full impact of the whip before yanking it free and sending her body spinning. She gasped as the burn in her shoulders increased. The large hands of his assistant gripped her hips, stopping her movement and steadying her before the whip flew again – curling around her breasts and upper back. She cried out despite herself, she hadn't wanted to give him the satisfaction of hearing her cry but the brutal whip was too much to bear. Another blow tore another cry from her lips. He paused in the beating and motioned for his assistant to gag her. Nodding, the assistant pulled a red ball-gag from his pocket and forced it into her mouth, harshly tightening the straps around her head.

'I don't want to hear her beg ... yet.' Jeffrey laughed and raised the whip again.

She was actually grateful for the gag that stopped her from crying out. After being left to spin several times, the assistant held her hips to stop her and then stepped back, watching as his Master delivered another blow and then another, twenty in quick succession that sent her spinning round and round. By the time he lowered the whip the ball was filled with spittle that dribbled down her chin. Hands steadied her again, preparing her for the next blow and she shook her head in dismay, her desperate eyes on Jeffrey. He studied her, nodding to himself, 'You really could take more, couldn't you?'

Another twenty blows scored her twisting body as the assistant stood back and watched her spin. When the Master finally curled the whip, Mia's head slumped forward, her chest heaving, her whole body aflame from chest to thighs. He left her hanging there for several minutes before he approached her and removed the gag. She sucked in a hungry breath, gasping and fighting the urge to sob, refusing him the satisfaction. With every breath the terrible burning eased a little, dying to a throb that seemed to echo with the beat of her heart slamming against her ribs. He circled her slowly, running his fingers through her hair, stroking her breasts and buttocks. After several moments her stopped in front of her and waited for her to raise her eyes to his – as he knew she would.

'You are not a slave,' he announced, 'Oh, you have been abused and you have been fucked like a slave ... but you are not a slave ... not yet.'

She stared back at him, still trying to catch her breath. Only the fear of a punishment if she angered him kept her from speaking.

'I will make you a slave.'

'Better men than you have tried,' she responded before she could stop herself.

He paused and stared at her thoughtfully, 'Do you mean Sergeant Kent?' Her eyes widened with surprise and that seemed to anger him more than her speaking out of turn, 'Do you think we have run a successful house for several years without knowing what we are doing?' He shook his head with disdain, 'Don't be a stupid whore, I can't abide it.'

She thought about his manipulation of her, the way he had managed to get her demoted to House Slave and the way that he now had her restrained so that he could beat her. 'You're no different from him.'

He laughed then but there was no humour in his tone, 'Be careful,' he said, 'do not think that my current interest in you means that you are spared the rules of this house. I will have your respect or you will suffer the consequences.'

She stared back for the briefest of moments before she lowered her gaze. She had every intention of fighting him but as she had decided previously – there was no point being stupid.

Jeffrey started to circle again, 'Your policeman has abused you ... that is all, you are not his slave.'

Mia thought about Kelly, the young slave who was owned by one of Kent's female colleagues. They had met on that first night that she had fallen into Kent's clutches and on several occasions since then. She had seen similarities between Vicki and Kelly – in the way that they submitted to the whims of their dominant – she understood now why Jeffrey was saying that she wasn't Kent's slave. Since being in this house she had witnessed various acts of domination and cruelty – and that was the difference, the domination. Kent was cruel but he did not dominate her – he just used her. For the first time since being in this house, Mia suddenly wondered if she had made the right decision in coming here to avoid Kent's wrath – she began to wonder if what Jeffrey had planned was far worse. It was quickly becoming apparent that Jeffrey wanted to make her a slave and Mia intended to fight him every step of the way – not just because she had sworn to herself that she would fight until her last breath, but because she feared that she wasn't as different from Vicki as she had tried to convince herself. And if she wasn't so different – could she really become Vicki? Could she submit so willingly to the whims of a Master? The very thought of it made her feel ill but beneath that was a strange and curious part of her that wanted to give it a try. She forced those emotions aside, she was still Mia. Mia – who had lived on the streets and fought every day just to survive. She had no idea how much time had passed but she knew that they would only keep her for a year – at least she hoped that they would keep to their contract. And when that year was over, she would need every ounce of strength if she was going to stay away from Kent. If she lost that now – if she submitted now – then she would never survive when all this was over.

She slowly raised her eyes to his, forcing defiance into her gaze even as she knew she would be punished for it. It was easier than she thought –perhaps because she saw Kent in the man before her and she had been longing for a chance to defy him, if only to prove that she still could. This man might not be the policeman who had dragged her into this world, but he was the next best thing and she was tired of being forced to live like this. She stared back at him, unable to speak the words that she heard in her head but they shone in her eyes, 'You will not break me.'

His eyes ran over her body and the numerous welts that were turning purple, speckled with red. The welts smothered her from neck to calf and her stretched, lithe body wore it well. Her full breasts had taken the whip particularly well and he took his time studying those welts and the way that her nipples had hardened and swollen to twice their normal size. She was aroused but fighting even the most basic of urges. It was a promising sign and one that he shared with her, 'I will make you come under the whip.'

She found her voice as she shook her head, 'No – never.' She was surprised by the strength and conviction that she heard in her voice. But then – why shouldn't she be convinced. She had spent the last thirty minutes suffering beneath the coils of the most vicious whip that had ever fallen upon her skin and felt nowhere near close to climax – were he to continue then even the barest amount of arousal that she could feel tingling at her pussy lips would be driven from her by the pain. The side of her that was curious, her hidden self that enjoyed the feel of the cuffs at her wrists and anticipated being fucked while restrained, that side did not appreciate the whip and took no pleasure from the pain.

'Every slave comes under the whip,' he announced.

She had no idea if his words were true or not and had no intention of questioning him on it. Instead she said, 'Then you were right, I am not a slave ... and I never will be.'

He stepped closer, 'It is easier than you think to make a slave, all you need is that flicker of desire, that longing to be restrained, the desire to be dominated ... and the spark is lit.' His hand stroked her cheek, 'And then all you need is one more ingredient ... fear.' He stared deep into her eyes, 'Once I have control of your fear, I have control of you.'

'I will not be your slave,' she announced but her voice faltered.

'How many times is that now?' Jeffrey asked.

Mia frowned, not understanding the question but then his assistant responded and she realised that the question had not been aimed at her. 'At least ten times, sir.'

Jeffrey nodded as he forced the ball of the gag back into her mouth, tying it firmly. 'Then we shall have three lashes for each of those ten.'

Mia shook her head in despair, groaning against the gag.

'And I shall add another ten because, my whore, you keep forgetting your place and whether you believe that you are a slave or not, you are a whore in this house and there are rules to be obeyed.' He held his hand out and Mia began to tremble as she watched him raising the hood to her head. He paused, studying her carefully and then he smiled, 'It appears I have found your fear.' The hood closed over her head, smothering her and making her tremble uncontrollably. Sound was muffled and she had to hang in fearful anticipation, not knowing when the first blow would come. Seconds dragged like hours and she could feel her panic rising with every passing moment. When the whip finally curled around her middle, despite the burning agony that engulfed her tortured skin, it was almost a relief. The wait for the next blow was just as long and the relief just as intense when it came. Ten of the punishment blows were delivered in this way – the pause between almost intolerable followed by the ecstasy of agony and relief. By the tenth blow, nothing existed for Mia but the darkness and the white pain that seared through it. After the tenth blow, he picked up his pace, mere seconds passed between each terrible strike. Her body twisted and bucked under each blow and the pull of the whip as it was yanked from around her body. Disorientated and feverish with pain, Mia had no idea where the next blow would land – she had only the terrible certainty that it would come. By the twentieth blow, her groans from within the hood had all but ceased. When the final blow fell, she made no reaction. After the whip had fallen from her body for the last time, he snatched the hood from her head, expecting to find her unconscious. But her eyes were half open and although listless, she was still aware and managed to focus her gaze on him. He lifted the whip again and delivered another blow, watching her reaction carefully.

'Amazing,' she heard him say, 'the more she suffers, the more she resists.'

'Master?' Jeffrey's assistance queried.

'I see now why Thomas was so keen to have her in front of the cameras. Her body is wired quite differently to other slaves. I have seen this before on occasion ... but this one ...'

If he said anymore she didn't hear it as she finally succumbed to the exhaustion that swamped her senses with darkness.

*

She was aware of her body stinging and aching long before she had fully woken and as her consciousness slowly returned she was seized by the terrible sensation that she was being beaten again. She felt her body tense and twist in anticipation of a blow that never came. She slowly opened her eyes, allowing herself a sigh of relief when she realised that it was just the residue of her last whipping that still stung her flesh. She tried to lift her head, groaning at the ache in her neck and shoulders, the stiffness suggested she had been suspended from these chains for some time. She tried to move her fingers but her hands were numb and she couldn't feel anything above her elbows. Her legs felt heavy and it took all of her strength to move her feet, to lift her toes. The sudden change made her ankle bones ache and she murmured something that even she didn't understand – perhaps a curse. There wasn't a part of her that didn't hurt or ache and she wanted to weep under the sheer weight of it all. Suddenly something touched her leg and she jumped as fingers pushed her thighs apart. She looked down and gasped as she watched the hand sliding the smooth domed head of a dildo towards her pussy lips.

'Please ...' she whispered but even she was unsure whether she was imploring them to stop or begging them to continue as fast as possible.

The domed head continued to tease her labia lips, slipping between them and rubbing against her clitoris. Shuddering, her head fell backwards, the ache in her neck forgotten. The vibrator hummed into life and delicious ripples ran through her most sensitive areas. Those ripples ran through her entire body, making her skin shudder. She gasped as the movement made the numerous welts sting anew as if they were being delivered freshly to her skin. But rather than nullify the sensations that warmed her pussy the pain only intensified the feelings until she was gasping over and over, her pleasure increasing to almost unbearable levels with no end in sight.

'Oh God ...' she heard herself say, her chest heaving

as both pain and pleasure fought for control over her body – had she been more aware, Mia may have seen the danger of giving in to the pleasure but after everything that had happened, she needed the release that was being offered.

The dome of the vibrator hovered at the wet opening to her cunt and her hips circled, desperate to feel the trembling phallus filling her hot pussy. 'Are you ready to come for me?'

Mia lifted her head and found herself staring into the eyes of the Second Master. She feared that if she said yes, then he would snatch the phallus away. He must have seen the fear in her eyes because he smiled, a nasty, evil smile that only increased Mia's fear.

'Answer me!' he demanded, pushing the phallus harder against her clitoris and making her gasp, 'Are you ready to come for me?'

With the vibrator humming against her clitoris it was impossible for Mia to think clearly and she had to fight through the fog of pleasure to whisper, 'Yes ... Master ...'

'And that is how you ask me?'

Mia swallowed, 'Master, please may I ... come for you?'

He studied her, his hand pressing the vibrator to her opening while his thumb slowly turned the dial.

'Oh, God!' Mia cried, 'Please, Master!' The humming at her pussy entrance was delicious, the pleasure overriding any pain that her convulsing body may have caused her – but it wasn't enough, she needed more. Suddenly the phallus was sliding into her and her thighs clenched as her legs lifted, urging him to thrust it into her as hard as he could but he held back, sliding it in slowly.

'Please, Master!'

When he had slid it all the way in he rubbed his thumb over her clitoris, making her cry out. He held her on the edge of the abyss – studying her eyes and the tears that were rolling from the corners as she silently begged him for release. Slowly he let the phallus slip from her aching cunt and she groaned in desperation – she couldn't take anymore. Suddenly he thrust the phallus into her, hard and fast and she cried out as her climax broke. But even as the intense pleasure seized her, a whip sliced her back, reawakening a thousand burning needles that pierced her flesh and made her scream in agony – but her orgasm was too powerful to stop and her body was torn beneath the extreme pleasure and the terrible pain. Another blow tore her breath from her lungs before she could scream and the whole time the phallus was being driven into her soaking cunt. She orgasmed over and over as her body was rocked by blow after blow from the whip. Finally she succumbed and drifted back into unconsciousness.

*

When she awoke it was to feelings of unbelievable relief. She had been released from the chains and lay on the softest bed that she had ever known. On the edges of her senses she could feel the ache of the countless whip marks that would become a stinging pain as soon as she awoke properly – but for now she let herself drift on the edge of consciousness, not yet ready to let go of the serene satisfaction.

'Get up!'

The command in the voice was enough to make her sit up. The movement made her head spin and she groaned as her stomach lurched.

'If you vomit on my bed I will flay the skin from your pretty arse.'

Mia moved to the edge of the bed and slipped to the floor, kneeling with her head bowed she fought against the nausea. Only when she was sure that she had it under control did she try to lift her head.

'Very wise, now stand up.'

Using the bed for support, she managed to lift herself onto shaking legs but she was unsure how long she would be able to support herself.

'A bath has been prepared for you,' Jeffrey told her, 'go and bathe.'

'Yes, Master.' she replied and stumbled towards the door. 'Thank you.'

'You have ten minutes and then you will come out here and show me the proper respect, slave.'

The terrible stinging and aching that smothered her entire body was enough for her not to argue, 'Yes, Master.'

She entered the bathroom and slowly approached the tub that was half-full with lukewarm water. Slowly, she climbed in and let herself sink below the water. She couldn't help the breath that hissed through her teeth as her whole body protested with a thousand different stings but after a few moments the stinging eased and her aches started to do the same. There was nothing for her to wash with and so she just lay in the water, watching the clock mounted on the far wall. Her mind was empty, her thoughts still. She watched the second hand ticking round and the minute hand click onwards. When eight minutes had passed she lifted herself from the tub. There was a towel left on the edge of the basin and she gently patted herself dry, trying her hardest not to reawaken the pain of the welts that smothered her body. When she was dry she looked in the mirror and felt her breath freeze in her throat. Her body was bruised and battered but her eyes glittered with life. She had never been beaten like that before, never beaten into utter submission. She had imagined that it would have left her looking haunted and lost – but she had never looked better. Frowning, she turned so that she could study her back and buttocks. A warmth spread over her chest, something akin to pride. Shaking her head at these new sensations, she turned for the door. In the room beyond was a man that she hated as much as Kent and for very similar reasons. The sudden desire to stay in this bathroom forever was suddenly overwhelming and it took all her strength to turn the door handle – her ten minutes were nearly up.

She left the bathroom with her head bowed and, after closing the door, she held her hands behind her back, awaiting instruction.

'Approach the bed.'

She did as she was told, each step heavy but at least she was free of the chains. Whatever he asked her to do now could not be any worse than that.

'Kneel on the floor.'

Mia dropped to her knees at the foot of the bed, lifting her head slightly as Jeffrey moved so that he was sitting in front of her. His legs were naked and she took a tiny glance up. Above his flaccid penis was a sagging stomach ... she had no desire to look any further and cast her eyes down again. Behind her she heard chains rattle and she tensed with fear, suddenly expecting to be grabbed from behind and hauled back into those chains.

'Be still now, slave, you'll have your fun soon enough.'

It took Mia a moment to realise that he wasn't talking to her but someone behind her – currently suspended within the chains that had held Mia. Had she dared, she would have looked over her shoulder but with the Master so close, she wasn't that curious.

'Get started, slave,' Jeffrey ordered, twisting his fingers in Mia's hair and pulling her head towards his groin. She opened her lips to his penis that hardened quickly as her breath stirred the skin. She used her fingers to lift him and drew her lips down his head, pushing back the rolls of skin and revealing the sensitive area beneath. She took him as deep as she could, rolling him from one side of her mouth to another. He shuddered and groaned and she warmed with satisfaction. This master must have had the mouths of many slaves at his cock, yet he was aroused almost instantly by her attentions. It drove her on. She forced herself to take him deeper – as deep as she could, possibly deeper than she had willingly taken any man.

'Oh fuck, she's good ... better than you.'

The chains rattled behind Mia as she made him groan again. She drew back and allowed some of her spittle to run down his length before swallowing his length easily and with a hunger to satisfy.

'I'm going to have to get her to teach you a few things.'

This time the rattle of chains was accompanied by a muffled whimper and Mia had to fight down the urge to glance over her shoulder. She denied the urge by taking him deeply again, forcing herself not to gag on his length as she held him for several moments. Sensing his increasing arousal, she worked hard at his cock, eager to have him come so that he would be finished with her.

'I wonder if she will be able to drink all my come without spilling any.' he sighed and gave a small laugh, 'I seem to remember that you have failed to do so of late.'

Mia didn't hear anything else as she worked hard at his penis – using every trick that she had learned to ensure that Kent and his friends were done with her as fast as possible. The tricks worked on him just the same and she started to feel his cock swell and quiver. She held him deep, drew her teeth back along his length and then thrust down again in time to feel the first jet of his come hitting the back of the throat. She drank it down quickly, ignoring the weight of it in her stomach as she forced herself to swallow the rest. The sound of his satisfaction made her efforts worthwhile. He quivered and then lifted his foot to push her away. Gasping in pain, she rolled several times and then quickly lifted herself up, resting on her hip. She found herself at the feet of the hanging slave and slowly looked up, her eyes travelling the length of the lithe, tanned body. When she reached the slave's face she gasped as Vicki stared down at her, her eyes filled with tears and heavy with arousal.

Mia cried out as she was roughly grabbed and dragged back towards the bed. Crying out again as she was thrown down onto it. The Second Master was on her immediately, sliding his still hard cock into her tight cunt. Had the pain not been so intense then Mia might have marvelled at the sexual stamina of the man who now fucked her – but each blow drove her battered body into the mattress and she gasped over and over again. His hands found her thighs and lifted them to his shoulders, penetrating her harshly. Her stomach cramped and she cried out as she was deeply pierced. The sound of his groin slapping against her was louder than her whimpers that had faded as she became light-headed. Through the haze of her pain she could feel her orgasm mounting to near unbearable levels.

'Do you need to come, slut?' he asked breathlessly.

'Yes ... Master,' she groaned in response.

'Then you had better ask me properly.'

She swallowed, biting back the words that burned her throat. She saw herself as she had seen herself in the mirror in the bathroom, was reminded of the pride that she had felt and the strength. She had thought that her strength had deserted her – she was wrong. He continued to pound into her and she fought against the building pleasure, denied herself the release – just to prove to herself that she could.

He stared into her eyes and although she didn't look at him, he could see the defiance there. 'I shall make you come under the whip ... I promise you that.'

A cold sheet of fear suddenly smothered her, dampening the arousal. She turned her head to the side, tears wetting the bed clothes beneath as he suddenly reared back and pulled free. She gasped as she felt splashes of hot come smothering her stomach and breasts. When his gasps had faded he grabbed her hair and pulled her off the bed, forcing her to her knees on the floor.

'Watch now ... see what I shall do to you ... and then you will be mine.' He climbed from the bed, scooping up the bullwhip from the floor and uncurling the long strand of harsh leather. Vicki watched him approach, her eyes wide, her full lips stretched thin by the ball-gag that filled her mouth. He moved to stand beside her and the two slaves locked stares. They held each other's gaze as he lifted the whip and then, as if sensing what she could surely not see, Vicki closed her eyes and clenched her fists. The whip curled around her naked waist, the very tip of the whip slicing downwards to slice a curve over her pubic bone. Her eyes flew open in an expression of both pain and delight. He yanked the whip free and set her spinning, not waiting until she was still before he delivered another devastating blow to her breasts. Her nipples were crushed beneath the coils of the whip and as he pulled it free, dots of blood appeared around the hardened buds. Another blow and then another ... blow after blow coiled around her naked, spinning body. Striping her from shoulder to calf, just as he had Mia. Sweat stood out along her forehead and beaded down her spine as her body quivered in anticipation of each blow. Mia watched, fascinated and deeply aroused as she witnessed Vicki's submission to the whip and her own dark desires. Suddenly Vicki gave a muffled cry and fell limp, her head lolling forwards as her thighs were soaked by her own juices. Her chest heaved and her gasps were desperate, as if the pleasure had not been enough and she was desperate for more.

Jeffrey slowly coiled the whip and rested it against his thigh as he moved to stand in front of Vicki. Reaching behind her he unfastened the ball gag as he asked, 'Did you ask me if you could come?'

The slave lifted her head, her eyes wide with fear, 'Master, I'm sorry ... I -'

'Silence,' his voice was quiet but held a dangerous tone. 'Did I ask for an apology, you worthless fucking whore?'

She stared just over his shoulder, not wanting to lower her gaze but not making eye-contact either – that would surely make her punishment worse.

He stroked the coils of the whip down her breasts, making her shudder, 'You are pleasured too easily.'

Mia stared at the welts that lined the slave's body and

couldn't help but think that her climax had been far from easy.

'I wanted you to be a demonstration for that whore ... but you have demonstrated nothing but your own weakness beneath the whip.' His harsh voice brought both tears and excitement to Vicki's eyes. 'Let's try again and this time ... show some restraint!'

Mia flinched as she watched the coils of the whip fall from his hand and realised that he was about to whip Vicki again. She was about to say something, to beg him not to, but then she saw the expression of anticipated delight on Vicki's face and the breath froze in her throat. She stared at the slave – her view unhampered as Jeffrey moved to stand behind her. Vicki lifted her head, awaiting the first blow – she looked beautiful, serene ... alive. Her fingers clenched into fists, her beasts lifted, nipples hardening in anticipation. Her thighs quivered, expectant and hopeful of the pleasure to come. And as the whip flew towards her, Vicki heard its swing and closed her eyes, her lips turning up into a radiant smile. The whip curled around her ribs, slicing under her stretched breasts and tearing a cry from her lips. He set her spinning again but this time he waited for her to stop before delivering another blow, this time to her thighs. After ten blows, Vicki was breathing heavily, her gasps almost desperate. Jeffrey coiled the whip and Vicki gave a small groan of disappointment.

'Patience, my slave,' her master half laughed as he approached the wall where the chain that held her was tethered. He placed the whip in the rack beside the winch and then slowly lowered the chain until Vicki could place her feet flat on the floor. After securing the chain he chose another whip and approached her. The whip he now held was similar to the first but, judging by the fewer coils, at least half as long. 'Spread.' he ordered and then waited until she had spread her thighs as far as she could before he let the end of the whip fall to the floor. A flick of his wrist and the whip snapped across her shoulder blades, forcing her head back as her body arched. Once she had settled, he delivered another blow with the same response and then again. Each time Mia had to fight down the urge to go to her and clasp her breasts that were thrust forward, so enticing was the sight of her arching body. The next blow landed on her buttocks and while her body arched, her head fell forward. Mia became fascinated by the way the slave reacted to the different blows, like eddies in a lake stirred by different objects cast over the surface.

He had been beating her without pause for almost ten minutes when Vicki suddenly gasped, 'Master, may I come?'

The blows that followed punctuated his speech, 'How badly do you want to come, my pretty whore?'

'Badly, master.'

'How many more blows could you take before you come?'

'Five?' Vicki groaned.

'Count ten more blows and then you may come.'

'Thank you, Master.'

'But come before that ...' he left the sentence unfinished, there was no need for the threat other than to enhance Vicki's passions.

The whip sliced her buttocks, 'One ...' her breasts, '... two ...' her shoulder blades, '... three ...' she had counted her way through five blows before Jeffrey changed position slightly. He paused, allowing her to fully anticipate and then flicked the whip between her legs. The leather sliced her swollen pussy and she screamed loudly, tossing her head and sending droplets of sweat flying in all directions. He continued to whip her pussy even though her cries of pain stopped her from giving the count. When she had recovered her voice she gasped, 'Eight!'

'Six,' he corrected and whipped her again, waiting until she responded with the correct Seven, before continuing. Her pussy took the rest of the blows as she counted them out. 'And now you may come.'

'Thank you, Master ... ahhh!' He had moved around the front to whip her breasts, the first blow sent her over the edge and she screamed in delight, quivering and shuddering as juice sprayed from her clenched pussy lips. He continued to beat her until her legs gave way and she hung limply from the chains.

He turned to Mia, curling the whip again, 'That will be you soon.'

Mia stared at the limp slave, fighting down the urge to shake her head. If she argued with him she had no doubt that she would instantly be back in those chains and despite his size, the second Master still appeared to have plenty of stamina and strength in his whipping arm.

'I will lay my slave beneath you so that you can spray your juice all over her when you come ... and then you will lick it off her as I fuck your arse.' Behind him, Vicki groaned and he smiled, 'Even my slave likes the idea.' Laughing, he cast the whip onto the bed and left the room.

Mia sat with her head bowed, tears prickling the corners of her eyes as she felt the weight of her current situation bearing down on her.

'He will break you.'

Mia looked up at Vicki, wiping her eyes with the back of her hand, 'So – I should just submit?'

'That will be the end result anyway,' Vicki replied as she adjusted her position to stand properly on her feet, rather than hanging from her wrists. 'If you submit now, it will make things easier for you.'

'I can't.'

'Why?'

'I have never submitted to anyone in my entire life – I won't ... I can't ... start now.'

They stared at each other and the gulf between these two women was suddenly apparent. They found themselves thinking about their own lives and the events that had led them to this point – then, staring at each other, it was as if they were staring through the looking glass to see the exact opposite of everything they knew. For Mia, she could see Vicki's privileged upbringing and a desperate need to escape it. Vicki only felt alive when she was serving and suffering. How different was that to Mia's harsher background – even before she had fallen into Kent's clutches. Worlds apart, they could only imagine what it was like to see this world as the other did.

'We're not so different,' Vicki announced, making Mia frown. 'Tell me when you have ever felt more alive than you do now.'

Mia shook her head but even as she did, she knew that she was lying to herself. She did feel alive. 'It doesn't matter what I feel,' she sighed in response, 'even if I do feel alive now – if I submit, I will die inside.'

'Really?' it was more of a gentle challenge than a query.

Mia stared at her, anger shining in her eyes.

'You're upset with me?' Vicki asked, more of a gasp, as her eyes lit with excitement.

Mia sighed, even in hanging in chains Vicki was more free than she was. Mia was amazed, as she had been many times before, at how easily Vicki showed her emotions. Excitement, fear, arousal, it was all written so perfectly across her features and she didn't even realise that she was doing it. Mia wondered if that was what made her a good slave – did a good Master read those signs and use them accordingly? In Mia's experience a Master looked for nothing in a slave – all they wanted was sex and pain, degradation and submission. But then – Vicki wanted nothing more. Such freedoms were alien to Mia and she feared them. The thought of being unable to hide her emotions made her feel ill – what would Kent have done to her had he seen what she truly felt while he fucked her. He saw fear and pain in her eyes but that was all – she refused him anymore. He had certainly never seen submission – nor had he ever seen excitement. She wondered if that were because of her strength or because of his failings as a Master. She shook the thoughts from her mind, damn it, Kent was not her Master – he was just the bastard that took what he wanted from her.

'Are you okay?'

Mia looked up at the sound of Vicki's voice but didn't know what to say in reply.

'It will be hard for you ... but you will submit.'

'I am only here for a year, if I can survive until then ... then I ... I ...'

'What?' Vicki asked, a sad smile playing over her lips, 'You'll go back to your life as if nothing has happened? You'll forget all about this place?'

She nodded, not trusting her voice to hold the conviction that she desperately wanted to feel.

'If that is what you want then I suggest you submit fast.'

Mia frowned, lost in the apparent contradiction.

'Submit to my Master or the scars he will give you will ensure you will never forget him.' Vicki stared back, her eyes intent and pleading, 'It's easier than you think.'

'For you maybe.'

'You have the strength to do it and survive it.'

'And that's all it takes? Strength?' Mia had wrestled her own thoughts on that very subject, warring between seeing Vicki as weak and as the strongest person Mia had ever met.

'It's all just fantasy.' Vicki sighed, closing her eyes and flexing her fingers, the chains clinked above her and she quivered at the sound, 'You have to have the strength to live in the fantasy, to ... enjoy it ...' she sighed again, shifting her hips and Mia realised that Vicki's arousal was growing as she spoke. Mia was both surprised and disturbed by it ... until she noticed the dampness between her own legs. 'You must take what little pleasures you can ... when you can.' Vicki lazily opened her eyes, 'If you will not submit to my Master ... then at least submit to your own desires.'

Before either slave could say anymore, the door opened. Mia fell to her knees, crossing her hands behind her back and hanging her head. She jumped as a small pile of clothing was dropped at her feet.

'Get dressed, you have duties to attend to.'

Mia recognised the voice of Jeffrey's assistant but didn't move until after he had moved away. She stood slowly and dressed in the leather waistcoat and small thong that showed her to be a house slave. As she was led from the room, she glanced over her shoulder at Vicki who stared back – both of them were sure that this was not the last time that either of them would witness the torture of the other.

Chapter thirteen: house slave

Finally, the daily punishments ended and she was left to perform the duties of a house slave. In the back of her mind was the warning that any misdemeanour would add time to her contract and she worked hard to behave and stay out of the way. For the most part it worked as the men around the house chose others to submit to their desires. There was no escaping the Second Master though and he frequently had her brought to him. She began to wonder if this was the reason why she was left by the others and worried that he had used his influence to keep her to himself. When she was called to him he always beat her mercilessly and fucked her how he pleased. His aim was the same – to make her come under the whip – and he used a variety of techniques, all of which had so far failed ... he had yet to realise how close she was actually getting. To start with he always beat her before he fucked her but now he chose to enjoy her first and then beat her, giving him the chance to enjoy her further once he was done. The initial fucking had become more arousing and she found herself willingly opening herself to him – whether he requested her mouth, pussy or arse. She told herself that it was because of Vicki's advice – to take what small pleasures she could when she could – but the last time he had fucked her she had lost all sense of who she was. He had finished the beating and released her from the frame, throwing her onto all fours. Taking her from behind she had shuddered with desire, desperate to feel the barest ounce of pleasure that would ease her pain. He had been particularly harsh with the whip and she had let herself succumb to let herself escape, for a time she was his slave. For just a few minutes she had no recollection of Kent or his colleagues, of Thomas or Vicki. He had fucked her brutally and she had climaxed with abandon and suffered the punishment without complaint. It was only afterwards that the realisation of what had happened struck her and she sobbed herself to sleep, curled into a ball in the corner of the slave's dormitory.

It was with some relief, a few days later, that she saw another of the Masters approach her as she was cleaning. He was not a House Master but she had seen him often enough. He was handsome and strong and she felt a rush of pride that he had picked her to swallow his cock. She used everything she had to satisfy him. She swallowed his length, despite the fact that he was longer and thicker than Jeffrey. She used her hands to squeeze his balls and, unbidden, played gently with the star of his anus. He had climaxed with a thrust of his hips and she had swallowed his juice without spilling a drop. He wiped his cock in her hair and then turned and walked away. She was pleased to see her efforts rewarded that evening when, between courses at dinner, he beckoned her. She brought the decanter of wine with her, assuming that he wanted more but he merely waved at the table. Setting the decanter down, she climbed onto the table in front of him, presenting her buttocks when commanded to do so. She gasped as he poured the wine between her buttocks and used it to lubricate her tighter entrance. Laughing with the Master beside him, they took it in turns to slide various implements inside her. She had no idea what and had no desire to know. They soon tired of the amusement and he slapped her buttock, ordering her to pour them both wine before telling her not to leave as they would be wanting her servitude after dinner.

She waited in the corner of the room while the Masters and their guests finished dinner. She stood with her head bowed, lost in simple thoughts, and didn't realise that the meal had been finished until the Master who had taken her earlier that day touched his fingers to her chin and lifted her head. There was something strangely tender in the way her touched her and she slowly lifted her eyes to meet his.

His smile held genuine amusement, 'I shall have to punish you for that indiscretion.'

She quickly lowered her gaze, 'This slave apologises, Master.'

He laughed, 'I'm sure you do ... as I am equally sure that your indiscretion wasn't as innocent as it appeared.'

His companion appeared at his shoulder, 'What's this, Jake? You're talking to the whore?'

Jake glanced at him and sighed, 'I like to appreciate before I satisfy.'

'And I like the taste of a good wine, but that doesn't mean that I have a conversation with it as it gets poured out the bottle.' He laughed and wandered back to the table, shedding his clothes as he went.

Jake turned back to Mia, 'You will have to excuse Charles, he is ... unrefined.'

Charles laughed as he removed the last of his clothes and leant back against a chair, his arms crossed.

'By way of apology, I shall allow you to choose your tool of punishment.'

Charles snorted but seemed more amused than annoyed.

'I offer you the crop, the flogger or ...' he fingered the buckle at his waist, '... or my belt.'

Mia swallowed, 'If it pleases you, Master ... the belt?'

He tipped his head slightly to the side and smiled, 'As you wish, my lovely slave.'

Mia felt her nipples harden at his words and she squeezed her thighs together, gasping softly at the wetness she felt there.

'Let us make an agreement then,' he rubbed his chin and then, with a smile, took her hand and walked her to the table, 'I will give you fifteen lashes with the belt in a place of your choosing. If you can then ... without begging me to stop ... take five lashes in a place of my choosing, then I will allow you your first climax of the evening.'

Mia saw no way that she could refuse the agreement

– what would he do to her if she did? Slowly she nodded, 'I agree, Master.'

'Excellent,' he breathed and began to unfasten his belt, 'Tell me, little slave, where shall I beat you?'

'Master, please whip my buttocks.' He seemed disappointed by her response and Mia had the strange reaction of wanting to take back her words and suggest somewhere more to his liking. She knew better though and instead said, 'Master, I offer any part of my body to you. If my choice – '

He stared at her and half smiled, 'You're a strange one, aren't you?'

'Master?'

'Well – I have seen you with the Second, you despise him and fight him at every turn. Yet here you are offering me any part of your body.' He laughed, 'Dear Jeffrey would have a fit if he knew.'

Charles sighed, 'For Christ's sake, Jake, can we just enjoy the whore? I have to go home tomorrow and I wanted my last night to be a special one.'

'Oh, it will be,' Jake responded as he slowly turned Mia round. 'Bend and grip the chair arm.'

'Yes, Master.' She moved to stand beside a chair that had been pulled back from the table. Bending at the waist, she stepped backwards until her back was parallel to the floor and her buttocks presented. Her hands closed over the wooden arm of the chair, her knuckles white with anticipation.

'If you fall to your knees, the agreement is at end. Understood?'

'I will not disappoint you, Master.'

He laughed as he curled the buckle end of the belt around his hand, 'I'm sure you won't.'

The first blow was delivered with an upsweep of his hand. The leather sliced across the under-curve of her buttocks, making her gasp as she was sent up on her toes. The next blow was swift in coming, delivered downwards to snap across the top of the mounds. The next – sideways – slicing across the centre of her arse cheeks. Tears prickled in the corners of her eyes as she focused on a mark on the floor a few feet ahead of her. She bit her lip as she sensed him raising the belt again. It found the underside of her buttocks and she realised that he would beat her in the same pattern as the first three blows. By the time he had completed the five revolutions, Mia was weeping softly, her tears rolling down her cheeks. Her pussy was soaked, throbbing and desperate. The beating had been so ... perfect. She had never felt anything like it. She was being beaten for his pleasure but at the same time it was for her. She had chosen the belt, she had chosen the location and if she took the punishment well, she would be rewarded. It was a strange, wonderful sensation and she could hardly wait to feel the five lashes in the location of his choosing.

'Well done, my little slave.' His fingers stroked the raised welts and she quivered, sighing softly. 'Now then, where shall I beat you?' His fingers ran down her spine, 'Stand.'

She straightened and stepped back to give him space. Slowly, he circled her, studying every inch of her beautiful skin.

'I find myself torn,' he said softly as his fingers ran down her breast, making her gasp. 'Shall I mark these gorgeous tits or ...' his fingers travelled lower, dipping between her thighs to find the moistness there, '... should I really make you scream?'

'Why don't you ask the whore to decide?' Charles mocked, his hand gently sliding up and down his thick, hardened cock.

Jake stared at Mia, a small smile on his lips, 'Ah, now as much as I would like to, that was not part of our agreement.' He stroked her breast again, using her juice to write a cross on her right breast. When he was done, he dipped again to her pussy and then did the same to the other breast.

'X marks the spot.' Charles laughed.

'Lean back and grab the chair.'

'Yes, Master.' Mia did as she was told, her arms shaking as she tried to support herself in the awkward position.

'Bend your legs and plant your feet ... yes, that's good. Now straighten your arms. Excellent,' he breathed. His hands found her breasts again and he stroked the flesh, making her engorged nipples quiver with delight. He stroked the skin, raising goosebumps. 'These will take the blows even better now.'

'Thank you, Master.' Mia seemed as surprised by her words as the two men who laughed and smiled at each other.

'Can't you see how wonderful she is?'

Charles shrugged, 'I'll fuck her sopping pussy before I decide.'

Shaking his head, Jake lifted the whip, 'Lock your elbows,' he commanded and when Mia was steady in her position, the belt cut through the air. The leather strap flattened her breasts, the loud snap rebounding around them, quickly followed by Mia's pained gasp. He let the leather slide from her and waited until the flesh had stopped quivering before delivering the next blow. Mia stifled a cry, turning her head to the side and staring at the chair back, fixing her gaze on embroidered pattern. From the corner of her eye she saw the whip fall again and she tensed, crying out as the edge of the leather caught her aroused nipples. She waited for the fourth blow, tense with anticipation. It came quickly, searing her breasts and making her gasp. Her arms quivered as she fought to hold herself up – the strain on her shoulders was barely tolerable but she forced her arms to stay locked. The fifth and final blow landed with shuddering force that made her sag at the waist. She forced herself straight, knowing that she hadn't been given permission to move. She stared at the patterned chair and wondered what was different about Jake – why was she so willing to obey him after she had tried so hard to fight the Second at every opportunity? She jumped as his fingers stroked the lines across her breasts and then gently pinched her nipples.

'Spread your legs,' he commanded. 'It's time for your reward.'

Mia quivered with the effort of keeping herself up as she slowly slid her feet apart. She groaned softly as his fingers pressed against the outer folds of her pussy and closed her eyes as he dipped the tip of a finger inside her.

'You're soaking,' he breathed, 'and so wide.'

She felt his finger slide into her, his thumb rubbing at her clitoris, making her gasp and groan.

'You like that, my little slave?'

'Yes, Master, if it pleases you.'

He laughed softly, 'Whipping your tits pleases me, beating your arse pleases me ... sliding my finger into your soaking, wide cunt is hardly for my benefit now, is it?'

Mia didn't know how to respond. She heard Charles chuckle but Jake said nothing further as he slipped his finger free and then slipped three back. She groaned loudly, her climax mounting faster than she could have imagined possible. He thrust his fingers in and out roughly but so beautifully. He left no doubt that he was the Master, this was an act of power, to beat her and then make her come – that was the aim and she was to submit fully to his whims or suffer the consequences, she had no doubt of that. But the way he thrust his fingers in, the way he had beaten her, it had been to prepare her for the climax that tore at the edges of her senses, that crested and dared to break before he had given her permission to come. It was the most incredible feeling and one that she wanted to last forever. She felt whole, everything was so right ... she was so completely alive. All too soon she felt herself being pushed over the edge and she gasped, 'Master, may I come?'

He held his silence for several moments as his fingers continued to draw her climax out like a string of delicious pearls. Slowly he leant forward to whisper in her ear, 'Come for me.'

Mia threw her head back and screamed in delight as her orgasm ripped through her body. She quivered and shook under the intensity of it but somehow managed to keep her grip on the arm of the chair. She was lost in the sheer delight of it and barely noticed that Jake had made her stand. He led her to the table and forced her to bend forward over it. Moving behind her he slid his cock into her throbbing pussy and she cried out again as another climax washed over her, renewed by the deep invasion. His hands gripped her hair and he yanked her head back, causing her to gasp as needles seared across her scalp. With her head back and her mouth open in a silent scream of desire, Charles knelt before her and slid his cock between her lips. Instinctively she closed her lips over him and used her tongue to work at his cock that twitched and suddenly exploded in her mouth. Behind her she heard Jake groan and suddenly he pulled free and spun her round in one quick motion. She was forced to her knees and his cock slipped between her lips as his hands gripped the sides of her head. His come mixed with Charles' and dribbled out the sides of her mouth. She swallowed what she could but revelled in the feel of the warm droplets falling from her chin onto her bruised breasts. He let her go and she collapsed sideways, gasping and quivering.

She had no idea how long she had lain there before an awful and terribly familiar voice made her open her eyes.

'Are you finished with the whore?'

She looked up at the Second Master who strolled towards her, his intentions clear.

Jake stepped into his path, 'Actually, no, we are not finished with the whore. My friend,' he glanced at Charles who was lounging back in one of the chairs, 'has yet to sample the delights of her pussy and I would like to feel how tight her arse is before I finish with her.'

'How ... how dare you?' Jeffrey spluttered, 'Do you know who I am?'

Jake studied him in silence before responding, 'Of course. Do you know who I am?'

'Of course I bloody do,' Jeffery spat, 'The son of the First Master and that is all. You have no power here and certainly do not out rank me.' He pointed at Mia, 'She is my slave and I will have her this night.'

'She is a house slave and therefore open to all. The rules of the house state – to put it bluntly – first come, first served.'

'To pardon the pun,' Charles sniggered.

Jeffrey's mouth opened and closed, his face red with fury. 'Have her sent to my room when you are finished with her.'

'Would you like her washed and bathed first?'

'Just fucking make sure she is in my bed by midnight!'

Jake lowered his head in agreement, 'So be it.' He smiled as he watched Jeffrey leave, slamming the door behind him. 'Well then,' he said, glancing at the clock above the fireplace, 'since we only have an hour and a half left to us, I suggest we get started.' He bent and lifted Mia to her feet before he held his hand out to Charles, 'Hand me that bottle of wine.'

*

She knew that Jeffrey would take his anger out on her but she hadn't been prepared for how he would treat her. After several further climaxes during the remaining hour and a half that she spent with the two masters, the abuse that Jeffrey heaped upon her seemed so much worse. The following morning she barely had the strength to stand and every movement was an agony that made her gasp. She was given light duties but even as she wiped a mop across the entrance hallway, she felt her legs shaking and couldn't stop herself from falling to her knees. She couldn't move and just knelt with her head bowed, her gasps painfully shallow. A shadow was cast over her and she quickly struggled to her feet, leaning on the mop for support.

'Sorry, Master,' she whispered, fearing a punishment for slacking in her work.

A hand gripped her shoulder, 'Are you okay?'

She looked up sharply and straight into the eyes of Thomas who stared at her with obvious concern.

'Are you okay?' he asked again.

'Yes, thank you, Master.'

'I'm going to get you back,' he said, 'I promise.'

She stared at him, not fully understanding his words.

'Mia,' he said softly, 'don't give in to him. Just hang on, don't submit or I'll never get you back.'

'Are you going to fuck her?'

Both Mia and Thomas looked at the man who had spoken and it took Mia a moment to realise that it was Jake.

'No,' Thomas said softly and then louder, 'Do as you wish with her.'

Thomas turned and left as Jake led her to a room at the side. There was no one else in the drawing room and Jake led her to one of the oversized, leather armchairs. He lowered his trousers and then sat down, beckoning her over. 'Turn round.' She did as he ordered and waited while he slipped her thong to the side and then guided her down onto his cock. She gasped with pain as her bruised pussy was invaded yet again. 'Hmmm ... he was harsh with you, wasn't he?' His hands stroked the welts on her back and then pushed her forward until her hands rested on the floor. He used his hands on her hips to move her up and down, groaning as she quivered with both pain and arousal. He fucked her slowly and she found her thoughts wandering towards what Thomas had said to her. She imagined herself back on the movie sets and everything that that would entail. Did she really want to go back to that? Was being a house slave so bad? She quivered as his thick cock drove into her and her pleasure, for a time, overrode the pain. But just as she hovered on the edge of climax an image of Jeffrey swam through her mind. She groaned, her pleasure gone too far to stop.

'You may come,' Jake announced through gritted teeth.

She gasped, her buttocks quivering under his touch as her pussy vibrated with the need to come. Suddenly she felt the heat of his come filling her and that was enough to make her gasp with pleasure. When he was done, he slapped her buttock. She lifted herself up, steadying herself for a moment as the world swam. Then she slowly lifted herself off him and dropped to her knees. He stood and rearranged his clothing.

'Master,' she asked softly, 'did I please you?'

'Yes.'

She swallowed nervously, 'Then may I ask my Master a question?'

He seemed amused by her request, 'Go on.'

'Am I always to be a house slave? I mean, could the Second Master get something more from me?'

He considered her question, 'Master Jeffrey could petition the other House Masters for full ownership of you. If he was granted it, then that would override all other commitments that you have.'

Mia had no doubt that that would include the contract that she had agreed with Gary Marshall. The thought that she would belong entirely to Jeffrey with no chance of escape ... a cold blanket of fear fell over her.

'Is the interrogation over?' Jake asked as he stood and slipped the belt from the waist of his trousers, motioning for her to bend over the chair.

'Master?' Mia whispered, 'Please, I fear I cannot take much more.'

'You will take twenty lashes and be grateful for each one as it is better that I do this than report you to the House

Masters for your forward attitude.' He lifted the belt, 'And then you will take another five for daring to argue about your punishment.'

Mia wept softly as he delivered the blows – she had never felt so wretched.

Chapter fourteen: Revelations

'You look more and more beautiful beneath the lash,' Vicki whispered.

Mia turned to her sharply, 'Ssshh.'

They were kneeling at the end of Jeffrey's bed. He was currently lying in it, his arm draped over a visiting Mistress. Another Mistress curled into his back. All three of them had enjoyed the two slaves greatly and now slept soundly.

'He won't wake,' Vicki responded in a whisper, 'He enjoyed you too much to wake for at least an hour.'

Mia tried not to think about what Jeffrey and the Mistresses had done to her – mainly because her one allowed orgasm still ticked in her loins. They had left her far from sated.

'If he continues, he will break you eventually but you will not be his slave.'

Mia stared at her, confusion creasing her forehead.

'He will simply drive you mad,' Vicki responded matter-of-factly, 'It has happened before and the slave always ends up useless. They are kept as house slaves for a time ... after that ...' she shrugged.

'I won't let him do that to me.'

'But that's the thing,' Vicki sighed, shaking her head, 'he is better than that.'

Mia gave a soft snort, making her feelings regarding Jeffrey clear.

'Think what you like of him,' she responded, her look suggesting that she had noticed the change in Mia of late – she had become more stubborn. A subtle change that had gone unnoticed by Jeffrey but not by the experienced submissive. 'He did not become the Second Master by luck.' She looked up to where he slept, 'He has bent many a slave to his will, easily and without effort.'

'So why am I so different?' Mia sighed. A voice in her head kept telling her that if she just submitted to him, then he would stop torturing her. The realist in her convinced her otherwise. Even if she submitted, he would continue – why break her and not enjoy her submission? He hadn't turned from Vicki after he had broken her and had even begun to use her as a means to torture Mia. She sighed again, 'I cannot submit to him.'

Vicki nodded, 'I know ... but what neither of you realise is that it is him that you will not submit to.'

Mia stared at her – hadn't she just said that?

'You will submit to a Master, one day, but ...' she glanced at the bed, '... it will not be him. At least, not if he continues as he is.'

'I don't understand,' Mia hissed with frustration.

'You drive him to distraction. He covets your strength and your stubbornness. Why ... I don't know ... but you have sent him crazy with desire to break you and in so doing he has forgotten all he has learnt as a great Master.' She shook her head through lack of understanding and the ability to explain herself properly, 'He said something a while ago, something about you being wired differently, do you remember?'

Mia shook her head, 'No. What did he mean?'

'I have no idea – I am not clever enough to understand the complexities of a slave and how those complexities are viewed by a Master.' She sighed again, 'But perhaps that is what drives him to have you so completely. I have no doubt that if he treated you as he treated me at the very beginning, you would quickly be his.'

Mia swallowed, 'And will you tell him this?'

Vicki laughed, making both slaves look nervously at the bed. They stayed silent as Jeffrey stirred. Vicki shook her head with amusement, the fear fading when their Master did not wake, 'Tell my Master how he should train a slave?' She bit back another laugh, 'I love pain, my darling, but I am not mad.'

They fell silent again for several minutes before Mia turned to Vicki again. 'Am I ... different?' She asked the question softly, afraid of the answer.

Vicki was thoughtful for a moment, 'I have met slaves like you before – slaves who can take more punishment than others.'

Mia was surprised by the statement – it hadn't occurred to her that she could take more punishment than any other slave. Although now the facts were presented to her, she could see the truth in the words.

'Slaves like you are rare ... Thomas must have seen it from the start, that must be why he petitioned for you to become a Movie Slave so early.'

'And now look at me,' Mia whispered wretchedly.

If Vicki felt any remorse about being the one to put Mia in her current position, she showed no sign.

Thoughts of what had happened and Vicki's position as a Movie Slave made Mia frown, 'How is it that he has been able to enjoy you so much recently? I thought that Movie Slaves could only be enjoyed once a month.'

Vicki glanced at the bed when one of the Mistresses rolled over. When she was still again, she replied, 'I don't know. I hadn't thought about it. It is not my place to question the workings of this house.'

'Nor is it your fucking place to talk while your Master sleeps.' Both slaves jumped as one of the Mistresses sat up and glared down at them. 'I expected more from the slaves of Master Jeffrey.'

'These slaves beg forgiveness, Mistress,' Vicki said hurriedly.

'Well just be thankful that I am too exhausted to punish you properly, although be sure that your Master will hear of this when he wakes.' She waved towards a flogger that had been tossed onto the floor. 'Take that in there and deliver twenty lashes each.' Mia, who was closest, stretched her hand out to grip the handle, still slick with her juice. She closed her eyes, remembering the feel of the ribbed leather as it was slid into her. 'And do it properly,' the Mistresses commanded as she lay back on the pillows, 'I shall check your buttocks in the morning and if they are not properly marked I shall deliver double the punishment myself ... before your Master shares his anger with you.'

'Yes, Mistress,' the slaves said together and hurried out of the room. The door to which the Mistress had directed them led into a large dressing room. Wardrobes lined the walls, each door a mirror that reflected their naked forms back and forth endlessly. In the centre of the floor was a square stool and Vicki moved to it as Mia closed the door behind her.

'We must be quiet,' Vicki whispered as she knelt and leant over the stool, presenting her buttocks to Mia, 'Or they will surely punish us further.'

Mia felt the whip in her hand, suddenly too heavy to lift. It hung by her side, the strips of leather tickling her naked thigh.

'What are you waiting for?' Vicki hissed, looking over her shoulder.

'I've never done this before.'

'So?' When Mia continued to hesitate, Vicki added, 'If that mistress is still awake and doesn't hear the sound of that whip then she's going to -' The strands of the leather striking her arse stopped her and she hissed through her teeth. 'Harder,' she gasped, 'you must mark me or we're both for it!'

Mia shivered as the retort of the next blow quivered down her arm. Her stomach rolled as she lifted the whip to deliver another lash.

'Yes!' Vicki gasped, quivering with delight., 'Oh god, yes!'

Closing her eyes for a moment, Mia delivered the next five lashes quickly, eager to finish the task as quickly as possible. Vicki gasped beneath each blow, wriggling her buttocks when Mia stopped. 'Please, give me the rest ...

quickly!'

Mia realised that Vicki was watching her reflection and that was adding to her arousal. She delivered the last of the blows in quick succession, making Vicki gasp and half-cry with desire. When she had delivered the twentieth blow she let the whip fall to her side.

'No!' Vicky hissed, 'Please – don't stop!'

'But, I ...' she began but Vicki's arousal was clear. Damn her – how dare she put her in this position? She raised the whip and thought about everything that had happened. It was Vicki who had tricked her, made love to her, and then left her to the mercy of the Masters as a House Slave. Perhaps the best way to take her revenge was to leave Vicki to suffer the arousal with no release but Mia couldn't do that – and she didn't want to. Her anger vibrated down her arm and she heard Vicki gasp a moment before the whip came down. She must have seen the anger in Mia's gaze because she tensed and then cried out loudly when the whip found her bruised flesh. She stifled another cry as her climax ripped through her, tossing her head. She froze as she watched Mia lift the whip again, 'Don't stop ... please don't stop.'

Mia continued to beat her, feeling her own arousal grow as she watched Vicki climax over and over again. After several lashes, Vicki raised a quivering hand, 'Enough,' she gasped.

She lowered the whip and glanced at herself in the mirror opposite – the breath caught in her throat and she froze. She looked beautiful. Her naked body was covered in sweat and her breasts quivered as her chest heaved.

Vicki slowly climbed to her feet and slipped the whip from her hand, 'Lie down.'

Mia slowly dropped to her knees, tearing her gaze from her reflection.

'You just saw what the Masters see. You're gorgeous.'

She didn't respond as she lay over the stool, crushing her breasts. She stretched her hands forward, pressing against the floor to support herself.

'Ready?'

'Just do it.'

'I shall add five lashes for that!' Vicki smiled, making Mia glance over her shoulder, 'Oh, don't worry, I'll make it worth your while.'

Before Mia could respond, the whip found her buttocks and she gasped, hanging her head. After three more blows Vicki told her to lift her head and watch. Mia had no idea why she obeyed the command of the fellow slave but she lifted her head. A sudden warmth spread through her as she watched the naked slave raise the whip. She watched its decent and enjoyed the look of her buttocks as they were moulded by the flogger. She closed her eyes to savour the feel of the flogger against her flesh. When the initial sting of the blow had faded she opened her eyes to watch the next. By the time Vicki had delivered twenty-five lashes, Mia's pussy was throbbing for attention and Vicki wasted no time in sliding the handle of the flogger between the folds of her pussy. Mia bit her bottom lip, her buttocks quivering. Vicki's fingers found her clitoris and Mia's juice suddenly gushed from her. Vicki dropped to her knees and lapped at the juice, her own fingers sliding into her pussy. Several minutes later, the gasping slaves curled up together and slept, their limbs entwined.

And that was how they were found the next morning. Both were woken by hands that gripped them harshly and they shuddered with fear as they were dragged out of the dressing room. They both assumed that Jeffrey had been told about their indiscretion the previous night and that they were to now face his wrath. Their fear grew as they were dragged through the bedroom and then through the house. They were taken to the great hall where the five masters waited for them.

They were made to stand in front of the seated masters, their hands behind their backs and their heads bowed. Both trembled with fear, unsure of what was going to happen next.

The First Master spoke, 'State your case and make it quick.'

Mia half lifted her eyes as she heard Thomas say, 'Thank you, First Master.' She caught sight of him as he walked to stand in front of the five masters and then lowered her eyes again. 'I wish to petition the House Masters to allow this slave to return to her rightful place as a Movie Slave.' Mia dared to look up, dared to hope that he was talking about her. He was and he stared right at her as he continued, 'Will the Masters hear me out?'

'The fuck we will!' the Second shouted, 'How dare this fucking wanker even be given the chance to speak?'

'Calm down, Jeffrey,' The First said calmly. 'I wish to hear him out.'

'He is a fucking employee! He is under contract the same as those fucking whores!'

'Let us hear what he has to say,' the Third suggested and received nods from the two Masters who had yet to speak.

'Fine,' Jeffrey sighed angrily. 'Speak then!'

Thomas nodded, 'Thank you, sir.' He paused and then continued, 'Sirs, I ask that the slave known as Mia be returned to me and earn this house money as a Movie slave. She is wasted as a house slave and should never have been demoted to that role in the first place.'

'The whore fucked that slave who now stands beside her – not for the benefit of the camera,' the Fourth Master announced. 'This house has rules and she broke them – are you suggesting that she shouldn't have been punished?'

'If she had done something wrong, I would have no argument – but that slave was betrayed and tricked into believing that she was permitted to take pleasure off camera.'

The First visibly bristled, his harsh gaze falling on Vicki, 'Is this true?'

Vicki licked her lips nervously, 'Master, I -'

'Answer the fucking question! Did you lie to your Masters when you told us that she had instigated the whole thing?'

Tears rolled down Vicki's cheeks as she slowly nodded, 'Yes, Master.'

'How fucking dare you!' his fury rolled across them, making them both shrink back, 'Did you act alone?'

Vicki swallowed, 'Please, master, this slave begs you not to make her answer that.'

'You will answer me,' the First said slowly, his voice vibrating with fury, 'or I will make you tell me – and, my dear Vicki – you will not enjoy it.'

A tiny sob escaped Vicki and she whispered, 'Please, master.'

Thomas held his hand up, 'I can answer for her.'

'Then answer.'

'Sir, she was working under the command of the Second Master.'

Jeffrey snorted, 'For god's sake, Thomas, do you really think that anyone is going to believe that.'

'Vicki!'

She jumped at the sound of her name and looked up at the First before quickly lowering her gaze, 'Come here.'

She climbed slowly to her feet and approached the First, falling to her knees at his feet.

'Look at me.'

She raised her eyes to his.

'Were you following the orders of Master Jeffrey?'

She swallowed a sob, 'Yes, Master.'

'So fucking what!' Jeffrey yelled and threw his hands in the air, 'I am the Second Master of this house – I have the right to do as I please.'

'If that were true then why act to underhandedly?' the Fifth asked.

'I agree.' The First turned to him, 'This house has rules for a reason. We are not the Mistresses of the Slave

House, we do not play these games!' The other three Masters nodded their agreement. 'We do not manipulate and manoeuvre – that is why this house has remained the most successful. I will not allow petty games to threaten our position.' He glared at the Second and then at Vicki, 'Your part in this will not be ignored, slave and you will be punished.'

'Yes, Master.'

'And as for you,' he turned to Jeffrey, 'I have become increasingly concerned by your behaviour and this has just confirmed my concerns. You will leave this house and not return for six months.'

'You're banishing me!'

'I am, if my fellow Masters are in agreement.' They all nodded and then the First continued, 'And upon your return you will be the Fifth Master. Until then, my son, Master Jake, will take the place as the others all move up.'

'And what makes you think I will return in six months?' Jeffrey demanded as he stood.

'That is up to you.'

He clearly wanted to say more but his fury kept him silent.

'You have one hour to be out of this house – we will forward on any belongings that remain.'

He turned to the First, 'Just one thing before I go, Richard, you speak to me of games and manoeuvring, yet here you are promoting your own son into the seat of a House Master.'

'A seat that you may have upon your return in six months' time.'

'You will be begging me to return within a week – and I shall have my rightful place as Second returned to me.' He didn't wait for a response but just turned and left, slamming the door behind him.

The First studied Vicki in silence for several moments as he considered her punishment. Eventually he said, 'For the next five days you will be whipped daily, in the great hall for everyone to see.'

'Yes, master,' she sobbed.

'You will be placed within the whipping frame and remain there all morning – open to any who choose to use you.'

'Yes, master.'

'Each afternoon will be spent with a House Master, each of whom will decide upon a suitable punishment.'

'Yes ... master.'

'Take her away.'

Weeping softly, Vicki was led from the room.

'Master Richard,' Thomas said softly, 'Now that the matter is resolved, may I take the slave Mia?'

The First shook his head, 'No, I wish her to see out the rest of today as a house slave. You may have her tomorrow morning, when I have finished with her.'

*

Several hours later, Mia gasped as her body was sent spinning once more by the whip that wrapped around her breasts. Richard was using a stock whip on her – thin and sharp – he delivered it with consummate skill. Her breasts were marked and red, evidence of the hot wax that he had smothered her with before whipping the flesh clean. The whip wrapped around her waist, flicking at her groin and making her groan.

'You have a great tolerance for pain,' he announced as he tugged the whip free and watched her spin. Another blow – this one to her thighs. 'My son tells me that he has enjoyed you greatly of late. I'm sure he will be greatly disappointed to learn that you are to return to the films.' She gasped, her chest heaving as the whip found her stomach. 'I can see why Master Jeffrey wanted you so badly ... you never did submit to him, did you?'

'Master,' Mia gasped and fought for breath so she could speak, 'I did everything that Master Jeffrey asked of me.'

The whip found her breasts again and she gave a small cry. 'Yes, but you didn't submit.'

'I don't know how to.'

He laughed then, a strange sound that warmed her inner thighs. 'Strength and innocence wrapped up in a whore's body.' He shook his head and curled the whip, tossing it onto the bed. His breath was hot against her neck, 'I have no desire to see you broken. I think you are perfect the way you are.'

She felt a rush of pride in her chest, 'Thank you, master.'

He lowered her to the floor and released her wrists. 'On the bed, spread your legs.'

She did as he commanded and waited for him. He climbed onto the bed and drove into her, making her cry out with the sudden invasion. He fucked her hard, brutally – caring only for his gratification. When he came a few minutes later it was with a grunt of satisfaction. She was left quivering with painful arousal that didn't go unnoticed.

'Don't worry, we have plenty of time yet.' He lit a cigarette and studied the glowing end. 'Present breasts.'

Chapter fifteen: The truth

The blonde knelt between Mia's spread thighs and guided the dildo into her soaking cunt. Mia tipped her head back, groaning with desire. Her hands pulled against the chains that had her secured to the floor as she writhed beneath the delicious fake cock.

'You know what to say.' Thomas' ever present voice echoed around them.

The slave held the dildo inside Mia and slowly twisted it, making her groan again. 'Just tell me where your friends are and I'll let you come.'

Mia lifted her head and hissed through gritted teeth, 'I'm not going to tell you a thing.'

'Resistance scum!' She yanked the dildo free, making Mia cry out. She stood, 'Damn, it's hot in here.' She unbuttoned her uniform jacket and slipped it from her shoulders. She was wearing nothing beneath and her large, full breasts glistened with sweat. She grabbed the crop from the table in the corner of the interrogation room and moved back to Mia.

Mia watched her return. 'You're too late anyway. My friends are already on their way to the target. Ahhhh!' The crop sliced her nipples, making her buck upwards. Another blow to the centre of her breasts drove her down again.

'Where is the target?'

'I'll not tell you anything!'

Ten blows in quick succession had Mia gasping for breath.

'That's good!' Thomas' voice, 'More like that.'

'Fuck you!' Mia snarled although it was unclear who her anger was aimed at.

Another ten blows and Mia was writhing beneath the crop, twisting and pulling against the chains that held her wrists. The blonde beckoned the male guard who had been standing in the corner of the room, 'Take her ankles.' He stood with his feet on either side of Mia's head and then bent to grab her legs, hauling them up so that her back was rounded and her buttocks lifted. The blonde rested the crop on the twin mounds, 'I'll ask you again ... where is the target?'

Mia shook her head, 'No.'

The crop fell across her buttocks and then the backs of her thighs, making her scream as a torrent of blows sliced her flesh.

'Okay.' Thomas said softly, 'Let's go to the final stage.'

A new flurry of blows fell and Mia screamed, 'Please! No more! I beg you!'

The blonde nodded and the male guard let go of her ankles before returning to his place in the corner. She cast the whip aside and grabbed the dildo, kneeling once more between Mia's thighs. Mia sobbed as the dome pressed against her pussy, 'Please, don't ... anything but that.'

The dildo was slammed forward and Mia's hips lifted to greet it, sucking it in deeply. She cried out, tossing her head from side to side. 'Please ... oh God!'

'Tell me where the target is and you'll feel so much better.'

'I can't ... please ... stop.'

The dildo was thrust into her again and again, driving her to the point of climax only to stop when she was at the very point of release.

'Just tell me what I want to know ...' she thrust the dildo forward, her breasts quivering with the effort, '... you know you want to.'

'The North West bridge!' Mia screamed and thrust her hips upwards.

'Good girl.' The blonde lifted Mia's ankles, forcing her knees onto her chest as she drilled the dildo into her. Mia screamed, her climax seizing her immediately. Her scream turned to a high-pitched whine as the blonde suddenly pinched and rubbed her clitoris. Suddenly a spray of clear fluid jetted from Mia and the blonde leant back to allow the ejaculation to smother her breasts.

'Excellent ... let's cut it there.'

Lost in the quivers of her climax, Mia barely noticed when her hands were released and she was taken to the showers to be cleaned.

'Ten minutes, then I want her back on set ready for the next scene.'

*

It was several hours later that Mia was stopped in the corridor on the way out of the film studios.

'I want to speak with you.'

Mia managed to lift her head and stared at Thomas, 'I need another shower.'

Normally she knew better than to speak to one of the Masters like that but ... Thomas wasn't exactly a Master and she was exhausted.

He studied her filthy, bruised skin. She was smothered in come – some of it hers but most of it belonging to the seven men who had just enjoyed her for the benefit of the cameras. 'Very well – please shower and then one of the men will bring you to me.'

'Yes, sir,' she sighed.

She was given soap and shampoo and – for once – the water was hot. She scrubbed until her skin glowed pink and then washed her hair three times to get the sweat and semen out of it. When she was done she was given a towel to dry herself off and then followed Thomas' assistant. With a small sigh she realised that she was being led back to the studios. The assistant opened a door and ushered her inside before closing it behind her. She was left alone in a bedroom. A four-posted bed dominated the space and looked so inviting that Mia couldn't resist sitting on the edge. She waited. Several minutes passed and when no one came she lay back on the mattress, telling herself that she would hear the door open and would be able to jump off the bed.

She stirred but didn't fully wake as a hand stroked her inner thigh, moving slowly upwards. She groaned softly as the fingers traced a line around her leg and then over her hip. A tiny quiver ran through her body as the fingers tickled her side and then gasped as nails gently scratched the side of her breast before fingers squeezed her nipple. Suddenly she saw a vision of Vicki and the memory of what had happened made her eyes snap open.

'It's okay,' Thomas said softly, drawing circles on her breast with his fingertips, 'We won't be disturbed.'

She studied him in silence. He was naked and lying on his side, stretched out beside her. Her eyes flicked over his body – toned and nice. Her gaze went lower to his semi-erect cock and her eyebrows flicked up in surprise. Even partially aroused he was huge – thick and long. She felt a rush of heat at her neck and he must have noticed because he gave a small laugh.

'All in good time,' he smiled.

'I don't think so,' Mia responded and sat up, pushing his hand away.

'I could order you.'

She glared at him, 'You're not a Master – technically I don't have to do anything you say when the cameras are off.'

'Who says they're off?'

She looked quickly around the room, imagining a hundred hidden cameras all watching.

He laughed again, 'I'm joking – there are no cameras.'

Her look clearly stated that she didn't believe him but instead she said, 'What do you want?'

'You, Mia.'

She had expected the response but the sound of his voice, the warmth she heard and the way he said her name

... she felt herself moistening. 'And what do you want from me? A good sucking or do you just wanna spank me and then fuck me?' A look of sadness flashed across his face and Mia instantly regretted her words. An apology flew to her lips but she bit it back – damn it, why should she apologise? After everything he had done to her.

'I just want you. No orders. No pain. Just pleasure.'

She thought of Vicki again, 'And then you'll hand me over to the House Masters for punishment? I don't think so.'

'I would never do that,' he replied quickly, 'God, Mia – how could you think that of me?' He was genuinely shocked and Mia had to bite back another apology. She shook her head with frustration, just as angry with her reaction to him as she was by his incessant games. 'I would never hurt you, Mia.'

She allowed herself a laugh, 'No, but you'll happily give your orders and watch others do it for you.'

He lowered his eyes for a moment, 'I cannot apologise for our roles in this house. You have your role to play just as I have mine.'

'And what is my role at this moment? Hmmm? Stupid little whore who is too stupid to realise when she's being set up? Oh, sorry, I've already played that.'

'You had no way of knowing that Jeffrey was capable of such things – God, I could hardly believe it myself when I got back and discovered what had happened.'

She stared at him, she didn't know what to believe but she did know that she wanted to believe him.

His hand moved slowly to her breast, 'I promise you two things, Mia. One, there are no cameras filming us now and, two, the House Masters will never find out about this.'

'Why should I believe you?'

'Like you said, I am not a Master. You have no idea what they would do to me if they found out about this.'

Mia was stunned into silence. Eventually she said, 'So

why are you doing it?'

His only response was a small smile that melted the last of Mia's resolve. His hand moved up from her chest and cupped behind her neck, pulling forward. Their lips met and Mia responded to his kiss with a passion that stunned them both. They feasted hungrily on each other, their tongues meeting and driving together. He pushed her back onto the bed, his hand sliding down to cup her breast. As his hand moved lower his lips moved to her neck and she sighed as his teeth nibbled at her sensitive flesh. Suddenly his fingers were at her pelvis and sliding through the moist folds. She gasped, pushing her hips up to meet his probing fingers that slipped deftly inside her. She ground her pussy against his hand, forcing his fingers deeper and gasping against his neck at the sweet feeling of him rubbing at her inner walls. His palm rubbed against her clitoris and Mia arched her back, pushing her head into the mattress. His lips found her throat and kissed and licked the skin before slowly kissing his way down her body. She groaned, with disappointment and anticipation in equal measure, as his mouth slid over her pussy lips, his fingers gently spreading them so that he could smother her opening with his lips. He sucked and licked at her entrance, making her squirm and gasp. Then suddenly his mouth was gone from her pussy and his body was sliding over hers. In one easy movement his cock was inside her and Mia gave a small cry of delight. He smothered any more noise with a kiss that left her head spinning. Gently, he reached back to grasp her thigh, lifting her leg and holding it behind the knee to increase the angle and depth of penetration. Her hands found his shoulders, pulling him back down and kissing him before moving her lips to his neck. He quivered as she nibbled at the most sensitive spot between neck and shoulder. He filled her completely, the sweet friction like nothing she had ever felt before. He groaned softly as he started to move, sliding back slowly and then forward again, pinning her to the bed and making the breath hiss in her throat. He moved so slowly that it nearly drove Mia mad with lust. Using her foot on the bed, she pushed and rolled them over until she was on top of him. His cock was so big that she could keep him inside as she moved and he smiled at her with obvious pleasure. She began to move, lifting herself up and then dropping back down, rocking back on her hips to take his full length as deep as she could. His eyes widened with surprise, his chest heaving with desire. His fingers found her hips and her lifted her up and then pulled her back down, making them both gasp. She wanted to ride him harder, faster, but the build up was too pleasurable for them both that she fought to restrain her desires ... for just a little longer. Suddenly he was gone from inside her and he was rolling her back, flipping her over and pulling her up onto her knees. He gripped her hips and guided himself in, groaning as she pushed back. His hands stroked her buttocks as he started to thrust once more, making her grip the covers beneath her. She tossed her head and groaned with each delicious thrust. He slowly built the power of his thrusting until he was quickly slamming into her. She buried her face in the mattress to stifle her cries. And then she could feel the orgasm building, wave after wave of delicious pleasure rolled over her. She heard him groan, sensed the same build up in him. The sound of his pleasure only aroused Mia all the more and soon she was thrusting her buttocks back against him, as desperate to feel his come explode inside her as she was to feel her own orgasm break. He tensed and the first spurt of ejaculation pushed Mia over the edge. She threw her head back and screamed silently as she felt him quiver and explode within her. She cried out as his fingers found her clitoris and rubbed firmly, causing spray after spray of Mia's own juice to soak the bed beneath them.

When they were spent, they fell forward, disengaging to lie side-by-side, panting softly. When he had regained his breath, Thomas said softly, 'I've been waiting a long time to do that.'

Mia gave a small laugh, 'Why?'

He stared into her eyes, 'Because I love you.'

She stared back and in that blissful moment of peace that he had given her, she knew that she had fallen for him. Despite the danger, despite the risk ... she would love him back.

Chapter Sixteen: Affair

Mia watched as the slave was suspended from the chains in the centre of the room. The slave was surrounded by cameras – at least twenty crammed tightly together. There were no operators for the cameras but they moved none the less, shifting from side to side, lenses moving in and out to capture every droplet of sweat that ran down the slave's smooth skin. Thomas appeared, a red flogger hanging from his fist. He moved to the slave, his lips meeting hers and devouring her with passion. His hand gripped her breast, teasing the nipple to life. Then his hand moved lower, sliding between her thighs and stroking at the moistness. Then he pulled back and stared into her eyes, 'I love you,' he whispered and before she could respond, he raised the flogger and lashed her breasts. He beat her mercilessly until she lost consciousness. A few minutes later another slave was hanging in the chains, her lips smothered by his as his hand found her pussy. 'I love you,' he told her a moment later and a moment after that, the flogger found her flesh. She too slipped into unconsciousness and once she had been removed, he approached Mia. She followed him willingly and allowed him to hang her in the chains. She waited as he moved to stand in front of her. Her lips parted as he moved to her and she groaned softly – lost in the intensity of the kiss. She groaned again as his fingers found her pussy. He pulled back. 'I love you.' She knew what was coming next and the anticipation made her skin quiver. The flogger found her breasts, hurting her more than she could ever have imagined. The pain seared through her as blow after blow found her flesh. She looked at Thomas through tear-filled eyes – his love would save her from the pain. But when she looked at him he just stared back blankly – bored. She sobbed as the realisation – she was just another slave, just another piece of meat to suffer for the cameras.

'Please,' she whispered but he didn't hear her.

He continued to beat her, never tiring. She sobbed over and over, her despair growing with each blow. The darkness started to pull at the edges of her senses and she welcomed it – desperate to escape his bored expression as much as she wanted to escape the flogger.

'Mia.'

Thomas' voice tugged at her but she fought against it, forcing herself to accept the darkness.

'Mia.'

With a cry she awoke, slapping at the hands that gently shook her.

'Mia, it's okay, it's okay.'

'Thomas?' She rubbed her eyes and looked round, the last webs of sleep falling away.

They had found a shadowed corner in the back of an indoor set and, atop some musty cushions and blankets, they had made love. It was several days since Thomas had announced his feelings for her and, during the stolen moments since then, she had found herself falling for him. But now, with the images of the dream still scratching at her mind, she realised that she could no longer ignore the fears and concerns that plagued her waking moments.

'Why?' she whispered softly.

'What?' he asked, his arm sliding around her shoulders, fingers stroking her arm.

'Why me?'

'I don't understand,' he replied but his tone suggested otherwise.

'Do you love me?'

'Yes.'

'Then ...' Suddenly she couldn't ask anymore, suddenly she didn't want to know the answers.

Thomas took a deep breath, 'Then how could I do those things to you?'

She nodded slowly, not trusting her voice to answer.

'I am under contract too – I must do what the House Masters command,' he replied simply, 'If I under perform ...' the sentence was left unfinished. Eventually he said, 'Well, you can appreciate what would happen.'

In recent days she had come to realise that Thomas was different to the Masters and he had hinted as much. But that didn't explain why he had been so cruel to her. She managed to find her voice and asked him why.

He sighed, 'You're special.' He rested his cheek against her, 'It was just luck that I picked you out of that line – but when I saw you, when I saw how you reacted ... I knew you were special.' He continued to stroke her arm as he spoke, 'But I also saw that rebellion in you. I knew that if I didn't make you stand out, if I didn't make you perform – then your rebellion would have seen you demoted to a house slave for the length of your contract ... and I would have lost you.' He sighed again, 'In truth ... I made you suffer because I was being selfish and I just wanted you with me – that was as close as I could get to you.'

Mia turned to look up at him, 'Vicki says that I am special ... Master Jeffrey said that I am wired differently ... what did he mean?'

Thomas studied her, 'You have a great tolerance for suffering and for pleasure. In a different world you would be Vicki now.'

Mia shook her head firmly, 'No.'

'If you had had an easier upbringing, then yes – you would be Vicki.' He held her to him again, 'Your introduction to this world was brutal and because of the way you have lived, your only choice was to fight back. But underneath all that, your body is learning to love the domination.'

She shook her head again, refusing to believe him.

'With the right master – you would be an incredible slave.'

'No more talking,' Mia whispered, tears rolling down

her cheeks.

He nodded his agreement, 'But know this – it is who you are that I love, Mia, the person I see now, the person I see inside – it's all you and I love you.'

She lifted her face to his and kissed him firmly before falling back onto the blankets and surrendering herself to him.

*

Mia stared out through the windscreen at the large full moon that hung overhead. The stars were bright tonight and she wound down the window a crack to smell the fresh, cool air.

'You look beautiful by moonlight.'

She turned, a smile playing on her lips. Vicki was sat beside her in the passenger seat, her arm resting on the car door, her other hand playing with the hem of her short skirt. Mia's eyes shifted slightly to the side to stare through the passenger window at the car next to them. Although it was a few metres away, the sounds emanating from it would leave anyone within hearing range in no doubt as to what was happening within.

Vicki followed her gaze and the wound down her own window, giving a small laugh, 'At least they're enjoying themselves.'

Mia glanced around the clearing, spotting the outlines of several vehicles. As she watched, an engine started and a car moved off, only its brake lights glowing as the driver somehow navigated his way back to the road. In the red glow from the brakes, Mia caught the silhouettes of several individuals clustered around the edge of the clearing. 'It's a popular spot,' she breathed.

Vicki leant over, revealing a plunging cleavage, 'You've not done this before, have you?'

'Is it that obvious?'

She smiled, her hand resting on Mia's thigh and then

slowly travelling higher. Mia closed her eyes and sighed as her fingertips brushed the damp material high up between her thighs. 'Hold that thought,' Vicki whispered and there was a rush of cold air as she opened the passenger door.

'Where are you going?'

'I need to pee ... won't be a sec.'

Mia watched through the open door as Vicki moved into the edge of the wood and slipped behind a tree. She smiled to herself, tilting her head back and closing her eyes as she let her hand drift between her legs. She played her fingertips gently over her crotch and sighed.

A few moments later the car shifted as someone climbed into the passenger seat. Smiling, Mia turned and opened her eyes. She froze.

'Don't make a sound.' He was about Mia's age with dark eyes that seemed to stare straight through her.

'What do –'

His hand clamped over her mouth, pushing her back against the door, 'I said ... no noise.' A knife appeared in his hand and hovered near her throat. 'Get out the car.' Mia grabbed the door handle and his next words made her heart hammer in her chest, 'Don't try anything stupid – we have your friend.'

She climbed out of the car and moved to the front when he beckoned her. She stood, shivering with cold fear, as he slipped a bag over her head.

It took an eternity to walk through the woods but eventually she was aware that they had entered a building. The bag was snatched from her head and she felt her breath catch as she stared at the sight before her. Vicki was on her knees, naked with her hands cuffed behind her back. She knelt, immobile, as a man thrust his cock into her open mouth.

'Couldn't you have waited?' the young man who held Mia's arm asked with amusement.

The man who fucked Vicki's unresisting mouth glanced

over, 'Nah ... she just looked so inviting.'

A few moments later, Thomas' voice echoed around them, 'That's good – now let's see it go all the way down her throat.'

The sound of his voice – which had once made her feel sick with anger – now warmed her pussy and made her nipples harden. She tried not to think of him as she watched Vicki struggle to take the full length of the cock. Mia knew that Vicki would have no problem swallowing his length but as she watched the other slave struggle, she remembered the instructions that Thomas had given them as they were seated in the car.

Vicki gagged and coughed as he withdrew his cock, laughing. 'Please,' she gasped, 'let us go!'

The man looked at his companion, 'Uh ... no.' He grabbed her head again and forced himself between her lips, sighing as she struggled to take him again. 'I do love a virgin mouth.' He groaned as the thrust a few more times and then, with a sigh, he pulled free. 'Best not come too quick, wanna make it last.' He turned to Mia, 'You still dressed?'

Mia didn't know what to say in response and just stared back dumbly.

'You deaf?' the younger man who grabbed her demanded as his fingers tightened on her arm, 'Strip ... or be stripped.'

'Don't strip.' Thomas told her.

'Please,' Mia looked pleadingly at the man beside her, 'I just want to –'

His finger slipped into the neck of her t-shirt and she cried out as he yanked downwards, tearing the material straight down her front. His nails scratched her skin as he shredded the last of the material and then ripped her small shorts open, making her stumble as he yanked them down her legs. She stood before them, wearing just a white thong and small white bra. They studied her hungrily before the older one said, 'Finish it off.'

The younger man dug his knife out of his pocket and used it to slice the straps of her bra and the thin cord at her hip. Her underwear fell away and the men both smiled, 'She's some catch,' the younger announced as he put his knife away.

'Nah,' the other turned back to Vicki, 'I like this one.' He walked over to where she knelt and stroked her hair, 'She told me she was virgin.'

'Seriously?' he laughed and fixed Mia with a cold stare, 'What about you?'

She swallowed, 'I ... I ... Yes, I'm a virgin.'

'Why the hesitation?'

Mia's gaze flicked to Vicki but she didn't answer.

He laughed, 'You two?'

'Them two what?'

He glanced over his shoulder, 'They're not exactly virgins.'

The older man began to slip his belt from his waist, 'You lying to me, girl?' In a swift movement he had pushed Vicki onto her front and knelt on her back while he curled the belt around his wrist.

'Don't!' Mia cried but was grabbed before she could do anything.

The first snap of the belt was as sharp as Vicki's high-pitched cry. She struggled to get out from under him but he held her firmly as he delivered another nine quick blows to her quivering buttocks. When he was done, he stood, 'That'll teach you to lie to me.' He turned on Mia, 'You got something to say?'

She looked down at Vicki who was sobbing on the floor. She shook her head but he seemed far from appeased. Nodding at a battered table on the other side of the room he followed slowly as Mia was pushed over it. The younger man held her wrists, dragging her face down across the table.

'Please,' Mia whispered.

'Good,' Thomas' voice whispered around them, 'more

of that.'

'Please,' she said again, 'I'll do anything.'

'Really?'

She struggled, her breasts scratching over the rough surface, 'Yes ... just, please, don't beat me.'

He eyed the belt in his fist as his hand stroked her buttocks. After a moment he smiled nastily and raised the belt, 'We're pretty much gonna do what we want to you anyway ... so ...'

The belt came slicing down and Mia threw her head back to scream loudly – the blow hadn't really hurt as much as her reaction suggested but, as always, she had her direction from Thomas. The thought of him made her heart thump against her chest and then, suddenly, it wasn't the older man beating her but Thomas. She closed her eyes and saw Him lifting the belt behind her and bringing it down across her rapidly reddening buttocks. She saw Him lift the belt over and over again. Felt His sweat peppering her back as he exerted himself with every terrible blow. And then she imagined Him, casting the belt aside and undoing his trousers, moving in on her and ...

'Get up.' A fist twisted in her hair, making her gasp as she was yanked backwards and thrown to the floor beside Vicki. The other slave had been released from her cuffs and she reached out to hold Mia in a quivering embrace as they both stared up at the older man. 'So, my brother Jimmy tells me that he reckons you two have fucked each other. That true?' Neither girl answered, prompting the older brother to lift the belt, 'Want me to beat an answer out of you?'

'Yes,' Vicki said quickly, licking her dry lips, 'we have ... fucked ... each other.'

'Well then, how about a demonstration?'

Jimmy clapped his hands together, 'Damn it, Mark, you're a fucking perv.'

'You complaining?'

'Nah,' he laughed and waved at the two girls, 'Well,

fucking get on with it.'

Mia turned to Vicki, a tiny smile playing across her lips. They leant towards each other and kissed gently, tongues probing softly.

A sudden snap and a cry from Mia as the belt sliced her shoulder blades. 'I said fuck each other!'

Before Mia could respond, Vicki had moved her onto her back, her hands gripping her breasts. She gasped, raising her leg as Vicki licked her way down her stomach and across her pelvis. Then suddenly her tongue was at Mia's pussy and her back arched. She had no time to consider how wet she was before Vicki's fingers were inside her and she was crying out with passion.

'Let her come.' Thomas ordered and then any other noise was lost beneath Mia's cries of desire. Vicki thrust her fingers into her as she sucked and nibbled at her clitoris. Her other hand found her breast and pinched the nipple.

'Oh God!' Mia suddenly cried out, her back arching and her hips quivering as she climaxed. Her body was rocked by the power of the orgasm but she had barely recovered before she was being lifted up.

Lost for a moment in the afterglow of her climax, it took another blow with the belt before she realised what was expected of her. She lifted herself onto her knees and the leant forward to bury her face between Vicki's thighs. The slave gasped, her pussy lips quivering around Mia's tongue. She worked hard at Vicki's pussy, eager to afford her the same pleasure that had been given her.

Suddenly she tensed as she felt large hands grip her hips and lift her up. A thick cock pushed against her soaking pussy lips and she groaned against the pussy before her as she was deeply filled.

'Fuck, she's tight,' Mark snarled.

'What do you expect from a virgin pussy?' Jimmy laughed, moving to stand beside him, stroking his cock.

'Yeah, well I'm too fucking big for her.' He pulled free, making Mia gasp. 'Here, you have her, I'll have the other one when she's come.'

His words seemed to arouse Vicki almost as much as Mia's tongue. Mia lapped at her juice, groaning as another cock penetrated her, the man's fingers digging into her hips. He rode her hard and fast, coming quickly and spreading his come over the red and white lines that the belt had raised on her skin. As soon as he was done, Mia was pushed to the side and Mark fell onto Vicki. She tried to back away from him but he grabbed her thighs and yanked her back. He knelt, pulling her up onto his cock and impaling her, making her scream.

'Yeah,' he growled, 'That's fucking better!' She struggled and sobbed beneath him and although Mia knew it was just an act for the cameras, Vicki was incredibly convincing. He fucked her for several minutes before he pulled free and rolled onto his back, pulling Vicki with him. He thrust into her and then used his feet to push her ankles apart. 'Wanna join me, bro?'

Jimmy laughed as he sank down between her thighs and forced his cock in on top of the one that already filled her. Vicki screamed loudly but the juice that gushed from her spoke of more than pain. Jimmy groaned as he managed to slide all the way in, 'Get over here and sit on her face – she'll show you a good time.'

Mia did as she was told, sitting astride Vicki's mouth and gasping loudly as the other slave's tongue immediately slid inside her. She cried out as Mark's finger played at her soaking opening before slowly sliding into her arse.

The frantic fucking continued for several minutes and it was impossible to tell who had climaxed first – Mia or Vicki – but by the time both men had shot their seed into her, Vicki had fallen limp, lost in a delirium of pleasure.

'That's good,' Thomas announced, 'that'll do.'

The four disengaged from each other and stood, panting, awaiting their next instruction.

'Okay, Jim, Mark, take the blonde slave to the showers and all three of you get washed. The other slave is to stay there, I've got more planned for her.'

Without argument, the three filed out of the cabin and Mia was left to stand alone, wondering what Thomas had planned for her next.

When the door opened, she was surprised to see Thomas enter. He closed the door behind him and smiled at her, 'The cameras are off.'

'Good.' She wanted to run to him, to embrace him and kiss him ... but there was something that she needed first. She turned and lay face down over the table. Spreading her legs she glanced back at him, watching as he shed his lower clothes. And when he sank into her ... it was so much better than she could have ever imagined.

Afterwards they sat on the floor and held each other. Mia had never felt so warm and content.

'There's something I need to say to you,' Thomas said softly.

'Hmm?' she had to force her eyes open or she would have willingly fallen asleep.

'We're planning another big project.'

Mia felt her chest constrict, 'Like the Prison?'

He nodded, 'Yes, but bigger.' He turned so that he could look into her eyes, 'Mia, you're not going to see or hear me while it's being filmed.' She frowned but he didn't let her speak. 'I can't explain anymore than that right now but I wanted you to know that ... even though you won't hear me, I'm there. I'll be watching and I promise you, I won't let any harm come to you. Just know that I'll be there.'

She nodded slowly, 'Okay.'

He cupped her face in his hands and kissed her tenderly, only breaking from the kiss to whisper, 'I love you. Never forget that.'

Chapter Seventeen: Whorestown

It was three weeks later that Mia found herself standing in the middle of the Wild West. They had been here for ten days and she was still amazed by the sheer complexity of the area. Real houses and shops lined the dusty street, horses were tied up outside the bar and there was even a sheriff's office – that was currently abandoned. They had flown here in an old military transport plane and had then ridden for what seemed like hours in the back of a truck. When they arrived they had been immediately assigned their roles. Mia had often wondered if this place had once been a 'themed' town. It was all so real and with nothing but rough desert and rock all around them, it was hard not to get caught up in it all.

'Morning, Miss.'

She turned at the leering man who tipped his hat as he passed. 'Morning to you, sir.' A wind blew along the main street and she bent to brush sand of her ruffled petticoats. Split up the front and gathered at the sides to reveal her firm thighs and black lace underwear, stockings and suspenders, the costume left no doubt as to what her role in the town was. A corset had been tied tightly around her chest, lifting her breasts and giving her an impressive cleavage. Elbow length gloves clung to her arms like a second skin. Her hair had been scooped up on her head and more make-up than she had ever worn in her life had been skilfully applied. The 'dressing house' was the only place in the town that wasn't continually monitored by state of the art hidden cameras and Mia was required to go there every morning to check her clothes and make-up. Once she emerged, as she had this morning, she had only one destination – the whore house. Situated next to the saloon, it was – unsurprisingly – the most frequented building in the whole town.

Even at this early hour, the first of the day's patrons had arrived. She nodded at them as she entered and headed for the stairs but was stopped by the Madame – Roxanne.

'Where are you going?'

'My room ... I have customers.'

'And that is how you speak to me?'

Mia took a deep breath and lowered her gaze, 'Sorry, Madame Roxy ... may I please go to my room to prepare for my first gentleman?'

'Your room is being cleaned. Attend your gentlemen down here.'

She glanced at the two men who sat and watched her, smoking and sipping coffee. 'I am to entertain them both at the same time?'

'Is that a problem?'

'No, Madame, of course not.'

Roxanne dismissed her with a wave and turned to harangue another of her whores.

'Gentlemen,' Mia smiled as she approached them, 'how are you both this fine morning?'

'Hot and horny,' one replied – Mia knew him only as Jacob. The other grinned – he was Karl. She moved to sit on his lap and he slipped his arm around her waist, squeezing her tightly. 'Let's go upstairs.'

'Madame has asked me to entertain you down here, my room is being cleaned.'

Karl leant forward, 'By that pretty young maid?'

'I don't know, sir ... but I can assure you that once the room is cleaned -'

Karl cut off her words by grabbing her hand and dragging her to her feet, 'Let's go.'

He dragged her towards the stairs and as they passed Roxanne, Mia called, 'Madame, has Vicki finished with my room?'

Roxanne studied the three of them in turn before her gaze settled on Karl. Slowly she held her hand out and he grunted as he retrieved notes from his pocket, slapping them into her palm. He grunted again as he climbed the stairs, dragging Mia behind him.

He entered Mia's room first and gave a small laugh, 'Well, well, well ... what have we got here?'

Vicki looked quickly from Karl to Mia, 'I'm sorry ... I shall finish cleaning later.' She was dressed in a simple, plain dress. Her hair tied back in a ponytail and her face flushed from her duties.

As she approached the door he stuck his arm out to stop her, 'Where you going, pretty?'

She stared at him, 'Sir?'

'I've paid for the both of you for a whole hour and I reckons we should get started.' He grabbed her harshly and threw her onto the bed.

'Sir, please!' she cried as she tried to roll away from him, 'I'm just the maid.'

He hauled her back and pinned her beneath him, 'And I've been watching you clean for a long time now.' He lifted her dress, revealing no underwear beneath and quickly lowered his trousers. Mia half turned away as he forced himself into her, making Vicki scream. He rode her harshly while Jacob slowly undressed and then climbed onto the bed, tipping Vicki's head back and sliding his cock into her mouth.

Jacob groaned as he slowly thrust between her lips, savouring the feel of her. After a few minutes he looked up at Mia, 'Whisky.'

Nodding, Mia turned to the small dressing table and poured two glasses, taking them to the bed. As she approached, Jacob reached down to rip open the front of Vicki's dress, revealing her beautiful breasts. He took the glass from Mia, swallowed a large gulp and then poured the rest over her chest. She jumped at the feel of the liquid on her skin and gagged on his cock. Suddenly Karl snarled and thrust firmly into her, holding himself deep as he climaxed. He withdrew almost immediately, leaning back against the bedstead and smiling as he watched Jacob thrust into her mouth. He beckoned Mia who brought him whisky and a slim cigar. 'Clean her up ... inside and out.'

Mia leant over Vicki's prone body and licked the whisky from her chest – enjoying the taste of the hot liquid on her tongue. Vicki writhed beneath her and Jacob laughed as he rode her movements, fighting to keep himself in her mouth. 'She's a lively one,' he laughed and motioned for Mia to move lower, 'Go on ... I wanna see if I can ride this mare when she really bucks.'

Mia leaned over the bed to seek out Vicki's pussy. With whisky still on her tongue, she sought on Vicki's clitoris. The blonde bucked upwards, groaning against the cock that slipped into her throat with the movement. Mia continued to lick at her pussy, using all the tricks that Vicki had taught her to make the slave buck and writhe. Vicki's fingers clawed at the bed, her nails tearing at the sheets.

'Fuck me ... she's a wildcat!' Karl laughed as he watched Mia slip her fingers into Vicki's welcoming cunt. He held the glass out to Mia, 'Take a mouthful and then lick her out.'

Mia slipped her fingers from Vicki, smearing the slave's juice across the glass as she took a large mouthful. She handed the glass back and then bent to suck Vicki's clitoris, dribbling whisky between the creases of her pussy. Vicki climaxed instantly, writhing and shuddering. Jacob pulled free of her mouth and her scream of delight echoed around them as he came across her breasts. Mia continued to lick and suck at her pussy, drawing another shuddering climax from her. When she was done, she sat back and Vicki rolled onto her side, sobbing and trembling.

'What the fuck is the matter with her?' Karl demanded.

Mia glared at him, 'She's young and inexperienced ...' She let the fantasy of the roles that they had been given flow through her and she rested a gentle hand on Vicki's shoulder, 'Let her go now – you'll have more fun with me.'

Karl licked Vicki's juice from the side of the glass, 'No, I don't think so.'

Mia climbed onto the bed and crawled towards him, lifting his semi-erect penis and gently stroking it. She bent to flick her tongue over the end and looked up at him when he sighed.

'She isn't a whore of this house ... she's just the fucking maid,' she said.

Karl looked over her shoulder to where Vicki lay – she had fallen silent but still trembled. 'I'll be having words with Madame Roxy – that one has potential.'

'Forget her,' Mia whispered and drew his penis into her mouth, instantly feeling it harden. She sucked him for several minutes before he suddenly lifted her off him.

'Take your panties off.' Mia did as she was told, slipping her panties off from under the petticoats to reveal the neatly trimmed pussy. He climbed off the bed and led her round so that he could bend her over the metal bedstead. She gasped as the iron frame dug into her stomach and reached out to hold the corner posts. He lifted her petticoats and, with a swift movement, slid into her. She stared blankly at Jacob as she was ridden. He stared back, sipping more whisky as his own arousal started to grow once more.

After a few minutes of watching Mia being fucked, Jacob leant forward to rub his fingers between Vicki's legs. She jumped but didn't move. He lifted his eyebrows as he smeared Vicki's juice over his cock and then looked up at his companion, 'Give her here.'

If Karl was annoyed by the request, he didn't show it. He pulled free and smacked her rump, 'Go on.'

'Take the petticoats off,' he commanded, 'I want your arse.'

Mia did as she was told and as she approached the bed, Jacob harshly kicked Vicki off. The blonde cried out as she hit the floor and Mia quickly bent to her, 'It's okay, you go on now.'

'Thank you,' Vicki whispered, wiping a hand across her eyes. She stood and went to move round Karl who grabbed her arm, 'Where do you think you're going?'

She looked up at him fearfully as Mia answered, 'Just let her go ... like I said, you'll get more out of me.'

Karl glanced at her, 'Yeah? Like what?'

Mia climbed onto the bed as Jacob lay down and lifted his cock towards her. She smeared her own juice around her anus and his cock before she slowly lowered herself onto him. He groaned as he was gripped by her tight passage, Mia wincing as he filled her deeply. When he was in her, she lay back on his chest and spread her legs, her meaning clear as she stared at Karl, 'Is she really worth your time?'

Karl smiled but didn't let go of Vicki. Instead he propelled her towards a chair in the corner of the room, 'Sit. I want you to watch this ... maybe you'll learn something.' He climbed onto the bed and Mia watched him as he stroked his penis. Jacob had already started to move within her and suddenly she was desperate for Karl to fill her. She braced her hands on the bed, steadying herself as he moved between her legs. Then suddenly he was in her and Mia threw her head back, gasping. The two men moved alternately the sensation of being emptied from one while filled in the other was incredible and soon Mia was gasping with rising passion. As their speed increased it became impossible to tell one sensation from another, making her cry out with each thrust. Breathless with desire her chest heaved as she fought to make the sensations last. But then suddenly she was coming and her scream tore from her throat. Jacob's teeth found her shoulder and she screamed again as his teeth sank into her skin, another climax ripping through her.

'Well, lookey what we have here,' Jacob laughed, 'The whore likes a little pain.'

Pausing in his thrusting, Karl bent his head to her breast and sucked her flesh, his teeth biting down. She screamed again, writhing in pain and so much more. The two men began to thrust again and Mia was lost in a delirium of pleasure. Jacob's teeth found her other shoulder and she turned her head to the side. A soft whimper made her open her eyes and she stared at Vicki. She sat with one leg hooked over the arm of the chair, her fingers rubbing at her soaking pussy. The two locked stares and then Vicki threw her head back, gasping as her juice jetted from between her fingers. The sight was too much and Mia screamed, her own climactic juices soaking both men who quickly followed, filling Mia with hot come.

The sound of the door being thrown open made them all turn in that direction as four men barged their way into the room.

'What the fuck?' Karl demanded as he jumped off the bed. Jacob threw Mia off him and she scrambled to her feet to stand in front of Vicki as the men lined up just inside the door, hands on holsters by their sides.

'Gentlemen,' a fifth man announced with a nod as her entered the room, 'sorry to disturb you good fellows but we need to speak to the ... ladies.'

Karl was about to say something in return when he noticed the shining silver star on the man's breast. He dipped his head, grabbed his clothes and then he and Jacob hurried out of the room.

The Sherriff approached Mia, tilting his head slightly so that he could see Vicki. Mia moved to block his view, 'What's this about?' she asked.

He stared back, his eyes cold, 'It's about the good folks around here getting their town back.' He appraised Mia for a moment longer before turning to glance over his shoulder, 'You know what to do.'

When he had left, the four men approached Mia and Vicki. Two grabbed Mia and hauled her to the side while the other two lifted Vicki who struggled in their grip. Both were roughly stripped and then marched naked out of house and into the street beyond.

A large group had gathered, more people than Mia had ever actually seen in the town stood silently, staring at a kneeling line of naked women. Mia recognised them all as whores from the house. Kneeling among them was Roxanne, hands tied behind her back and her head bowed. Mia and Vicki were similarly bound and forced to their knees at the end of the line.

The sheriff addressed the crowd of conservatively dressed men and women, 'Ladies and gentleman, today your town is handed back to you. Today women and children will feel safe in the streets. Gentlemen will be able to go about their business without fear of Satan's whores tempting their good nature.'

Mia wanted to laugh but instead bowed her head and let herself become immersed in the role once more.

The crowd mumbled an acknowledgement, their mood dark and vengeful. The Sheriff held his hands up, 'Now, I know that you'd like to see these women punished for what they have done to the good name of this town, but ... these fallen women deserve our pity.'

The crowed shifted, angry and unsure.

'I have it on good authority that these women were tricked into this undertaking, they no more wished to sell their good bodies than this town wanted them to. Only one of these women shall be punished this day ... the one who started it all and ran the den of evil pleasures.' He turned back to the line of women and Mia glanced to her right. She couldn't help but feel a sense of anticipation at what was to happen next – she wondered what punishment they had planned for Roxanne.

'You!'

Mia jumped as the Sheriff stood in front of her. She looked up, squinting at the sun, 'Sir?'

'You are the Madame of this whore house – are you not?'

'No, sir ... I'm just one of the whores.'

Blinded by the sun, she didn't see him move and his

backhanded blow caught her off guard, sending her reeling. Two of his deputies picked her up and put her back in line. 'I will ask you again – are you the Madame of this whore house?'

'No ... sir,' she said deliberately.

His eyes went to Vicki and he took half a step towards her. 'I was told that the Madame of this house was entertaining in the very room where I found you two ... and since I discovered you both, stained by the men and legs spread ... one of you must be the Madame.' He kept his gaze on Vicki but he spoke to Mia, 'And if you are not the Madame, then I guess she is. Pick her up.'

Vicki cried out as she was grabbed and lifted to her feet.

'Stop,' Mia sighed, turning to glare at Roxanne before she turned back to the Sheriff, 'I am the Madame.'

'Bring them both.'

A platform had been erected at the end of the main street and as they approached Mia felt her breath catch in her throat at the sight of the noose that hung from the centre of the beam. 'You've got to be kidding me,' she half-whispered as she was marched up the steps.

'Silence, whore,' the Sheriff announced angrily, yanking her arm, 'Accept your punishment with dignity.'

She was positioned beneath the noose that hung about a foot above her head. Her wrists were released from their bonds and then her arms yanked over her head. Her hands were slipped through the noose and the knot tightened until she was firmly gripped by the rope. She took a deep breath as she watched one of the Sheriff's deputies take a step towards a large lever. With a nod from the sheriff, the lever was moved and the trapdoor beneath her feet slammed open. She only fell a couple of inches but that was enough for her to yell as her arms were wrenched in their sockets. She kicked wildly as her body spun.

'Quieten down,' the Sheriff ordered as he steadied her

body, 'You'll have plenty to yell about in a minute.' As he spoke another of his deputies handed him a horsewhip. She had seen this type of whip used before – a crop with a braided leather leash attached to its end – but had never been on the receiving end. Now, as the Sheriff made a point of showing her the whip, she realised why even the submissive Vicki had cried for mercy as she had been beaten with it. He turned to the townsfolk who had approached the platform and now stood watching and expectant. Despite their austere clothing and apparent attitude, their collective gaze was hungry and malicious – there was no doubt that they fully intended to enjoy the spectacle that would be played out before them. The other 'whores' had been led away – all except Vicki who now knelt at the edge of the crowd. Her hands were still bound behind her back and a chain had been looped around her neck, the other end being held by the largest of the deputies.

The first blow of the whip was so unexpected that Mia froze for a moment, her body slowly spinning. Then the needles of pain forced their way into her consciousness and she gave a small cry. The crowd started to clap and cheer as the whip landed again and again. The sheriff didn't target any area of her body but just let the whip fly. The design of the whip was such that the crop landed first and then the braided cord wrapped around – extending the line of pain. Each blow was given in quick succession and it was hard to tell where any particular one landed. She bit down on her cries refusing to give them the pleasure of hearing her suffer. It seemed to make no difference, they enjoyed the sight of her pain just the same. The Sheriff didn't keep count of the blows – his intention being to beat her until she begged for mercy. She would give him no such plea. She twisted beneath the whip, her body smothered in welts that glistened with sweat. Soon her hair was sticking to her face and neck in wet rats' tails. She tossed her head, giving a small cry as the whip found her breasts. The next her thighs and then her buttocks. With each blow the pain grew worse but she could hold off – she would not cry out!

It was several minutes before the Sheriff, panting heavily, lowered the whip and Mia hung her head – satisfied that they had not broken her. She heard a second set of footsteps and assumed that it was another of the deputies coming to let her down. She half lifted her head and frowned when she saw the Sheriff with the crowd, Vicki's chain gripped in his hand. Mia turned slightly and gasped when she saw the large deputy lifting the horsewhip. She closed her eyes – tears squeezing from the corners with the sudden realisation that her punishment had barely even begun. He struck her too quickly and too many times for her to keep count. His extra size and strength meant that the blows fell twice as hard and soon, despite her desire not to, she was screaming as the whip lashed her skin. Sweat poured off her body as she writhed and spun beneath the whip – the pain in her arms and shoulders only adding to the agony.

'Please ...' she gasped when he paused to adjust his stance, '... no more.' The whip fell again and she screamed loudly, writhing uncontrollably. 'Oh, God! Please!'

He paused, perhaps looking to the crowd for confirmation of what to do. The crowd pulsated with the anger that was far from sated.

'Give her more!' someone shouted.

'The whore deserves more!'

'Beat the whore!'

'Make her suffer!'

'Beat the devil from her!'

The slice of the whip smothered the rest of the shouts and she screamed, tossing her head from side to side. With no end in sight, she became lost in a delirium of pain. She could feel her senses clouding at the edges but every time she dared to hope that she was losing consciousness, the whip found her breast or some other more sensitive area and brought her round again. After several more minutes it didn't matter where the whip landed – she could feel no individual blows and her head fell forward as she slipped into unconsciousness.

She was brought round again by a bucket of freezing water. Gasping and coughing as the water slid from her skin, she stared at the hungry crowd who applauded her awakening.

'God has shown us the way ... she deserves more ... beat the whore ...'

The heavy-set deputy was replaced and as the newcomer started to beat her, Mia thought that she heard Vicki's voice. It was hard to tell as her senses faded again but she thought she heard Vicki begging them to stop – or perhaps it was her own voice that she heard. Darkness took her soon after and this time, despite the freezing water, she could not be revived.

*

Mia came round with a cry, her body aflame. She writhed and lashed out, desperate to get away from the agony that had seized her. A voice tried to soothe her and eventually the words got through. Her chest heaved and she opened her eyes, finding herself staring into Vicki's blue eyes. The sight of the blonde slave calmed Mia and she relaxed slightly, groaning as her body protested at even the slightest movement. She cried out as Vicki touched a wet, cool cloth to one of the welts on Mia's back.

'Sorry,' Vicki whispered and gently patted the cloth against her skin.

'It's alright,' Mia said through gritted teeth. As Vicki continued the cooling water eased her pain a little and she relaxed again. She lay on her front with her eyes shut, feeling herself awaken slowly. As she came round the pain eased slightly and she slowly opened her eyes. Vicki turned to wet the cloth and Mia gasped as she saw the angry welts that lined Vicki's back. The slave turned back, realising why Mia had gasped. She started to gently pat the cloth against Mia's skin again. Tears shining in her eyes, Mia asked, 'What did they do to you?'

Vicki wiped her own tears with the back of her hand, 'It's nothing.'

Mia slowly took Vicki's wrist – despite her pain, Mia had been trained to fall into whatever role she had been given and to stick to it regardless. 'What happened?'

'They ... I ...' she sniffed, 'I couldn't just let them keep whipping you like that ... I begged the Sheriff to stop ... but they ... they said I was a whore too and ...' the tears rolled down her cheeks, 'They left you hanging there while I leant over the platform and ...'

'It's alright,' Mia whispered when Vicki's voice broke. She gave a small smile, 'Thanks for trying.'

Vicki looked up at her, 'They're right though, aren't they? I am a whore.'

Mia shook her head, 'No, don't you listen to them.'

'But ... but what those men did.'

Before Mia could answer there was a loud bang as something struck the bars of the cell. Both slaves jumped and turned to see the Sheriff, the handle of the horsewhip held against the bars. 'You're awake then.'

Mia bit back a sharp answer and bowed her head, 'Yes, sir.'

He studied them both, his eyes giving a clear message – he was deciding which one he wanted.

'Sir,' Mia said softly, 'may I have a drink?'

Slowly he lowered the whip and turned to the small table on the other side of the office. He poured a glass of water and returned, holding the cup through the bars. Groaning softly, she managed to get to her feet and shuffled over. She took the cup with a small thank you and sipped the water, coughing as it seared her dry throat. She turned to hand the cup to Vicki but was stopped when the whip handle snapped down on her wrist.

'Did she ask for a drink?'

Mia looked at him, 'Please, sir ... I'd be most grateful.'

'Alright.' He moved the whip and then, as Mia gave Vicki the cup, he unlocked the cell door. Vicki shrank away as he entered and Mia moved to stand in front of her before falling to her knees. He moved to stand in front of her and unfastened the front of his trousers. 'Do it nice and I'll get you some food.'

'Thank you, sir,' she whispered and slipped her lips over his thick cock. She took him deeply and sucked him hard, grimacing at the taste of his sweat. She had learned a lot since being at the Movie House and had learned many tricks to make him groan and sigh. It didn't take long before he groaned loudly and his cock quivered as he shot his come down her throat. He slowly withdrew and tucked himself away as Mia wiped her hand across her mouth. Suddenly he leant down and grabbed her hair, making her gasp as he yanked her head up, 'If you tell anyone about this ...' He left the threat unsaid as he threw her aside, making her cry out as her battered body hit the floor. He turned and left the cell, running the whip handles along the bars and whistling as he went back to his desk.

A few minutes later one of the deputies arrived and opened the cell door. He set a tray of bread and two cups of water on the floor before he turned to Mia, 'Well?'

Sighing, Mia hauled herself to her knees and crawled towards him. He came quicker than the Sheriff and left them without saying another word.

The bread was stale but at least it was food. They ate in silence, sitting beside each other and drawing comfort from the closeness of the other.

When they were finished, Vicki asked softly, 'What are we going to do?'

Mia leant back and closed her eyes. 'I don't know.'

They both looked towards the cell entrance at the sound of a key in the lock.

'Put these on,' the deputy told them and dropped a pile of sacking into the centre of the cell. He stood, leaning against the cell bars and watched as they pulled the rough sacking dresses over their heads. The two slaves looked at each other, sewn onto the front of each was a red W. 'So no one forgets what you are,' the Deputy announced, 'Follow me.'

Mia leant against Vicki as they followed the deputy out of the cell and into the main area of the Sheriff's office. The sheriff was sat with his feet on the desk, smoking a thin cigar. They were led over and made to stand in front of him, hands behind their backs and their heads bowed. He studied them in silence for several moments before puffing smoke and announcing, 'Well, it took all of my powers to convince the good people of this town to not expel you into the wilderness. What do you say?'

'Thank you, sir,' they said together.

'As of tomorrow, you and the other whores will repay your debt to this town.' He puffed on the cigar, 'Each morning you will report to Mrs Cooper, the town chairman's wife. She will deliver five lashes to your whore asses and then you'll be given you your duties for the day. After you have completed your duties you will be brought back here for the night.' He leant forward slowly, 'And what happens within these walls remains within these walls ... is that understood?'

The two women nodded.

'Take them back to their cell.'

*

'Remove your dresses.'

Mia and Vicki slipped out of the sacking and that been roughly fashioned into a dress and stood naked before Mrs Cooper and her two assistants, middle-aged women who looked just as grey and austere as she did. Their hair was scraped back into buns, they wore no make-up and their dark dresses covered them from neck to ankle. Mrs Cooper beckoned Vicki, 'Grip the edge of the desk.'

Vicki moved slowly forward and bent to grip the desk,

presenting her smooth round buttocks. Mrs Cooper lifted the cane from the desk and moved to stand behind Vicki, resting the strip of wood against her buttocks.

'Can you count to five?'

'Yes, Madam.'

'Then count ...'

... Snap ... the cane flattened her buttocks and Vicki gave a small cry, 'One! ... Two ! ... Three!' A pause as Mrs Cooper moved to that she could deliver the last two blows from the other side, using a harder, back-handed stroke. 'Four! ... Five!'

Vicki gave a small sob as she was ordered to stand. She was handed her dress back once she had out it on, Mrs Cooper studied her. 'Do you regret you decision to become a whore?'

Vicki looked up at her as if to defend herself but the look on the woman's face made her lower her gaze, 'Yes, madam ... I am sorry.'

Mrs Cooper seemed satisfied, 'Good. The best thing for you is to work those evil passions out of you. Go with Mrs Trent and she will take you to the blacksmith who needs someone to pump his bellows.'

'Yes, madam, thank you.'

When Vicki and one of her assistants had left, Mrs Cooper approached Mia. She circled her slowly, studying the multitude of welts that smothered her body. She winced as Mrs Cooper ran the cane along a particularly harsh welt that sliced her shoulder blades. Mrs Cooper stood in front of her – she was at least half a foot taller than Mia and used her height to good effect as she stared down at her. 'You enslaved those poor girls and let evil corrupt them.'

Mia looked up at her but, just as Vicki had, she saw no point in arguing and lowered her gaze.

'But I am not without mercy.' She traced a welt across Mia's breast with the cane, 'I will not assign you any duties today and will not give you your daily punishment for the coming week. However, I will double your daily punishment the following week to make up for it.'

'Thank you, madam.'

She turned to the desk and laid the cane down. Turning, she lifted a piece of wood. 'Can you read?'

'Yes, madam.'

'What does this say?'

Mia cleared her throat, 'It says whore, madam.'

'Yes, it does.' She lifted the wood and hooked some string over Mia's head, leaving the sign to hang over her breasts. 'You will stand in the middle of the town so everyone can see that justice has been done.'

'Yes, Mistress.'

Mrs Cooper's other assistant led her out of the house and into the centre of town before smiling nastily at her and walking away.

Within an hour Mia was pouring sweat as the sun grew higher in the sky and by midday she was starting to sway with heat exhaustion.

'Stand still you filthy whore,' one of the townspeople snarled as they walked past. She ignored them – it wasn't the first comment thrown her way and not even the worst. In the four hours that she had been stood there she had been cursed and spat at and had tried her best to ignore it. But it was getting harder to ignore the need to pee and almost cried with relief when she saw Mrs Cooper walking down the street. As the woman neared her, Mia called, 'Madam, please, may I speak?'

Mrs Cooper stared at her as if surprised to see her there. She walked over, 'What?'

'Madam, please ... I need to pee.'

She looked her up and down, at her sweat stroked skin and the dried spit that covered her. 'So? Pee where you stand, no one will notice you filthy whore,' and with that she continued on her way.

Mia wanted to scream after her, to scream at anyone that this wasn't real and she had had enough – but she knew better. There was nothing that could be done to her that could be worse than what the House Masters would do if she spoilt the filming. Even another beating like the one she had received the previous day would have been preferable. She managed to squeeze her bladder shut for a few more minutes before the cramp in her abdomen became too much and the first trickle of urine ran down her leg. She gave a small sob and closed her eyes as she relaxed and soaked the sand beneath her feet. Those who passed could hardly miss the dark stain and the sight of it brought more derision.

The sun continued to beat down on her naked, glowing red body and she could feel herself getting light-headed. It was an hour later that Mrs Cooper walked past again, pausing to study Mia. 'You will stay there until sunset.'

'Please,' Mia whispered through dry lips, 'may I have a drink?'

Mrs Cooper's lip curled in distaste but she sighed and waved towards the water butt outside the saloon. Two horses had been tied beside it and were currently drinking. 'One minute and then you will be back here.'

'Thank you, Madam.' Mia hurried as fast as she could to the water butt, falling to her knees and dipping her lips to the water. The water was hot – having been out in the sun as long as she had – but it felt good as it slid down her throat. She used her hands to splash her face and neck before she returned to her place in the centre of the town.

Two hours later and she needed to pee again. This time she didn't hold it but just let it go as soon as she felt the need. The sun had moved round and now beat down on her back. She could feel her eyes closing but didn't have the strength to fight it. She felt her legs give way and she crumpled to the ground, her eyes fluttering. She heard voices, someone angrily telling her to get up. A boot nudged her, then again. She wanted to move – she just couldn't. Another voice, telling someone to fetch Mrs Cooper and then Mrs Cooper's voice, demanding to know why she wasn't standing. Mia found enough strength to respond in a whisper, 'Please, madam, it's so hot.'

Sighing, Mrs Cooper told those who had gathered to be on their way. Then she bent to Mia and said, 'Sunset is in a few hours, you'll find it gets quite cold then. I shall see you in the morning.'

The town continued to move around her as she lay on the hot sand. Sunset came and the sky darkened, the temperature dropping quickly. Mia's sweat soaked skin and hair chilled her all the more and she shivered uncontrollably as the lights of the town were turned off.

In the near-darkness, Mia sensed someone approach. She groaned as she was rolled onto her back. Her legs were kicked apart and then a thick cock was sliding into her. The faceless man fucked her harshly, grunting as he came. He was barely gone from inside her when another took his place ... then another ... and another. Shivering and exhausted, Mia had no idea how many men had taken her, but by the time the sun rose the sand beneath her was dark and wet. She was hauled to her feet and carried to the water butt. Lifted, she was thrown into it. She came to the surface, choking. Then she cried out as rough hands used sacking cloths to scrub her skin clean. Then she was lifted out of the water and dragged to a nearby house to stand before Mrs Cooper. She had no idea what the woman said to her and her last memory was of the woman's furious expression as Mia collapsed to the floor.

*

She was lying on the floor of the cell, the Sheriff thrusting between her legs. A sudden desire gripped her and she lifted her hips to meet his cock. He grunted in surprise but continued to fuck her, slamming into her and making her gasp. She tilted her head back, pressing it into the floor as her climax seared through her. The Sheriff came soon after, pulling free to spray his come across her naked breasts.

'Filthy bitch,' he snarled as he rearranged his clothing and slammed out of the cell.

Mia rolled onto her side, her hand slipping between her thighs to tease the last of the climax from her loins. She sensed someone move and her eyes snapped open. She relaxed when she saw Vicki who was staring at her with an expression of fear mixed with arousal. Mia had no idea if what she was about to do was allowed or if they would both be punished for it – but she had to do it. She crawled towards Vicki, her intentions clear. Vicki spread her legs, lifting her sacking dress to gather it around her hips. The first touch of Mia's tongue made Vicki gasp and she bit down on the back of her wrist to stifle any further noise. Mia licked her way up the creases and then moved back to delve as deep as she could, her fingers plying Vicki's clitoris. The blonde came quickly, shivering and gasping. When she had calmed, she lay with her head on Mia's lap.

'It's good to have you back,' Vicki whispered.

Mia leant her head back against the wall and closed her eyes. She could remember little of the past few days, just flashes of images – none of them pleasant. The last thing she remembered clearly was being dumped in the water butt and then collapsing in Mrs Cooper's parlour.

'You were gripped by fever for the last two days and slept through the next day.'

Three days. She had lost three whole days. She sighed, shaking her head.

'Mia,' Vicki's voice was so low that Mia had to lean down to hear her, 'We have to get out of here.'

'How can we?'

Vicki slowly sat up, 'I have been getting close to one of the deputies – he says that he will help us.'

Mia shook her head, 'I don't think we can trust him.'

'What choice do we have?'

She sighed, the blonde was right.

'Tomorrow night,' Vicki explained, 'If you have your strength back, he will leave the cell door open and we can get out.'

'And go where?'

'Into the desert.'

'Do you know how cold it gets out there at night?'

'We'll keep each other warm.' Vicki took Mia's hands in hers, 'Please, Mia, we have to do this.'

Mia nodded slowly, 'Okay.'

The following night the deputy came to their cell. He fucked Vicki harshly, pushing her up against the cell door and lifting her leg to grip her thigh. When he had come he nodded slowly at her and then left, closing the cell door but not locking it. He extinguished the lamps in the outer office, leaving just one burning by the main door. They waited for about an hour until the town had fallen silent and then crept out of the cell. In the main office, Mia took a moment to look around and found a jacket and an old blanket. She slipped the jacket on and put the blanket around Vicki's shoulders. Then they hurried out of the building and out of the town.

They found some caves and the remains of a campsite. Using matches stolen from the Sheriff's office, they started a fire and huddled together for warmth. As they relaxed, the heat between them grew and they moved slowly, gently pleasuring each other. They whispered to each other in the darkness and stifled their cries before falling asleep, wrapped together in the blankets.

Mia squinted at the first rays of morning sun. She stretched and sighed as nails scratched gently down her breast. She shivered as the fingers mover lower, tickling and arousing.

'Vicki,' she whispered, 'we should get moving. If we ...' The words and her thoughts dried up as those fingers slid through the crease of her pussy. She tipped her head back, groaning. Then a body moved over her and Mia gasped as a cock gently slid into her pussy. Her eyes snapped open as the man lowered himself onto her. Blinded by the sun she tried to push him away but his hands gripped her hips and held her down, skewering her beneath him. He filled her and stretched her, making her groan again. And then their bodies were moving together, his lips at her neck, his hand at her breast. That was when she smelt his sweat and felt herself go light-headed with recognition. 'Thomas,' she whispered.

A soft chuckle at her ear that made her quiver and then he began to enter her in earnest. She dug her heels into the sand and forced her hips up, grinding herself onto him. He grunted with her and sighed as they both approached climax. When he came he fell onto her and she held him tightly, fearing that it was all a dream and if she let him go she would wake and be back in the Sheriff's cell.

'It's alright,' he whispered into her ear, 'I'm here to take you home.'

Mia let his words roll over her as she lay back and closed her eyes. He slipped off her and they lay together, letting the sun warm their bodies.

Eventually Mia asked, 'Is the filming over?'

He shook his head, 'No, but the characters are well established and I can leave someone else in charge. I have other projects to attend to back in Britain.'

She sat up quickly, 'And I'm going with you?'

He smiled, 'I have to take you back to the Movie House, yes.'

'What about Vicki?'

'She's staying here.'

Mia felt a lump form in her stomach but she knew there was nothing she could do about it. 'Why me? Why am I going back?'

He frowned at her, 'You don't know?'

She gave a small laugh, 'I have no idea.'

'You have to go back ... your contract is nearly finished.'

Chapter eighteen: Home

Mia remembered little of the journey home. She was too distracted by jumbled thoughts and mixed emotions to take much notice of anything. Mia and Thomas weren't the only ones travelling back which meant that they had to stay apart and that just left Mia with her thoughts. She thought of Vicki – she would never see her again. She thought of Thomas – what was next for them? She thought of London – what was waiting for her back there? Each question brought more questions and no answers. Eventually, exhausted, she fell asleep and dreamt dark dreams.

Once back at the house there was something of a relief in falling back into the routines within. For the next five days she was filmed for the most of each day and had plenty to occupy her, keeping troublesome thoughts at bay. That was something of a blessing because she was very much aware that those Movie Slaves who did not perform, or who were distracted, were punished severely and demoted back to House Slaves. As the movies continued unabated, she began to wonder if she had misunderstood Thomas and by the end of the week she had more or less forgotten all about it. Life continued as it had done and although she missed Vicki, she soon thought about her less and less.

*

The Master led his two slaves into the tattoo parlour and made them kneel at his feet while he sat and read a magazine. His slaves were dressed in strips of studded leather that accentuated the most private areas. Each wore a studded collar and the chain leading from it was clipped to their Master's belt.

'Master Gregor?'

He looked up as the tattooist called his name. He stood, tugging the chain at his belt, 'With me, slaves.'

They followed him, heads bowed as their Master and the tattooist exchanged pleasantries. They discussed the weather, the football and then finally the slaves who stood behind him.

'Two fine acquisitions,' the tattooist remarked as Gregor unclipped the chains from his belt, 'Who shall we do first?'

Gregor waved at the red-headed slave, 'Number six.'

The red-head looked up sharply, neither of the slaves had been told what was to happen to them and Number Six was suddenly nervous as she was led towards the leather chair. Specially designed, once sat in it the slave's arms were pulled to the sides and cuffed, her ankles the same. Once fixed within the chair, the tattooist used handles to adjust the position of the slave's legs, forcing them to bend at the knee and spread the thighs wide. When she was properly positioned, her shaven cunt fully displayed, the tattooist turned to Gregor, 'This one for a piercing or tattoo?'

Gregor stroked his chin, 'Piercing I think.'

The two men studied the slave and the tattooist nodded his agreement. As he went to prepare his tools, Gregor waved at Mia, 'Nine – show her some pleasure ... but don't make her come or you'll regret it.'

'Yes, Master.' Mia sank to the floor in front of the chair and began to work at the slave's pussy. As she licked and sucked at the quivering flesh, she was aware that if this slave was to be pierced then she knew what would be happening to her. She tried not to think about it and concentrated on arousing the slave.

In just a few minutes the slave was gasping and writhing beneath Mia's wonderful tongue. Sighing, Gregor used leather straps attached to the sides of the chair to secure the slave more securely. When he was done, the tattooist approached with a piercing needle and ring. He stood over Mia as Gregor said, 'Slide your fingers into her.' She did as she was told and the bound slave cried out. The tattooist moved into position, his fingers pulling up the hood of the slave's clitoris. Mia winced as she watched him position the needle. 'Make her come,' Gregor ordered. Mia slid her fingers in and out, making the slave gasp and then she buried her fingers deep and curled them, searching out the most sensitive inner spot. Mia felt the walls of her vagina contract and Gregor must have noticed some outward sign of her climax because he gave a nod and the tattooist slid the needle through her clitoral hood. The slave threw her head back and screamed, sobbing uncontrollably before falling into a dead faint. The tattooist attached the ring and as he moved to unstrap her, Mia saw the silver S hanging from the ring.

'Nine,' Gregor announced and waved at the chair.

Mia stood slowly. She had sat on the chair and been fastened into it before she had fully considered what was going to happen next.

'The usual?' the tattooist asked. At a nod from Gregor, the tattooist pulled over a stool and sat between Mia's thighs, a tattoo gun gripped in his hand. He used a disposable razor to shave the skin of her lower pelvis and groin. 'You better hold still,' he told Mia as he started the tattoo gun, 'because if I fuck this up, you won't be able to sit down for a month.'

Mia jumped, gasping as Gregor leaned over her and slipped two fingers into her cunt. She felt her juice quickly building and as the needle of the tattoo gun started to scratch along her groin, she gasped in pleasure. Gregor continued to finger her as the tattooist drew the outline of the tattoo, wiping the blood away with a tissue, smearing the residual ink across her pelvis. She had no idea what was being inked into her flesh but she could feel the outline being drawn across her pelvis, deep into her groin and inner hip. At the same time she could feel her passions quickly mounting and she tried to hold still as Gregor continued to work his fingers inside her. He was as much an artist with his fingers as the tattooist was with the needle-gun and Mia couldn't stop herself from climaxing a few minutes later. Gregor seemed amused by this and waved for the tattooist to continue working while he continued to finger her. She would climax twice more before the tattoo was complete.

Still shivering from her last orgasm, Mia cried out as the tattooist suddenly stood and slid his cock into her. He gripped her spread thighs and thumped into her soaking cunt. She lifted her head to stare down at his cock, it felt strange. He smiled at her reaction and withdrew so that she could see the thick ring that circled his helmet. Groaning with delight, she fell back as he drove back into her. The sensation of the metal ring inside her was incredible and soon she was coming again. The feel of her quivering body was too much for him and he slammed into her, his nails digging into her flesh as he came.

Gregor took her next, fucking her quickly and brutally, making her come yet again. When he was done they released her wrists and allowed her to sit up so that she could see the tattoo. She gasped at the sight of the ornate S that was forever marked onto her skin.

'S is for slave,' Gregor announced, 'don't you forget it.'

She was allowed to shower when they had finished the tattoo film and she sat beneath the spray, arms crossed over her legs, sobbing at the thought of what they had done to her. After everything that had happened, everything that they had done – this was the worst. They had beaten her, fucked her, abused her and almost broken her – but all that would heal. The bruises and welts had faded to be replaced by new ones that, over time, had also faded. The faces of the men who had fucked her – all faceless now and lost in a blur of passion and pain. Even the memories would fade, remaining only to haunt her dreams. But this ... she stared at the tattoo through tear-misted eyes ... how could they have done this to her, how could He have done this to her.

That night she was paraded before the House Masters who inspected the tattoo and nodded at its appeal. She was then forced to spend the night with the new Fifth Master, Jake, who tied her, legs spread so that he could study the tattoo as he whipped and fucked her.

In the morning, he used a camera to take a photo of her and then a close up of the tattoo. 'Now everyone knows who and what you are.'

His words had stung her more than the different whips he had used the night before and she had had to fight back tears as she was led from his room.

She didn't pay much attention as to where she was being taken and was only vaguely aware that they weren't heading back to the dormitory, but to the film studios. She was led into a room with just a sofa and made to sit down. Her escort left and then a few minutes later the door opened and Thomas entered. She jumped up, glaring at him, tears of anger rolling down her cheeks, 'I'll never forgive you, I thought we shared something, but ... you've marked me forever as a slave.' He moved to her but she pushed him away. He sighed sadly, grabbing her wrists and pulling her down on the sofa beside him.

'You've marked me a slave,' she said again, too tired to remain angry at him.

'It's more than that.'

'How can it be, Thomas?'

'Samuel.'

'What?'

'My name is Samuel, Samuel Thomas.' He stared at her, his finger tracing the line of the tattoo, 'Anyone else may see slave written here, I see something else.'

'Samuel?'

He smiled, 'I like hearing you say my name. At least I

heard it once before you go.'

'Go?' she asked and then it hit her, 'I'm finished?'

He nodded, 'Your contact ended last night ... you have been here a year and now they are letting you go.'

She stared at him and was suddenly swamped by an overwhelming sense of despair. 'Come with me,' she whispered.

'I can't ... I had to extend my contract so that the First would allow me to reveal what had happened with Master Jeffrey ... I have another year.'

'Then I will stay ... I will extend my contract.' She hadn't considered the implications of the words before she said them but once they had been given voice, she didn't want to take them back. She would extend her contract. She would stay with him. No matter what they did to her, it would be worth it for those stolen moments with him.

He shook his head, 'I can't let you do that.'

He took her in his arms and she rested her head against his shoulder. She heard the pain in his voice and knew that he had almost agreed, had almost let her surrender to him by taking another contract.

The gulf of despair seemed to swallow her. 'I will wait for you.'

He gave a small smile, 'No, you won't.'

She looked up at him and saw the sadness and the truth in his eyes. 'Will you come for me?'

'You'll forget me as soon as you get back to London.'

She shook her head and it was her turn to stroke the tattoo, 'Tell me you'll come for me.'

He stared at her in silence, his eyes hollow. Eventually he said, 'You had better go.'

Slowly she turned away. She didn't look back but she knew that he was watching her. It wasn't over ... she prayed that it wasn't over.

Epilogue: Betrayal

The train ride back to London was a blur. Her thoughts empty and desolate. She was met off the train and driven through the dark streets, staring out of the window at the city lights that flashed past. They arrived at their destination and she was led through a house that she vaguely recognised. Soon she was standing in the study where all this had begun a year ago.

Gary Marshall stood as she was shown into the room. He smiled as he appraised her, 'I've heard good things about you. I'm looking forward to seeing the results.'

She stared back at him, silent and emotionless.

His smile didn't falter, 'Oh, come now, they didn't break you up there, I know they didn't.'

Mia sighed, 'So, what happens now?'

Marshall returned to his desk and sat on the edge, lighting a cigarette. 'I assume this concludes our business?'

Mia frowned and then realised that he wasn't talking to her but to someone who had entered the room behind her. Before she could turn, a booted foot kicked the back of her legs and she fell to her knees. An all too familiar hand twisted in her hair and yanked her head back. 'And where the fuck have you been?' Kent spat in her face.

'We discussed this, Sergeant Kent,' Marshall announced, 'Don't ask her about the last year because she won't tell you.'

Kent snarled and pushed her head away, making her fall face first to the floor.

'I assume that this show of good faith will keep your nose out of my business?' Marshall asked.

Kent bent to grab Mia's arm and hauled her to her feet. 'For now,' he growled and then turned and marched Mia out of the room.

And now here's a sneak preview of 'S is for Slave' which will be released later this year!

Chapter One: Anguish

It was as if the last year had never happened.

Kent took her to some waste ground and threw her over the bonnet of his car. He yanked her trousers down her legs and forced her chest onto the hot metal. She groaned as he drove into her, his nails digging into the flesh of her buttocks. He fucked her harshly and she was too scared to feel even the barest hint of arousal that would have normally helped her to suffer his attentions. When he was done, with his come sliding down the inside of her thighs, he beat her buttocks with his belt. They were glowing red and smothered in welts before the first scream escaped her lips. This was the first indication of the changes that she had undergone in the last year – she was so much stronger. Her fear of Kent kept her from noticing herself and his fury blinded him to the change in her. She had always been strong and perhaps that was why he had enjoyed her so much – in time he might notice how strong she had really become, although it was doubtful if he actually would. Kent was not interested in her strength – there was little about her that he was interested in. All he cared about was what he could get from her and once he had satisfied his lust and his anger, he had a further use for her before the night was out.

He allowed her to rearrange her clothing while he smoked a cigarette. He watched her silently, his eyes narrowed. 'You will tell me where you have been for the last twelve months,' he suddenly announced, 'I will make you tell me.'

Mia kept her eyes down and didn't respond. She would not tell him where she had been – she was not sure she even believed that it had actually happened. It all seemed like a dream now.

He flicked his cigarette away and waved for her to get back into the car. He didn't check if she did, seeing no need as she knew what would happen if she dared to disobey him.

Thirty minutes later and she felt her chest constrict as they drove into a truck stop at the edge of the motorway. Her throat dried as she stared out at the assembled trucks and the fifteen or so truck drivers that clustered in small groups near the rigs. Upon seeing the police car approach, a few of the drivers turned and headed for their trucks while the others clustered into one smaller group. He stopped the car and got out. His appearance drove most of the other drivers away but three remained, watching with interest as Kent dragged Mia out of the car.